THE CADILLAC OF DETECTIVES

Book Twelve of the San Diego Police Homicide Detail
featuring Billy Jack Cadillac

WILLIAM BARRONS

iCrew
digital publishing

Chula Vista • Columbus

Chapter One

The Homicide Detail Co-Commanders, Lieutenants Julie Brightwell and Brian Alan, walked me over to the area set aside for Homicide Team 3's, six office cubicles. I saw each walled-in space had a normal-sized desk, with a computer screen and keyboard in the center. Each cubicle, had two office chairs.

"Sergeant Ray Snyder," Lieutenant Alan said with a smile, "let me introduce you to your newest Detective. He's Arturo Abrito and that thick, wavy red hair of his, let's you know right off, he's a Mexican, and proud of it."

"Couple of things about him, Ray: he's five feet eight inches tall and as you can very plainly see, he pumps iron and he's a martial arts guy. He's a graduate of San Diego State and our Police Academy. He worked as a Patrol Officer here for just over four years. He earned some commendations in those four years; so, you know you're getting a top-quality Officer here.

"His great-granddad, his granddad, his dad and himself, have all served in wars in the Marine Corps. So, it seems, he has military discipline sort of built in.

"He'll be twenty-eight-years old tomorrow. Let's see, that's Thursday, January 30th, 2014. Hey Ray, I happen to know that would have been Franklin Roosevelt's birthday, too. Ah, the President would have been a hundred-thirty-four, if he had lived," Lieutenant Alan said.

"Very funny, Brian," Lieutenant Brightwell said, cutting in… although she was neither laughing nor even smiling at his remark.

"You'll have to excuse him, fellows," she said. "Lieutenant Alan loves history. Art, you'll be in very smart and dedicated company, here in Team 3. This Team is famous for solving homicides; and usually, they somehow solve them more quickly than our other four Teams do. You'll make the fifth Detective on the Team to bring it up to what it's supposed to have."

"Thank you very much, Lieutenants," Sergeant Snyder said, "for bringing him over. We'll see how he measures up pretty soon. We just got word of a horrible homicide with a hatchet, of all things. Art, let me introduce you to four really excellent Detectives."

My name of Arturo came from my dad's gratitude for a Marine Platoon Sergeant who saved his life in the Iraq war. That Sergeant was a large and very brave Black man who was killed in action, just three days after saving my dad's life from an Iraqi gone mad.

Then Sergeant Snyder took me from cubicle to cubicle, introducing the other Detectives on the Team. They were Ray Mason, David Mann, Martin Garcia and Su Chi. Her last name was pronounced, like the word China, but with no "na," I remembered. That very pretty Chinese gal had told me long ago, how to pronounce her ancient name.

"Sergeant, Su and I have been acquainted for a couple of years," I said. "Su, I heard you were transferred over to the Elder Abuse unit. But now you're back?"

"Hi Art; it's nice to see you again," Su Chi said. "No, I haven't gone there; at least, not yet. Commander Macias supposes I'd do well, working with old folks. Sergeant Snyder, would you like me to clue him in to his job?"

"Su, that's a really good idea, since you two know each other already. I'm taking the other guys out right now to investigate that latest homicide. Damn! Someone actually clobbered a guy with a damned hatchet, up there in Kearney Mesa. You two will get involved later," the Sergeant said. Then he and the others disappeared.

"Art, here's your office," Detective Chi said, pointing to the semi-private space. "You can use your own smart phone, or the desk phone. You might want to spend a few hours studying the files in the cabinet there, and in your computer. That will let you know about some of the necessary procedures, and the record-keeping. By the way, how's Angela doing lately?"

"Su, Angela moved last June, up to Orange County, where she got a big boost in pay for teaching private school first graders. The truth is, I'm glad she's gone out of my life," I told her. "As you know, we lived together for a few months, and the last few weeks were full of tension."

"I hardly knew Angela, Art, but I would have thought she was sort of easy-going. But she got upset a lot?" Su asked me.

"No, not that, Su. It seemed she had been interested, in going up there to work in a private school, but I guess she wondered, if she could live without me. Well, she finally decided that hell yes, she could do just fine without ol' Abrito around her neck! She packed up her stuff and drove off while I was at work, just after her school let out for the summer. She left a goodbye note, and that's the last I've heard from her. Which, it turns out, is okay by me.

"And you, Su? How's everything going with you?" I asked.

She hadn't seemed to have changed in the few months, since we had been on Patrol together. She was truly, a classic Asian beauty, I always had thought. It seemed strange for someone with her natural beauty, to want to do Police work. But the Chinese lady—no, she liked to say she was Taiwanese, because of her ancestors—was an excellent Officer, strong for a woman, and about an inch shorter than me. She had mastered martial arts, too.

Her dense black hair was always perfectly parted in the middle, and combed straight down on each side, to where it curved inward, to a little above her shoulders. Her Chinese facial features were perfect. I knew she was a couple of years older, than my twenty-eight-years, but she looked more like she was barely, out of her teens. She was totally feminine, yet a good Cop!

Today being chilly, like the others in the Homicide Detail, she was wearing a nice grey business suit, necktie, white shirt, and a pleated skirt to the knees, that was sewn in back, to make them pants. She had perfectly formed long legs.

I had been forewarned, so I dressed well in a business suit, too; but mine was brown.

"You'll remember my mom died, couple of years ago, and now," she said, "my dad has Alzheimer's really bad. Damn; he's just sixty years old. My sister Lu has taken a leave of absence from her job at Ralph's grocery, to care for him around the clock. I help out a little, too. I'm the only breadwinner now. It's the saddest damn thing, Art, to see a good man like my dad, to become a nothing person," Su Chi said.

"Oh Su, I'm so sorry to hear that. I only met your dad once, but I sure was impressed with him. Well, I guess I'd better dig into those files to find out stuff, eh?" I said.

"Right. You'll find out about that latest homicide, on your computer. Here, I'll get it up for you on your screen, and then I've got things to do, as well," she said.

She opened the file on the monitor for me and left.

I sat down to begin learning about my new job.

Wow! A picture showed the male victim's right ear, nearly cut off, and dangling. That angled blow by the small axe, that could be used with one hand, must have knocked him out. A second photo showed his balding head, with a wide, three-inch-long wound, where the hatchet had penetrated his skull. That hit was dead center (so to say) in the bald spot. Doubtless, the blade entered deep into his brain, and that killed the man.

The word hatchet, meaning small axe, is from the French. In English, it should be "axet." Axe in French is "hatch." In English, "hatch" is an opening, especially in a ship's deck. If the guy had been struck by a regular axe, the wound would have been longer.

The victim's body had simply been shoved off a Balboa Drive sidewalk, into a bush. When daylight came, someone walking by saw it, and called 911. The Medical Examiner people had grabbed up the body, and brought it to their lab, by about 10:00 a.m. The man would be identified officially, and the time of death estimated, in a report from them, soon.

Ah, as I was looking at the screen, the MedEx announced the hatchet victim's name as Anthony Baines Garcia. He was an illegal alien, from Mexico. He had been arrested and deported twice, at least. They said he was five-feet-five inches tall and weighed a-mere-one-hundred-twenty-two pounds. He probably weighed a little more than that, before a lot of blood spilled out of his illegal head. His time-of-death was stated, as about 3:45 a.m. that morning.

I know that area of the city quite well, from living there, and from patrolling it. I'd think there would be practically no people, or cars, traveling up and down Balboa Drive, at that hour. I was on night Patrol for nearly a year, in that neighborhood. My folks had had a house there, and I had an apartment in the neighborhood for a while.

The victim had no wallet on him, and no money. He was only identified through fingerprints. He could be one of the nine thousand homeless, in "America's Finest City of San Diego."

A search of the State of California records showed, he owned and licensed a car. That gave up the man's address. But he had no legitimate driver's license. His car was a black Honda Civic, of 2006.

How did he come by the middle name of Baines? Probably there was an Englishman somewhere in his background. Garcia is perhaps the most common, of Spanish surnames. Our Black Detective on Team 3, the big man Martin Garcia, has that name.

While I was still in San Diego State University, my dad got a great loan offer, to be a Master Chef, and begin his own Northside of Chicago, Mexican restaurant. He moved my mom, two younger brothers, and two younger sisters, there. My family likes it there but that place, with its really awful weather, is definitely not for me. I visit them at Christmastime, and they come out here to paradise, for a couple of weeks in the summer.

With my nose practically on the computer screen, I didn't see or hear Su Chi, come up behind me.

"Art, I forgot to ask about your family," she said. "Darn, it is a genuine pleasure to see your beautiful hair again."

Su had often commented on the waviness of my red hair; I suppose, since her hair was as straight as can be. I must have had a Viking ancestor, one time or another, to inherit that red hair on my head and on my face. I've always been careful, to shave every single day, to avoid having a doggoned red beard. My siblings all have red hair too, as does my mom, but not my dad.

"Oh, they're all doing just fine, Su; I spent Christmas week back there with them. They have a pretty nice, two-story brick building on the North Side there. They live right over their restaurant, which is called Café Abrito.

"My brothers, and my sisters are singing waiters. One sister plays her accordion, another sis plays her violin, a brother has a guitar, and the customer's favorite, another brother amazes everyone with his banjo. They all sing for about three minutes, every half hour. The patrons love those singing waiters. And of course, they're all in Mexican costumes.

"My family makes very good money there. My dad runs the kitchen, and mom is the boss out front, seating guests and taking payments," I told her. "She worries about her kids in that big, noisy city."

"Oh yes, and I just got a handful of birthday cards; one from each one of them. Every one of them had a Home Depot gift card in it, just to show me they're all doing well. Six hundred bucks is a pretty good haul, so soon after Christmas, I've gotta say," I said.

"Oh Artie, I'm so glad to hear you and your family are getting along, even though you're so far apart. So, you'll be twenty-eight tomorrow, eh? Well, that's a Thursday and I'd like very much to help you celebrate your birthday, a couple of days late. Want to come to my house Saturday night, for dinner?" the beautiful Su Chi said, lighting me up on the inside.

"Wow! Hell yes, Su!" I said. "That is so very thoughtful of you. "Then we can scoot down to the Gaslamp, and live it up a little?"

"That seems like a good plan to me, Artie," she said. "Now, back to work here. Did you see the new information from the MedEx on that case?"

"Yes, I did, Su," I said.

"I got a call from Sergeant Snyder a bit ago," she said. "He told me they found out who called 911 about the body. He's an auto mechanic near there. The entire intimidating four of them went to talk to the guy, in his repair shop. It was pretty slick.

"The Sergeant asked the guy if he knew how many years in prison, a man could get for stealing a wallet, from a dead man. The guy immediately handed the wallet, over to him. Turned out, there was a little over, eighteen hundred bucks in it. Snyder recognized the dead guy as being a drug dealer, and knew he'd have plenty of dough on him. Pretty cute, eh?"

I nodded yes, and she went on to tell me how exceptionally sharp their Sergeant was. Then she assured me Detectives David Mann, Ray Mason and Martin Garcia, were also "really sharp guys."

"Su, with you on Team 3, I am absolutely certain I'm on the best Team in the world," I said... and then regretted being fresh with her. At work, she was always, always, "on the job."

Quickly, I added, "Does that mean the guy got clobbered with a hatchet, because somebody doesn't like drug dealers, a whole lot?"

"That could be, Artie. But it is interesting that the one who killed him, didn't think to profit from his death. I think it's interesting, that the dead man had the same middle name as our second President Johnson had," she noted.

"Oh yeah," I said. "President Lyndon Baines Johnson, was his name. I'd forgotten that, Su. Maybe the dead man was related somehow, to the Johnsons."

"Ah, here's the rest of the Team," she said as the four men, gathered around my cubicle.

"You doing alright here, Art?" Team Leader Sergeant Ray Snyder asked.

"Yes, sir," I answered. "I've been looking over this new case on my computer. Is the Department going to update the older computers here?"

"Not likely, Art," he said. "Those we have perform okay, anyway. Well, we found out that illegal alien Garcia, has an apartment near where he was killed. We've got a search warrant request in, so we can go look it over. We should have it right after lunch, and we can all get up there. The man being a drug dealer, he might have some interesting stuff there. We found his car, so we'll get permission to inspect that, too."

"So, it didn't appear to be a robbery attempt, Sergeant?" I asked.

"It could have been Art, but maybe someone came along just then, and the perp had to disappear," Snyder answered me courteously.

"I know that area fairly well Sergeant, and it seems strange to me that a guy… especially a drug dealer, would be walking along Balboa Street, at 3:45 in the morning," I said.

"The only guess I can come up with Art," he said, "is that the guy agreed to meet someone there, at that time, for a sale. Those drug dealers, and their customers don't usually follow normal hours, or normal conduct, of course. Anyway, the guy sure got himself made really dead, for whatever reason he was there. He must not have felt a thing, what with the first chop at him, probably knocking him out. The second blow must have been, really a hard one."

Come lunch time, we all traipsed over to the cafeteria. It was made clear: all six of us had to "go Dutch," and pay for our own fare. It was a nice buffet.

I got an egg salad sandwich which was thick enough for two people. I'm a devoted coffee drinker, black with a little sugar please, and those two items satisfied me just fine. I saw that Su Chi bought the same sandwich as I got but drank coffee with so-called "cream" in it. Musing to myself, I thought hey, we two might very well be compatible.

In the months when I hadn't seen her, I had thought of her sometimes, but I was terribly busy cleaning up the house I bought. "Out of sight, out of mind," I suppose.

All six of us were no sooner back at our desks, when Sergeant Snyder ordered us to all go inspect the dead drug dealer's apartment, and his automobile. The search warrant had been issued. My Ford Expedition could hold eight people, so I volunteered to take the whole Team.

The dead man's apartment, was but two blocks away from where he got a hatchet to the head. We found his car in the carport behind the building he lived in.

"Dammit to hell!" Snyder said as he opened the guy's apartment door.

It sure was a messy damn place, with trash on the floor everywhere. Even a kitchen table was covered with the same stuff, as was on the floor. But half eaten food too, was in bowls and really cheap plates. It seemed the guy didn't give damn, about putting trash, in trash containers.

He was overmatched however, by the former ancient owner of the house, I had bought and worked to clean, for the last arduous five or more months.

But we weren't there to condemn the memory of the man, for his lack of caring for his house; actually, it was merely a small studio.

There was a "Murphy Bed" swung up against a wall. I reached up to grab the handles and then pulled it down.

Shockingly, the bed was made up neatly. It looked as though it had never been slept in.

"Hey Art," David Mann said, "let's you and me, lift up this mattress."

With the bed flat on the floor, we did that, and we shouldn't have been surprised; but much of the space under that, was covered with little "baggies." That was a common way for drug dealers to sell, $20 portions, of various powdered drugs. For a guy who was the exact opposite of neatness, the baggies were spread out in an almost orderly fashion.

"We might have known," Sergeant Snyder said, looking at the drugs. "Don't bother with that, fellows, because the Narcos are on the way; should be here really quick. Let's check that closet there. Marty and Su, you two should check the bathroom."

The man's closet was jammed full of clothing. Some of the jackets, shirts and pants were hung up on hangers. The floor was covered completely, with what had to be, his dirty laundry.

Two shoe boxes were on the single shelf, above the clothing rod. One was on top of the other. I reached up and brought both of them down. They hefted as though full of size eight shoes, as the ends of the boxes said.

Taking the tops off of each of the boxes in turn, I was amazed that they contained not shoes, but money!

"Damn!" the Sergeant exploded. "Art, that looks like one helluva lot of money. You and David… you two should clear that crap off the table and count all that."

As the two of us began taking hamburger wrappers, little boxes and all sorts of "crap" off the table, someone loudly told the Sergeant, that he had found a very big stack of pornographic DVDs. He counted twenty-four of those nasty discs, he told everyone.

We put the dishes in the sink, complete with dried, and spoiled food on them. His eating tools were plastic, well used and not washed.

All of the trash on the table was put into bags, rather than being added, to the mess on the floor. Then David Mann took a dirty washcloth and cleaned the table. That table sure looked not to have had that done, in a very long time. Then I found a not so terribly dirty towel and dried the table off with it.

Only then did David Mann and I, begin counting the money. Mostly, it was in twenties. There were only twenty-one, one-hundred-dollar bills. Snyder and Su Chi watched as we counted, and both of them made notes, as we continued on. It must have taken half an hour, for the counting of the two boxes, packed almost neatly, and full of bills.

"Fellows, I don't recall any seizure like this, being so rich," Snyder said. "You two counted exactly $53,378; that is quite the haul. Plus, he had, $1,800 in his wallet. He could've bought a damn nice car for that fifty-five grand... but wait, of course it wasn't his money; it belonged for sure, to the Sinaloa cartel. All that damn pile of drugs under the mattress, also belonged to the Sinaloas. So, this guy here was a distributor, and not merely a dealer. The Narcos will be interested in this guy, dead or alive, that's for sure."

"Sergeant, the cartel probably had a hold on the guy here, such as, his entire family in Mexico could be wiped out, if he cheated them," I offered.

"Oh sure; of course," Snyder said. "Those cartel people care absolutely not for anyone but themselves. They've made the usually law-abiding, and gentle nation of Mexico, the leading country for violence, and homicides. Even war-torn Syria, or other sand-box countries, can't compete with Mexico for murders. Those drug smugglers are utterly ruthless."

His saying that, reminded me of my grandfather Abrito. He had left Mexico for the States long before all that ugly, nasty, horrific drug business, began to corrupt that country.

"Ah, here's the Narcos now," the Sergeant said as two men walked in.

The Narcotics Section Detectives were dressed in blue jeans, casual shirts and jackets. Their pistols and badges were in plain view on their belts. We Homicide Detectives were all dressed, as though we were successful businessmen—with one very attractive businesswoman.

In fact, Detective Su Chi was dressed nicely. She was nicely slender and carried herself with grace. I couldn't help it; I thought more and more, that she was truly beautiful.

The entire Team 3 was hauled to the spot in my 2011 white Ford Expedition, that I bought used, to haul trash from my newly purchased house to the city dump. Everyone mentioned the largeness of it on the inside. It would seat eight adults nicely.

I explained to them, the reason I bought such a big car, was because I expected to be remodeling my Craftsman Style house, and I had to haul loads of long boards, etc. The huge Ford has turned out to be a pleasure to drive. But I haven't got rid of my five-year-old Mustang yet. I'll probably sell it, because I'm going to need lots of money pretty soon.

Sergeant Snyder got involved, in talking with the Narcos. He handed the dead man's car keys to me, and several of us went out to check on that.

We found the black 2006 Honda Civic, in the parking lot. I unlocked it, and immediately opened the trunk, so it could be looked into. It looked as though that trunk had not held anything… not even trash, since it had been bought.

Search as we might, we found no money at all in the car, but in both the center console and the glove compartment, there were, in each place, about a dozen tiny baggies, containing white powder.

Naturally, the front and the back floors of the Honda, were messy with food wrappers, empty milk cartons, and soda cans. Neither in his studio apartment or in his car, did any of us see evidence of alcoholic drinks. But the guy apparently was never told by his mama, that it was a good thing to be tidy and clean.

Besides the drugs, we found the car's title, and other records in his glove box. The car would be shortly towed, to the Police Impound lot. There, the Narcos would again check to find drugs. They would put a dog to sniffing for the stuff. If the pooch indicated he smelt something, they might virtually take the car apart, to dig the junk out.

Oddly, Detective Chi found in the back of a dresser drawer, a stash of money rolled up, in the guy's clean undershorts. We guessed that money, was to be his own. It was all in twenties and amounted to $1,360. That seemed a minuscule amount of money, compared with the other dough we found. In that drawer, he had packages of sox, and underwear, still in their wrappers. Maybe he never laundered anything; perhaps he replaced with new stuff, whatever he "had worn plenty long enough."

When we were through with the car, I gave the keys to the Narcos. It was their baby from then on. Before we left, I saw them open even the hood of the thing. They must have figured we Homicide characters, were too dumb to check for drugs there. But we had.

We got in the Expedition, and I drove Team 3 back to our Headquarters office.

Sergeant Snyder invited me to sit beside him, as he "filled out the file," on the dead man, Anthony Baines Garcia.

Wow! Snyder could type really fast. I watched as his fingers flew over that keyboard. Hell, I learned to touch-type, away back in grade school. But I don't think anyone ever encouraged me, to type like my Sergeant could. I know there are speed-typing courses available, where you do a lot of monotonous drill. But hey, it seems to me it would be worth it, trying to get my speed up like the guy I'm sitting beside and watching here.

"Art, you'll notice that I don't show a motive for this homicide," he said. "Very often, at this stage of an investigation, we don't have any idea, of a motive. But motive is all important. If we can nail that down, chances are, we've got our suspect. You'll want to remember that."

"Thanks for that, Sergeant," I said, acknowledging the lesson.

However, in fact I know a great deal about the homicide business. I had just graduated from high school, and got to Marine Boot Camp here in San Diego, when a friend of our family was murdered. He owned a large and popular bicycle shop in Kearney Mesa, and I knew him well. It took a couple of months before the murderer was charged. It had been a case of robbery. Detectives then found the suspect had bought a new car… he paid cash for it… and an investigation showed the robber, to have committed the murder.

After three years in the Marines, I got out, went four years to San Diego State University, and studied for a criminology major. Then I went through the San Diego Police Academy and was assigned as a Patrol Officer. I had done alright on Patrol. Really tough guys, thought I might be a push-over, at a mere five-feet-eight-inches, so they had to be disabused of such a notion. I won four hard-earned… I mean, *very hard-earned,* commendations, while a Patrol Officer. So, it wasn't as though I was altogether ignorant, of what to do as a Detective. I had meant it to be my life's work to obtain justice in homicide cases, and by golly, here I am.

As a Patrol Officer, I had been shot at, at least six times. But I only got a minor wound… in my left leg… once. I shot more accurately than those damn fools did, shooting at me.

At noon on Thursday, January 30th, 2014, Sergeant Snyder gathered up the entire Team 3, to have a birthday lunch, for my twenty-eighth birthday. All of those on the Team 3, really did make me feel, like I was among friends. They all seemed to be good eggs to me… especially a certain slender one, who happened to be just an inch shorter than me.

As usual, we all went "Dutch," but someone must have popped for the large chocolate cupcake, with a lit candle on it, for me. I made a big thing of wanting the candle to last all afternoon, but of course, I was testing their patience. Finally, I blew the thing out. I even cut the cupcake up into six pieces so we'd each enjoy a bite of it.

Detective Su Chi was no wallflower. She spoke up about the time, two years before, when she was on Patrol in North Park. She pulled over a guy, driving erratically down University Avenue. The guy rolled on a bit too far, and went up on the sidewalk, and stopped against a trash barrel. As Chi came around to the front of the man's car, to check the crushed barrel, the man got out.

"It was obvious the man was on meth, or crack cocaine, or something," she said. "He had no shirt, nor shoes, nor socks on. Damn, he was really muscular and tall. After a while, I was sure he was ten feet tall. He spoke nonsense. I couldn't grasp a word, he kept jabbering."

"Anyway, he paid no attention, to what I was ordering him to do. He kept walking toward me, and I kept backing up. I was afraid I'd have to shoot him, to get him to stop. He had followed me, jabbering away, around his car, and up on the sidewalk. I was sure tazing him, would only make him even crazier.

"Just then here comes Officer Abrito, literally flying through the air, hitting the guy in his back. He pushed the guy face down, on the ground, and had the cuffs on him, in seconds. Then he stopped the guy from flailing his feet around, by cuffing his ankles, too.

"I mention this, gentlemen," Su Chi said, "so that all of you will know, our birthday boy here, is one tough Police Officer."

"Oh, my gosh, Su," I said, "you can bet every single one of these Officers, have done that exact same thing, time and time again. But thanks, Su. I'd forgotten how, you and I met," I said.

With the happy birthday lunch over with, we returned to our offices.

None of us on Team 3, could remember anyone going about clobbering people, with a one-handed, small axe, that we, speaking French, call a hatchet. We speakers of English speak many languages, because of English borrowing thousands, of other languages' words.

Neither of our Commanders, the Lieutenants, could recall such homicides, either. People were made permanently dead, lots of different ways, but hatcheting them to death, was not a usual way. Guns, knives, clubs, hammers, machetes and poisons, seem to be much more favored, than hatchets, for sending someone off, for all eternity.

The only thing gorier than a hatchet homicide, would be decapitating, I suppose.

We sat or stood by our Sergeant's cubicle, while all of us puzzled over that puzzle. Why in hell, with all the many forms of weaponry available, would someone croak another human, with a damned hatchet? No one had an answer, except… "Well, you see, this here hatchet was right there and handy, and…" But somehow, that didn't quite fit, either.

The hatcheted victim Garcia, sold drugs. Indeed, we figured after a while, that he sold them wholesale, to other dealers in San

Diego, as a distributor… presumably for the Sinaloa cartel who it was known, were the masters of the Baja peninsula. They murdered men and women, virtually every day, to keep their control.

The Sinaloa cartel's crimes of homicide totaled—almost certainly—some thousands of victims. That was just so they could exclusively smuggle their poisons, across our border and get richer and richer, for doing so. Thanks Americans, for your continued financial support, of those evil devils!

It turned out, I spent much of my birthday, going over mostly cases that had been solved. That was so I could learn the proper procedures for the files, so others could quickly, and easily find information on a computer, in a standard way.

Team 3, 4 and 5, were all on duty ten hours a day, four days a week. Our current schedule ran from Wednesday, through Saturday. Teams 1 and 2, had the duty Sunday to Wednesday. The two Lieutenant/Commanders also split their week like that. Importantly, the entire Homicide Detail of two Lieutenants, five Sergeants, and twenty-five Detectives, were present on Wednesdays. That was so duties could be apportioned among them, and information passed around.

Saturday was proving to be dullsville, all morning. My thoughts kept wandering to dinner time that evening, with Su and her two years' older sister, Lu Chi. Both of those women were attractive, intelligent, and I knew they both dated men. But so far as I had heard, only the older sister, Lu, had been married… and that knot had come untied, rather quickly.

Absolutely forbidden in our business, was anything at all like romance between Officers, during working hours. That would be bad form. That could cause real problems. It simply was not done.

Right at noon, a Police Patrol in a City Heights alley, reported a homicide. The Officer said the man died, of a large wound to the top of his head.

This time, the six of us in Team 3, went in two vehicles. Su Chi took David Mann and me, in her two-year-old white Chevrolet Impala, four-door sedan. I sat in the back, and I was surprised, how very nice the car was. Inside and out, the car was immaculate.

Yet, General Motors had gone bankrupt, about six years before, and required a huge loan from the government, to resurrect them. Well, they sure were making very good cars these days. And they were profitable again, despite the overwhelming ocean-sized-floods, of car imports, from our former enemies, Japan and Germany; oh yes, also from our friends, the South Koreans.

We three Detectives got out of the car, and saw a large black man, lying on his side, at the edge of the alley pavement. He had a great amount of black wool on his head, so it was not easy to see his wound. All of his hair, was completely blood-soaked. Blood had also washed over his face and wetted his black tee shirt.

"Officer, have you seen any weapons around?" I asked a Patrol Officer.

"No Detective, I haven't," he replied. "I was driving down the street there," he pointed, "and a kid hailed me. I stopped, and the kid told me he saw a dead man in the alley. I drove here, saw the corpse, and called it in. That's the total extent of what I know about this."

"Okay; thanks for that," I told him, as I got down close, to the man on the ground.

The man's head wool was so thick, and so totally saturated with blood, that I could not actually see, all of the wound. But it did appear to be centered, in the top of his head. Blood was by then, barely coming out of the wound. I supposed he had to have been killed, within the hour.

Sergeant Snyder had a camera, and he took some pictures of the corpse itself, and of the surrounding space. All of us had our eyes on the ground, as we looked for... well, some sort of clue. Our usual search would be especially for shell casings, but this was obviously not the ordinary shooting case.

"Looks to me like a hatchet homicide again," Sergeant Snyder told his Team.

I thought he had to be guessing, because I looked at the top of the dead man's head, from only inches away. Damned if I could actually see much of the wound itself, through all that bloody mess there, in that ultra-curly hair.

A young Black girl walked up slowly toward us. She looked to be a teenager.

"Youse all is Detectives?" she asked.

Someone answered, "Yes."

"This man here, why, I knows him. He's got the apartment, below where I live. He be called Jimmy," the girl said.

"Thank you miss; thank you very much," Sergeant Snyder said to the girl, and then turned to Su and me.

"Hey Abrito and Chi, why don't you two, go with this nice young lady, to see where his place is? I'll call right now for a search warrant. The rest of us will be checking out the guy's pockets," he said. "Oh yeah; and give me a buzz right away, about the address."

Much of the city of San Diego, doesn't have alleys. This one in City Heights was pretty much lined with garages, while some lots merely had a place for cars to pull into the back yard. And some backyards were fenced in, with green grass, and lots of pretty flowers.

"What's your name, miss?" Detective Chi asked the girl.

"Florence," she answered.

"Ah; Florence," Su said. "That is such a pretty name. I know that's from the Italian language. I'm sure it means, someone as nice as flowers."

"I didn't know that, Detective. Thanks," the girl said, with a smile on her nice face.

The rather attractive young Black girl, led us down the alley about four lots, where she turned to walk between cars parked, on asphalt pavement, in a building's back yard.

"This car here, be Jimmies," the girl said, patting a Toyota Camry, parked in the yard.

Then she pointed to the rear door, of the first floor, of a three-story apartment building.

"That be Jimmie's place; but I see it's got a lock on it," she said.

"Thank you miss," I said. "We'll have a court order soon, to go in there to see if we can find any evidence, in the case of Jimmie's death. Is this the only door into his place?"

"Yes, 'tis," she said. "There's another 'partment in front, but they don't connect with Jimmie's. Me, my ma and my bro, we live right up there, above Jimmie's. We didn't like him very much. He plays his awful music too loud."

The girl left us and climbed up the stairs.

The address of the place was on a mailbox, next to the entry door. I called the Sergeant and told him about it.

I opened the lid of the mailbox, to see it was empty.

Then Su and I sat on the steps, waiting for the search warrant to be issued. Unless keys were found in the dead man's pockets, we'd have to break the padlock on the door to get in and overcome the lock on the door itself.

"Artie," Su Chi said quietly, as we plunked our butts down on a step, "did Angela leave you because of you buying that really old house?"

"I really don't know why she left, Su," I answered. "She was kind of strange at times. I think she left mostly to make more money up there, teaching kids in Orange County. Since she saw the house I bought later, I know she didn't like the idea of having my house in one helluva mess, while I worked a couple of days a week on it. In truth, I'll have to work on it for years, to get it done the way I want it."

"Can't you hire a contractor to get the changes done right away?" she asked.

"Oh sure; I could do that alright if a had about $300,000 in my pocket. A friend guessed it could cost that much. I already have a mortgage on it, what with paying only a bit more than a hundred-grand up front. But you know, I'm really lucky. I had a thorough inspection of the place before I committed myself. There's no termites, the foundation is sound, the basement floor even, has only a few cracks in it. Even the stucco seems to be okay," I told her.

"For a Craftsman Style house built in 1925, it was in good

shape except for being so damn awful dirty and filled with trash," I added. "I've spent about five months, with extremely hard work, to get it cleaned up. I sold tons of cardboard, wood pallets and aluminum cans.

"Honestly, I filled up three rented dumpsters with trash from it, but I cleared about three thousand bucks from recyclables. I wore rubber gloves and cleaned every square inch everywhere in that place. The windows in that house hadn't been washed in many years. I even rented a power washer for a lot of it. I power-washed the stucco outside, too."

"Okay, but what is it you want to do with it?" she asked.

"Well Su, I've got the blueprints… that's a miracle in itself. A Massachusetts architect designed it in 1925, for a guy named Peters. As you enter from the nearly house-wide front porch, you're in a five-foot-wide hallway that goes, fifty-two feet down the center, from the front door to the back door. The main, second floor has ten-foot ceilings. There's a full basement with an eight-foot ceiling, I call the first floor. But oddly, you can only reach that lower level from the back yard; from under the small back porch.

"To your left along the second-floor hall, are four sizeable bedrooms and one tiny bathroom. On the south side of the house, there's a parlor room with a nice fireplace, a dining room and then the room called the kitchen.

"Now Su, I've only lived there for… oh, it's over five months now," I said. "The place was a really dirty mess. I've cleaned and cleaned and cleaned. I've discovered the doors, door jambs and trim, are all solid mahogany. That very precious wood probably came from Belize, next to Mexico; or it might have come from Cuba.

"Even in 1925, mahogany had to have been fairly rare and pricey. Also, there's an acre of paneling and wood trim in the house, and it's all mahogany. All the varnished surfaces were filthy, and the varnish is cracked. But underneath, the wood is still good. But it will take a lot of work to refinish all that trim and doors, etc."

"The house is thirty-two-feet wide and fifty-two-feet, front to back. The original owner must have had an automobile or two or three, because the garage on the alley is also thirty-two-feet wide, and twenty-two feet, front to back. It has three overhead doors and stalls. The garage was empty of a workbench, oddly. It seems to have been built at the same time as the house was, so that owner had money. Could be, he was a car dealer. And he must have come from back east, to have that very shallow basement included.

"Both of the roofs are probably good for a few years yet. The front porch decking needs to be covered. The main floor is heated with hot water running through baseboards. The gas furnace has been replaced some years ago. I'd not put in air-conditioning, but rather, I'll put up ceiling fans with light fixtures, in every room in the house," I told Su Chi.

"Interesting, the house is on a double lot, sixty-feet-wide by one-hundred-twenty-feet from the front sidewalk to the alley. Some of the neighboring houses are on thirty-foot-wide lots. The house faces west and along the south side of it—the kitchen-parlor side of it—there's a small wild canyon that goes into the City Golf Course. Because of that, there's a pretty good view through that small canyon, from the front porch, of downtown, the bay and even a bit of the ocean. The sunsets from the front porch are often spectacular," I told her.

"I got a bargain in buying the place because the basement was absolutely filthy and full of trash. The Florida guy who inherited it, never stepped inside the place, because his eighty-some-year-old hermit uncle had left it so dirty. He had no idea the house, with two floors, had a living space of 3,744 square feet; however, the lower half of the house had never been lived in. With him just looking through the dirty windows, I got the guy down from $350,000 to $290,000. I think that's a very good buy."

"Artie, you may not know it, but my sixty-year-old dad was a carpenter from the age of fourteen until just lately," Su told me. "He could have been able to give you lots of help. But when my mom died of the flu, of all things, couple of years ago... when she died, dad right away began to get dementia and then Alzheimer's.

Now he's a vegetable. So sad; so very sad. My sister Lu, I think I told you, has left her work to lovingly care for him full time. She's wonderfully patient with him."

"I'm sorry to hear that about your dad, Su. Does that mean you know something of carpentry, too?" I asked.

"Actually, I helped my dad on some of his projects, during the summer vacations from school. Lu wouldn't do that, but I thought it was interesting. I liked it. Thinking about your place, Artie, I do imagine it's way to hell too much for one guy to accomplish, in just a couple of days a week. There should be a large contractor's crew tackling all that. Wow! The plumbing and the electric alone; that's gotta be overwhelming right there," Su Chi said.

"Well Su, I know it's gonna take years to get it all done, and done right," I said, "but I'm not sure I could increase my mortgage, to afford to hire a contractor. Like I said, I already have a mortgage of a hundred eighty-five grand on it."

"Artie, I believe you could get your mortgage re-financed to an amount enough to pay a contractor to get the whole job done, and done quickly for you," she said.

We stopped talking to each other because some kids were gathering around. We explained to the kids that we were Police Detectives and we were waiting for a court's permission to enter the dead man's house. Inside, we would search for evidence, even though he was murdered down the alley, instead of inside of his apartment.

Without thinking to note the times, I thought it was maybe an hour before Sergeant Snyder and Detectives Mason, Mann and Garcia came by, to also wait for the court's okay.

They told us the Medical Examiner's people had been to the murder scene. They hauled Jimmie Bob Riley's body off to their Kearney Mesa labs.

Those of Team 3 that had stayed there by the body, could find not the slightest hint of evidence of how the guy got murdered, much less, who dunnit. They had searched his pants pockets to find $244 in his wallet. It was his driver's license that said his name was Jimmie Bob Riley. They found a ring of keys in one of his pockets.

Oddly, they spotted a bulge in the dead man's crotch. Checking that, they discovered a gallon size baggie inside his shorts. Inside the big baggie were sixty or more, of tiny baggies. A test showed the powder inside them was methamphetamine. The guy was a drug dealer.

All of us Detectives were alert to the fact that this was the second dealer or distributor of very illegal drugs, to be whacked on the head… most probably, with an axet; a hatchet.

We all were very much aware of the campaign engaged in by Commander Max Macias, to warn San Diegans against using those "chemical poisons," as he put it.

Sergeant Snyder spoke up to us as we sat there, waiting.

"We of this Team must keep in mind, the luminaries that have been members of Team 3. The late Chief Jack Leslie was first a Detective and then a Sergeant on the Team, years ago. The same goes for our new Chief, Kevin Williams. Commander Max Macias, too. Also, Captain Morgan and our two Lieutenants, all got started on this glorious Team 3. We've gotta measure up, people," he said. "Yes, we've gotta measure up and solve this latest mystery."

A Police Patrol was watching over our cars, down the alley where we parked them. It really did seem longer than it actually was, to get the court's permission to enter the dead man's place and his car.

Chapter Two

With the search warrant in hand, we unlocked the two locks on Riley's entry door. Two of the Detectives unlocked his Toyota to search it.

Inside, we found a small, single bedroom, apartment. Everything looked fairly clean and tidy. We Detectives immediately began looking for hiding places. Where would he have hidden stashes of drugs and stashes of money?

The four of us were fairly accustomed to doing such searches, but we found no money at all; nor did we find any drugs.

However, Detective Martin Garcia found a checking account bank book. Wow! That was extremely unusual of someone engaging in such obviously illegal work; that is, to deposit his "earnings" in his bank account. Yet, that was what Black man Jimmie Bob Riley did. The balance shown, when he made a deposit only three days before, was $12,476.50.

Those two investigating the Camry in the back yard, had some luck. They found all of twenty-three little baggies, with the usual white powder in them. They were under the driver's seat of the car.

"Alright Team 3," our Sergeant said, "let's give this place a thorough going over before we leave here today. Check everything."

Taking over the bedroom closet, I went through all of the many pockets of pants and jackets hung up neatly there. In a sense, I hit pay dirt by finding a so-called "pocket secretary" in a sport coat inside pocket. It was a weekly diary, begun at the first of the present year, 2014. In the back of it were names, addresses and phone numbers of people. Lots of people were listed, including those named Riley in Laredo, Texas. That town was infamous for having more drugs than anywhere, smuggled to and through it, from south of the border.

To the Narcotics Section, that little book could be truly, *invaluable*. As I ventured into the living room, I spotted the end of a box, barely visible under the sofa. Pulling that box out, I saw inside that there were several pocket secretaries from previous years. Also, there were old check books. Did drug-dealing-crook Riley actually keep records for the IRS? That seemed most unlikely.

Anyway, the Narcos would have a grand time looking into the connections of this Riley with others of his clan and dozens of other people named, too.

However, nothing any of us found had so far led, whatsoever, to a killer of the wooly-headed Jimmie Bob Riley or with the balding Anthony Baines Garcia.

When we returned to Headquarters, we found the Medical Examiner had declared Riley's death was due to having been hatcheted to death. He was hit one time, with the blade going well into the brain, and that was plenty enough to do the man in.

Homicide Team 3 ended up our Saturday and the work week, with two new homicides; and nowhere near, was there a solution to them.

Detective Chi asked me to follow her Chevy Impala to her home, to have a birthday dinner. There was no need to change clothes for the occasion, she said. I told her I knew of a flower shop on the way there and that I absolutely must stop to look them over. Of course, while she waited outside in her Chevy, I bought a dozen perfect-red-roses for her and while I was at it—

what the hell—I bought a dozen, multi-colored-bouquet-of-tulips for her sister Lu.

Then, back in my car, I followed her again. I realized I had no idea where she lived. It turned out she lived in the house she grew up in, in the development called University Heights. Near the north end of Park Boulevard, she turned left on a street. In a couple of blocks, she stopped in front of a nice house and got out of her car. I parked behind her and got out, too. Most of the houses with their lawns and flower beds there, were well taken care of, including the Chi's, as I saw.

There was no university anywhere near University Heights. But the developers of that area many years before now, supposed the San Diego Normal School—where teachers back then were taught to be teachers—would someday become a university. But when the institution grew to become a college and then a university, it was located far to the east in the city, off College Boulevard.

On the grounds now of the old Normal School—off Normal Street—are the San Diego School District administration buildings.

Su Chi let me in the house and re-introduced her sister, Lu, to me. I had met her once, some time ago. The sisters resembled each other although the older of the two, was a bit overweight.

They much exaggerated the perfection of the two bouquets as they put them in vases.

"Artie, I'd like you to meet our father," Su said.

I followed her to their dining room and there sat the father of the girls, at their table.

He was balding, quite skinny and fully dressed in a nice, clean shirt, pants and shoes. Of course, he looked to be Chinese. Sitting there, he stared straight ahead. He paid no attention at the moment to his daughters or to me. He sure looked a whole lot older than his sixty years.

"Dad, I'd like you to meet Artie Abrito," Su said.

To my surprise, he turned toward me and held out his hand.

"Artie is good man, Su says," he said.

"Thank you, sir," I said as I grasped and shook his awfully limp hand. "I'm very pleased to meet you, Mr. Chi."

Both Su and Lu expressed profound surprise that their dad spoke.

"Art, those are the first words out of him in several days," Lu Chi said. "He must have overheard what Su was telling me about you. Wow! Dad actually spoke up!"

Their father said no more after that. He sat... wouldn't you know, respectfully, *at the head of the table*... stiffly, waiting patiently to be fed. I wondered if he still could feel hungry. I watched as the girls brought food to the table... and a beautifully done birthday cake. I made a big thing of counting the candles... to be sure there were absolutely no more than twenty-eight of them on it.

What was most interesting to me was to see the two sisters, sitting on each side of the man, feed him his macaroni and cheese dinner. After he chewed a few mouths full of food, they'd hold up a glass of milk to his lips, for him to drink.

The rest of us had a salad, perfectly broiled top sirloin steaks, mashed potatoes and peas. They also provided delicious biscuits, right out of the oven... a real treat for me.

When we had all finished that food, Su lit the candles on the cake. Again, it was interesting to see the old man's reaction as he stared at the burning candles and grinned a little. I thought he might be remembering other birthday cakes, on other happy occasions, in his lifetime.

Standing up, I walked over to blow the candles out. I was handed a cake server to cut and dish out the three-layer strawberry cake. Su shared her piece of cake with her dad. He managed to chew and swallow it, but his grin and sense of recognition were gone again.

I helped Su clear the table and get the dishes rinsed and in the dishwasher.

Lu Chi brought a photo album out of her mom and dad and the girls as kids. That was fun, to see a bit of their family history. Their parents had both been good lookers.

"Artie, if you don't mind too much, I'd far rather go see your house than to go dancing tonight. Can we do that, please?" Su surprised me by asking.

"Why yes; of course," I said. "It's already dark outside, but the lights are on pretty good in that house; even in the basement. Okay Su, let's go!"

There was a little delay for Su to park her Chevy in their garage. Then she climbed into my Ford Expedition and I headed south on Park Boulevard. I turned left on University Avenue, took that to 30th Street, went south to the neighborhood called South Park (because it's south of the larger North Park, I presume). I went down an alley so I could park in my garage. The garage door opener swung up the middle door of the three doors. Lights went on inside the garage.

"Su, you see those picket-fence-type gates on each side of the garage? Those are parking spaces, too. I'm going to put up a carport on each side of the garage. They will each have an overhead door, to open with a door opener, just as the three garage doors have," I said. "The carport on the south will be open on the yard side and the chain link fence side. On the north side, the carport will be open on the yard side but be pretty much against the neighbor's six-foot high solid wood fence. Technically, I found out by City rules, that counts as being open, too."

"Wow! Hey Artie, this is a really nice garage. So that's your Mustang," she said, seeing it parked in the right-hand stall. The left-hand stall was vacant. "I can see you'll have lots of workspace in here, too."

"Yes, and that helps to make this a really good property for me; you know, that I can saw up boards and sand things out here, instead of getting dust all over the house which I've had such a helluva time getting clean," I told her.

Actually, my house had been on the market for practically *only minutes*, when I bought it. Obviously, I was the only prospective buyer willing to clean up such an awful mess. I'm sure the house cost far less because of the trash and dirt piled up everywhere there. Perhaps no prospect besides me, realized the basement, filled solidly with stacks of cardboard and cans—which I call the first floor—could be made livable, too. I planned to turn it into guest rooms, but it could be rented out as a three-bedroom, three-and-a-half-bath apartment, as well.

We walked out of the garage into my back yard, where I told her I'd probably want to have a swimming pool and nice patio done some time far into the future.

A concrete walkway went from the garage to the eight steps up to the covered small porch, into the back of the second floor. Or, you could step to the right a little and take six steps down, to enter the first floor... which we did. I unlocked the first-floor door, turned lights on inside and showed her there wasn't much to see down there. Structurally, there was merely a five-foot-wide hallway down the middle, but only the thirty-two-inch-on-center-studs were there.

"There's the gas-fired, water-heater-furnace and an electrical panel," I said. "You'll notice the ceiling is eight feet up, which is very good. Back east, almost all houses have basements and I'd have to guess, the original owner had this one built so he could add bedrooms and so forth, for guests. But apparently, in the nearly one hundred years this has been here, it's only been used to store junk. That's what I found here; mostly stacks of cardboard and cans without end. I sold the cardboard and cans. And I filled up three rented dumpsters, cleaning up here and on the floor above," I told Su. "That included every piece of filthy furniture left by the deceased old hermit who lived here for probably fifty or more years."

"It sure is a big space, Artie," she said.

"Yes, it is, but you cannot believe how the junk accumulated over all those years. That's why I got a bargain on the place. It sure did look discouraging before. Oh well, it took an awful lot of effort, but by God, I got it done. I even had to rent a pressure washer to clean this floor and the walls. Now let's go up and I can show you what's up there," I said.

We walked out of there, I locked the door again, and we climbed six steps to ground level; then another eight steps up to the little rear porch. The porch light was of course inadequate, and I pointed out to my lovely guest, that I would be doing a lot with lighting.

Inside, I flicked a switch to light the hallway.

"Su, you see there are three magnificent doors to the left, to the kitchen, to the dining room and to the parlor. On the right side of the hall, there's that narrow door to the only bathroom in the place. Next, there's the four more beautiful mahogany doors to the four bedrooms. I haven't made any drawings yet, but I intend to change all along there to three nice-sized bedrooms. Each bedroom must have its own bathroom and a large walk-in closet.

"On the left here Su, I hope to take out this entire wall. I'll also take out the walls on each side of the dining room so, in effect, the kitchen, dining room and the parlor, will all be one great room. Taking out those dining room walls will certainly cause problems with the wooden floors, the walls and those beautiful ceilings. You see there's gorgeous cove molding all around.

"Here, let's look in the kitchen," I said, opening the hall door to that room. "I think these cabinets can be refinished and repaired and used in the basement kitchen. They appear to be solid mahogany, like almost every other thing of wood here. But I don't think they built kitchens way back in 1925 so complete as these cabinets are. These must be from the '70's. That refrigerator isn't very old… the stove isn't either. So, this kitchen can be transferred to become the first-floor kitchen. But that's a way off, for when I have both the time and the money to do those things," I admitted.

Next, I opened the door to the truly beautiful dining room which was absolutely barren of furniture. I ate from a second-hand stool at a kitchen counter.

We walked through a door to the parlor. It was almost empty also, but I did have a sizeable sofa and a small bookcase, jammed full of books with some books lying on top of it. The most striking feature here was the fireplace and Su actually gasped at the sight of it.

"That has got to be the most gorgeous fireplace I've ever

seen," she said, staring at it and the large window to the right, looking onto the front porch.

"Yes, it is," I said. "Especially, the mahogany mantle and those two twisted solid mahogany pillars holding it up. I don't like the idea of burning wood in there, because doing that has burned a lot of houses down and it pollutes the atmosphere. I'll convert it to a gas flame which is just as cheery and pretty as burning wood. Besides, you don't have to split gas and pile it up and sweep up that damned sawdust and ashes."

"Artie Abrito," she said with a huge smile on her beautiful face, "I absolutely adore your house already. I love it. I love it. But what challenges you face, to make it your dream home… your dream home and whoever it might be that you bless, to make your wife. You know you could do with a little help here."

"Oh yes; I know that," I said, while wondering if she was giving me a hint. I sure hoped she was. "But you know what, since Angela left… and I'm so glad she did… since she left, I've not dated one time. Not a single time. I've been hoping Su, that you and I… well, I've hoped you and I could hit it off. You are so wonderfully beautiful… and so easy to love."

She took me by surprise as she closed the small distance between us. She closed her eyes, pursed her lips… and I smothered her with kisses and heartfelt hugs.

"Su Chi, I tell you honestly," I said as I came up for a breath of air, "I have never really been in love before just now. *Su darling, I love you!*" I blurted.

We stood there kissing again and again. By and by, she kind of pulled away and asked me which of the bedrooms I was using just then?

We were soon in the room I had furnished with a used—but clean—full-size bed, a dresser and a chair. We paid no attention to the chair; nor to the dresser; just to the bed which accommodated us nicely when our clothes were off. It was heaven for me, to be between those perfect legs.

After the first of our love making, Su called her sister Lu, to tell her she would not be home that night. She spent only a few minutes on the phone, but enough to say her sister must see my place. She actually suggested Lu might bring her dad over; that he might be reminded of his carpenter days.

It seemed so pathetic to me, that she would have the forlorn hope that her father might be enough "with it" to enjoy seeing a carpenter's project. I had read somewhat about Alzheimer's, just out of curiosity, for I knew of no one personally who had that worst of diseases. There was no cure for it and as yet, no promise even of a future cure. When the mind is gone, it's gone.

Su seemed insatiable in bed and I could not get enough of her either. We hardly slept. The wonder is, our lips were still in place by morning.

We showered together in the tub behind a cheap plastic curtain. Washing her perfectly perfect body was sheer joy. We toweled each other dry and put our clothes back on.

"Ah, 'tis my turn to do the honors, darling girl," I said and hurried to the kitchen to make scrambled eggs, bacon and waffles in the toaster. Su made the coffee. We ate ravenously right there at the kitchen counter, sitting on a couple of used stools I got at a thrift store.

"I've gotta admit something, dear one," I said. "In the months I've lived here, I've been fairly well satisfied with the way things are, once I cleaned everything. But now, with the absolutely, positively, wonderfully love of my life to please, I've gotta get this place fixed up and do it right away. Monday, I'll look into getting a much larger mortgage and take your advice. I'll hire a contractor; that is, I will if I can get enough of a loan."

"You seem like you're kinda, sorta, getting serious about me," she said with a small grin.

"Serious? You imagine I might be getting serious about you?" I exploded. "I'll tell you how serious I've already got about you, darling Su. I love you… (and I dropped to one knee on the floor in front of her) and I want with all my heart to marry you and love you forever and forever! That's how serious…"

The beauteous one leaped off the stool and fell into my arms.

"Oh Artie, I love you with all my heart, too! Yes! Yes! I want to be your wife!" she said and oddly, tears were soon on her lovely cheeks.

After a few minutes of being kissed fervently, she pulled away. "I've gotta confess a couple of things, dear one," she said. "I didn't think to take a pill, like all young women do these days. I've had no need for birth control for a long time. So, be forewarned. You might be on the way to being a papa of some little wavy-haired kiddies. Also, I must admit… that I fell in love with you immediately when you saved me, from God knows what, with that giant mad man you knocked down and cuffed up."

"Okay, I instantly got feelings for you, too. And I sure do hope you're gonna make me a papa!" I said. "Do we have to decide just now whether we want a full dozen or just a half dozen little Abritos around?"

"Well now; aren't you the ambitious one," she said. "I think we ought to consider just one kid at a time. Okay my love?"

Still sitting on the kitchen floor with me, she turned serious.

She said, "You know I have a really sticky problem, dear. It isn't fair to have my sister totally responsible for our dad's care. He's mine too. At it is, she bathes him in the shower while she showers, too. She has to do that every day because he messes himself. She has to put him on the toilet and even wipe his butt. Imagine, she even has to hold his peter down, so he doesn't pee all over. She dresses him and he's got so now, that he doesn't under-stand how to help her do anything whatsoever.

"She feeds him, takes him for a walk everyday… and that's getting really difficult to do. I only help out by watching over him when she goes shopping or to a movie or something. Mostly, she's confined to the house and has only the television for company. I treasure Lu. She's is so very devoted to our dad."

"This may be an awful question, but do you girls have any idea of how long he might yet live? You don't have to answer that if you don't want to," I said.

"No Artie, that's okay. We don't really know but we both… and our doctor… think he can't last much longer. Some patients last for more years than our dad. He's getting worse every day,"

Su said. "Dammit Artie, it really is difficult to realize that just a couple of years ago, he was a loving, very hard-working, intelligent and even dynamic man. It is so very sad to see him as though he is nothing anymore," she said with tears wetting her cheeks.

Of course, I embraced her, feeling her pain in the decline of her father.

We got up and I showed her the front porch. All of the porch floor needed to be covered. It hadn't rotted since it was redwood. Some of the railing needed attention and perhaps replacement. The steps too, were not in good shape. In looking around, she noted that not a single flower was growing in the yard. I had, however, mowed the lawn consistently and the grass was in fair shape. The old hermit who had lived here, hired a gardener to care for the grass only.

"Artie," she said, "why don't we drive over to pick up my sis and dad and have them see our home to be? I'd like Lu to see it and it's possible, my carpenter dad might take notice of things."

We did just that and we found her sister to be enthusiastic about my and Su's future home. Her father, poor thing, had no idea where he was. He had zero interest in his surroundings and one of the girls had to hold onto and guide him, step by step. Both of them had to help him up and down stair steps. He seemed to have declined even from the day before, his daughters said.

We treated sister Lu and their dad to sandwiches and sodas for lunch. Shortly after that, Su helped Lu get their dad into Lu's car, and buckle him in. Su said she would gather up some clothing, etc., and drive her Chevy back. I gave her a garage door opener so she could park in the remaining stall back there; of course, she got house keys as well. It seemed so very natural that she would move in with me immediately… and stay forever.

That very night, Su convinced me that the 1925 Craftsman "bungalow"—as she called it—was certainly a treasure and deserved to have professional planning and construction. She knew of a young architect who was recently licensed and might enjoy applying his talents to such a project.

But all of that shouted out big bucks, to me. I worried about getting financing. Su seemed to think it would not be a problem at all. Well, we'll see about that, dream girl, I said to myself.

"Artie darling," she purred, "when do you think we should get married?"

"Get married?" I asked as though surprised. "Darling girl, I assumed we already are! Oh, but yes, I know there ought to be some sort of official ceremony. Hey! I would really love to have my entire family here for the occasion. Wow! Won't they be amazed to see what a perfect and beautiful prize I got for a bride! Oh, and all six of them are fully tied up with their restaurant in Chicago except for Sundays and Mondays. We could schedule it for those days. Ah, where would you like to have it happen, honey?"

"Why not in Las Vegas? I've been there to attend weddings twice, with friends. It was really quite touching, and those wedding chapels do the ceremony nicely," Su said.

"Sounds like a good idea to me," I said. "What about your side of the family?"

She said she had uncles, aunts and cousins in San Francisco and in Taiwan. That island nation off the coast of China was where her grandparents, on both sides, had come from. The family had been anti-communist and a part of Chiang Kai-Shek's forces. They had fled from Mao Che Tung's communist forces and mainland China in 1949. She thought it would be difficult for those on Taiwan to attend, but some of the San Franciscans surely would.

"I would not have told you this at all," she said, "but now that you've actually proposed marriage and declared your love for me, I have a secret. It's that my dad bought a couple thousand bucks worth of shares in Jeff Bezos' Amazon.com. That was when Bezos first began to sell books online. You probably know, Bezos hasn't paid dividends, but rather, has put the company's profits into expanding the company.

"Anyway, the stock has increased in value, incredibly, by some four thousand percent, I've heard. My sister has been given our house and I've been given that Amazon stock, by our dad. He did that when he knew his mind was going. The house is worth about

$500,000 and I don't know what the stock is worth; but it might be worth as much as the house, although I don't follow the market very much.

"I don't think I should sell the stock. From what I've heard, it will continue to grow in value. But I could use it as collateral for a loan, to help pay for fixing our house. What do you think about them apples, my man?" she asked with a huge grin.

"I'm grateful darling," I said, "that you already call this place, *our house*. Okay, we can see what develops there, although I could in no way, have expected you had some wealth. Also, I'm pretty sure the Police Department policy is such, that you and I can't work together. I suppose the thought is, that could cause personnel problems. One of us will almost certainly be transferred."

"Okay, we'll see about that on Wednesday," she said.

"You know what honey?" I asked. "I think you and I ought right now, to go find a suitable engagement ring… the whole set… for you and me."

She agreed to that instantly and we jumped into my pretty little Mustang and took in the jewelry stores in both Mission Valley Shopping center and at Fashion Valley. By the time one was found that we both liked a lot, we knew something about carats and prices and solid gold, gold-filled or gold-plated. Even so, the dainty little ring with the largish diamond, fitted to her finger, set me back over three hundred bucks; that included matching wedding rings.

But what mattered to me entirely, was that she was wonderfully pleased with those rings and inspected them lovingly, again and again.

We were planning to go out for a celebratory dinner when my phone rang, and I saw it was Sergeant Ray Snyder calling. No way, would I ignore his call.

"Yes, sir Sergeant!" I said into the phone. "What's up?"

"Art, I'm awfully sorry to trouble you on your day off, but we've had a double homicide today, in broad daylight, in City Heights. Two drug dealers have been hatcheted. Two of them! I'll give you the address if you'll come. I'll call the rest of the Team also," Snyder said.

"Sergeant, you won't have to phone Su Chi; she's with me. Give me the address and the two of us will get there as fast as we can," I said.

The Sergeant told me where to go and said Patrol Officers were standing by at the scene. Also, the Medical Examiner's office had been notified. Snyder would be there himself soon.

Luckily, Su had brought a couple of business suit outfits over from her house. I changed into my suit and tie also, and we were soon on our way in my Ford Expedition to City Heights.

The homicides happened at each end of a long alley.

The first victim seemed to have been seated on a milk bottle box, facing the street. He had apparently been waiting for a drug customer to come by as he sat there. Someone had obviously come from inside the alley, behind the man, and buried his hatchet down into the man's brain. The man pitched forward onto the concrete sidewalk and moved not an eye lash after that.

Incredibly, that was in broad daylight. However, no one admitted seeing that happen, so far.

Leaving Detective Su Chi there, with Detectives Garcia and Mann, I got back in my car and went down to the other end of the alley to where a group of Police Officers and Detectives were standing around. It was so very strange, in that the man who was face down on the sidewalk, had apparently been hatcheted from behind just like the other victim was. I imagined quickly, that it had possibly been two different hatcheteers. Again, the victims were said to be drug dealers.

Our Commander Max Macias, on television, had painted such people to be the scum of humanity, selling "poisonous chemicals," which were obviously dangerous to the user's health and even to their lives. It was hardly any wonder that dealers in those illegal chemicals called drugs, were not much cared about. But murdering them with a hatchet? To those of us enforcing the laws, homicidal hatcheting was not a recommended procedure.

"Hello, Sergeant," I said to Ray Snyder, standing next to the dead man. Detective Ray Mason was also there, along with a couple of Patrol Officers whose cars blocked entrance to the alley from the street.

"'Morning Art," Snyder said. "It certainly is a remarkable thing, to have two practically identical homicides on each end of an alley. And to have it happen in daylight, with innocent people nearby. I'm guessing, those guys with the hatchets, must have hidden themselves some way in each place. Maybe they were parked in a car.

"When they saw no witnesses around to see what they were doing, they snuck up to a spot behind the victims and sank their hatchet in their heads. Possibly though, one guy, with a car or even a goddamn bicycle, might have done it. Okay, you two Detectives are very smart, and I'd like to have you figure how it was done. Most especially, what sort of suspect could we look for, in these four hatchet homicides."

Mason didn't offer anything, so I spoke up.

"Sergeant, what I cannot imagine in these four homicides, is what the hatcheteer did with his hatchet, before and after he used it. Could he have carried it in his hand, ready for use? That seems unlikely. How about after sinking the blade of the hatchet into someone's brain? It would have been bloody, at the least. Okay, so did he have a backpack to carry it in? That's possible. So, all we have to do, is arrest every guy and gal in town, running about with a backpack on."

"Oh sure, Art; but that's not funny," Snyder said. "You've got a point there, though. No one would want their hatchet to be seen, at any time. It occurred to me to check every store in town, to find out who bought a hatchet. But hell, wearing a backpack, a guy would simply steal one off a hardware wall and stick it in his backpack. There must be thousands of those damn hatchets in San Diego; never mind the suburbs."

"My pa has an old hatchet; so has my grandpa," Mason told us. "Both of them have fireplaces and they chop kindling wood with their hatchets. I don't have a wood-burning fireplace; it's gas one; therefore, I don't have need for hatchet in my house."

"Another way it could be carried," I offered, "would be to simply shove the handle down inside of one's pants, with the blade holding it up atop the belt. He could cover it with his shirt tail or his jacket. If he didn't mind getting somebody's blood and brain matter on his pants and himself, that would be a simple way to keep it hidden. A guy could walk with a hatchet stuck down his pants… but no, I don't think you could peddle a bike with one there."

"Or he could hide the damn thing in his car," Detective Mason said. "That is surely what he does. He pulls up behind someone, he slips out of his car with his hatchet in hand, clobbers the guy and gets back in with his hatchet. That seems to me what had to have happened here in this alley, this Sunday."

Looking down the alley, we could see the Medical Examiner's van parked there. They were loading the body of that victim in the van. Within a few minutes, they had driven over to us, where the second victim still laid, face down on the sidewalk.

The Sergeant of Team 3 had already gone through all the pockets of the drug-dealer-victim by us. He found a five-shot mini-revolver of .22 caliber in one pocket. Another pocket held a wad of money which when counted, amounted to $282. Another pocket held his wallet and eleven little baggies with white powder in them. The wallet had no money in it, but did have his driver's license and importantly, the address of his apartment. Another pocket held a ring of keys, including a key to a nearby, parked Nissan sedan.

"I've already called in for search warrants for the apartments and cars of both victims," our Sergeant said. "This being a Sunday, the okay might come through quicker, as I've had it done in the past. Garcia, Mann and Chi will check out that guy's place while we check out this guy's here."

The victim on the other end of the alley was a short Mexican, here legally or not.

Of course, many, many photographs were made of the victim and the scene, as was always done at each homicide.

The one on our end was a Black man; a really, really big Black man. He looked to stretch out to about six-foot-six inches, so that made me wonder if his assailant was also very tall, to bludgeon him as he did. I'm merely five-feet-eight inches tall; could someone my height, have hatcheted that very tall man effectively, if the victim was standing? Oh, I thought it could be done. There was nothing there for the Black guy to sit on, except for his butt; maybe he stood while his head was split like a chunk of fireplace wood.

While we waited for the search warrant from the court, with the body gone, we cleaned up the blood and bit of brains on the sidewalk. Presumably, they would do the same on the other end of the alley.

Finally, the okay was given by a court and we three got in our cars and drove down the alley to the other part of Team 3 to let them know, also. They would go to an address on Wightman Street in City Heights. We would drive to an address on 36th Street, which might actually be in North Park. But first, we had to inspect the drug dealer's cars, both of which were parked at the curb, on the streets. Of course, Narcotics Section Detectives had been called and were present for the openings of the two cars. We'd be looking for guns and they'd be looking mostly for drugs. Also, two tow trucks were at the ready, to take those cars to the Police Impound lot.

Chapter Three

The Black man's Nissan car was clean on the outside and on the inside. There was not the usual wrappers and debris found in so many cars these days. Going through his glove compartment, the title and license papers were in order. There was a car manual too, and I looked to see he remarkably entered oil change and service records from the time he had bought it new.

In the glove compartment also, however, was a Glock-like semi-automatic pistol; although by a name I had not heard of. There were two extra magazines of ammos there too, as though he expected he could get in a gun battle. I didn't see any such thing as a license to carry that weapon, though; nor for the little .22 caliber weapon found in the man's pocket.

The Narcos guys found more baggies of drugs; they were in the center console. The trunk contained a spare tire only. Then the tow truck hauled the Nissan away. Later, the Narcotics Section guys would have a trained dog sniff around the car. If the dog smelt something, the car could very well be torn apart to get the drugs out.

We three drove over to north of University on 36th Street, with a Narcos Detective riding along, to find the dead man's apartment occupied by a White woman and a kid of about a year and a half. I judged the age by the way the little mixed-race boy waddled around his house.

Sergeant Snyder quickly told the woman about the man being killed. She instantly insisted she was his wife and the child was that man's also. The lady was way to hell overweight and her hair was obviously bleached blonde. Otherwise, her face was fairly pretty. Her blue eyes were large, but she painted her eyebrows on. She cried as though she might never stop. I was sure, from her appearance and demeanor, she was a drug addict. Poor woman. Poor child. That little boy would not likely have much of a life. Do druggies consider such consequences of their taking into their bodies the "lots of fun and harmless" chemicals sold on the streets?

The Sergeant somehow got through the woman's cries to tell her we were authorized to inspect the premises for drugs… and of course, we'd look for the money profited from drug sales.

Although the bleached blonde objected strenuously to our searching the place, we of course did it anyway. We found a stash of drugs, needles, tiny scales, spoons, and other drug paraphernalia in the top drawer of the bedroom dresser. Search as we might, we found no cash at all, and no hint of a bank account, nor a credit card account. No such information was found in the dead man's wallet, either.

The woman of the house would have to crawl to an agency and get welfare for herself and her child. She would only get supplies of drugs for her addiction, by prostituting herself, I supposed. The man's car would be confiscated also, so she would not have that, either.

It was pretty late on that February day when we were done with our work in our office. We told our Sergeant and the others that Su and I were now officially engaged to be married.

"Uh oh," Sergeant Snyder told us, "You may not realize it, but you cannot then be in the same Police outfit. Regulations won't allow it."

"Frankly Sergeant," Su said, "I had a notion that was the way it was. Maybe I'll just give Commander Macias his wishes and go to work at Elder Care as he wanted me to do. If I do, he said he'd promote me to Sergeant, and I should always wear my best clothing on the job."

"Honey," she said, looking at me, "I'll try to get the same work schedule as we have now. I think I can do that, so we'll have the same days off."

"Well hey guys, you do have our heartfelt congratulations!" Detective Mann said. "When's the wedding going to be?"

"David, we've not set a date just yet," I said. "But we'll be sure to let everyone know. By the way, Su suggested we tie the knot in Las Vegas. I'm sure my family will fly out from Chicago for that and we can all have some fun there. But right now, Su and her sister have a terrible problem in that their darling father has Alzheimer's disease and it has progressed terribly. That has to be our very first concern. Her sister is such an angel, in caring for their dad."

With that, we got in our—I found myself already calling my house and my cars, *ours*—Ford Expedition and drove to our garage. Dang it, it was already dark when we parked. I sure was glad our garage had three stalls.

A couple of friends of mine, married for many years, habitually ordained every single thing the two of them owned, as "Mine." They often got a new Cadillac, for example, and although it surely belonged to both of them, each of them said, "It's my Cadillac." They never even talked of their house as belonging to *them*; oddly, it was always, "My house."

Inside the house, I felt rather embarrassed to have so little furniture. But at least, our house was finally sparkling clean and trash-free. It suddenly occurred to me that we were rather shy of food in the kitchen, so I suggested we go out for dinner and then go grocery shopping.

We finally had a celebratory "engagement dinner" had it at the excellent Tom Ham's, on Harbor Island. After that, we shopped at a Ralph's Grocery and brought home several bags of food and drink. We watched the news for a while and could hardly wait, to "hit the sack!"

Monday morning, February 3rd, 2014, she was able to contact the young architect she had known, through her father's carpentry business. He told her he couldn't get to see us until the following Monday. But in the meantime, he said we should make a very, very extensive list of what we hoped to get done with our house. He would take it from there, he said.

So that is exactly what Su and I did all day and into the night, Monday and Tuesday. We also visited with her sister Lu to help with their father and to give Lu some time away from that house. I mowed their lawn, front, sides and back.

Su has a good video camera and she took endless views of our house, the way it is now.

We made notes on a lined tablet, that we would later edit and put on our computer to print neatly for the architect's use. Much of my concern was matching flooring and cove moldings when the dining room walls, and the hall walls were taken out. While we were at it, I asked for the design and contracting for three guest rooms, bathrooms and storerooms on our first floor. Also, there should be alarms and alarm lights on the front and back of the house and on the garage. All of the lighting inside and outside of the house, should be updated, we noted.

And what about preventing fires by having non-flammable insulation, for instance?

I described in detail also, how I wanted the two carports built, onto the garage sides.

Both Su and I asked Lu to bring their dad over for a Tuesday night dinner, but Lu refused. She said her dad was almost impossible to do anything with. He seemed even to have forgotten how to chew and swallow his food. She even had an awful time getting him to drink.

Both of the girls cried and cried, because their father had become worse than a zombie.

We returned to work on Wednesday and Commander Mathias had already been informed of Su's wish to return to the Elder Abuse Unit. He welcomed her there and promoted her to Sergeant with much good cheer. And the Commander congratulated me in winning the heart of a truly wonderful woman.

Once again, Homicide Team 3 was short one Detective. But luckily for us just then, there were no more hatchet homicides to deal with… not until Saturday morning.

That murder had occurred in the wee hours of Saturday, we found out. And again, it had happened in City Heights, *and in the drug-dealing victim's house.* This time it was a woman who had her head split open. Her wooly black hair was short on the top of her head, so we could see the usual hatchet wound there.

She was discovered dead by her Black father, when he got up that morning, ready to go to work. We found out he was fifty-one years old.

The victim's dad seemed like a regular guy. He had worked as a city bus driver for twenty-one years so far, he told us Detectives. He owned his home; the mortgage was paid off. He said his wife had become addicted to heroin and had overdosed and died, about six years before. Their daughter, to the man's utter disgust, had used drugs also, because of her mom. He assured us that he had no idea, that she peddled the evil stuff.

Yet there she lay, just inside the house, in the living room, with the top of her head split wide open. The blood on her head and on the white vinyl flooring was drying and it looked awful. She was fully clothed, stretched out on the floor, with her face twisted as though yet in pain.

The man's house was small, with two little bedrooms, one bathroom, and a quite nice and clean kitchen. There was a large coffee table in front of the big TV screen… it seemed, that was where they dined.

Sergeant Snyder asked the man about his daughter and the man let loose with his disappointments with her.

"Detective, I tried my best to raise the girl. Her mom wasn't very good at raising a kid. She just didn't give a damn. We only had this one here, thank the Lord. She was good in school until she got to be about sixteen. That's when, I guess, she started with those damn drugs, and she quit school.

"Even after her mom died, practically right there in front of her, would my little girl not give up shoving those damn needles in her arms. I sure didn't feel like turning her in to you Coppers. I thought she'd get tired of that life and get to hell away from that damn dope," he said. "Why hell, I don't think she ever had a real steady boyfriend; just junkies, like her."

"Okay sir, what's her name and how old is she?" Snyder asked.

"She's Jeannie Susan Jones and she just turned twenty-two. Just twenty-two, and she's dead already!" he said as he began for the first time, to cry.

Detective Martin Garcia wrapped his arms around Mr. Jones, trying to comfort the man. He walked the man into the kitchen, where the body of his daughter wasn't visible.

I heard him tell Garcia softly, "Now I'm never gonna have any grandchildren!"

Detective Ray Mason and I went into the girl's bedroom and found it a disorderly place. Her bed was a tangled mess with most of the covers and a pillow, on the floor.

Right out in the open, was a wide, shallow bowl on her dresser, filled with hypodermic needles. Some needles seemed new and others had been used. We found a stash of baggies containing white powder, right there in the top dresser drawer. Her wide-open purse with a wallet inside, was also atop the dresser. Opening that, showed she had three twenties, one fiver and three one-dollar bills. She had not done well, selling those "lots of fun and harmless" chemicals.

Her cell phone was also in her purse. We would turn that over to the Crime Lab, for the forensics of the Narcotics Section. They would find who she had called and who had called her. Or, in the secret world of the druggies, they would find phone numbers that might or might not be traced to individuals. They might find calls to and from her customers... *and most importantly, her drug suppliers.*

Ray Mason and I spent some time looking into her mess in a closet and we saw another disorderly place under her bed. At the age of twenty-two, the lady was certainly a troubled one. But with that hatchet plunging down into her brain, she had troubles no more… and no more the joys of life nor the joys of love.

The Crime Scene Investigators as usual, searched for fingerprints that could not be identified with either of the house's occupants. But it did in time seem to prove, that the killer had come in, buried the hatchet in the young woman's head, he or she yanked the hatchet out of there, and left. They could not find anything that proved to have been touched by the hatcheteer.

This was the fifth homicide with an axet and we still did not have the slightest hint of who was committing them. Nor, did we have a motive; except of course, that the killer had to hate drug dealers, even to the least of them, as was Ms. Jones.

The most valuable thing we came away with in this investigation, was probably the woman's smart phone. Finding out who she called and who called her, including possibly the hatcheteer, could be rewarding for both the Narcotics Section and the Homicide Detail.

When we five trooped into our Homicide Detail area, Lieutenant Brightwell called all of us into her office.

"Please shut the door, Martin," she said to Detective Garcia, who was the last to enter.

We crowded ourselves onto the sofa, facing the Lieutenant, seated behind her desk. Co-Commander Lieutenant Alan had that day and the previous two days off.

"Thanks for coming in, you Team 3 people," she said. "First, Sergeant Snyder, I want to know if, after five of these homicides by hatchet, you have any idea who could be doing it."

"Ma'am, to tell you the truth," Snyder answered, "we don't have the slightest idea yet, who could be committing these homicides. Obviously though, it's someone who hates drug dealers enough to risk being in prison for the rest of his or her life, for murder. I think it's almost gotta be a man doing it, because of the strength needed to whack the head so deeply as he does.

"The fifth victim, that we saw in City Heights today, looks to me to have been struck by the hatchet from in front of her. All four of the others, we were told by the Medical Examiner, were hatcheted from behind. Mostly they were sitting. The woman killed today, apparently was standing, when she was hit.

"I've gotta say, Lieutenant Brightwell, that would take some doing. I mean, surely the victim should've seen the blow coming; so why would the hatchet still hit in the middle of the top of her head, with the wound lined up front to back. Why wouldn't the wound at least be at an angle and not so well-centered? Maybe the killer is extremely tall. That's possible. But ma'am, I am so very sorry to say, that's all we know so far. Oh; which is to say really, that we hardly know a damn thing in this case."

"Thanks for that," she said, nodding to the Sergeant. "Despite the despicable characters being killed in this hatcheting series, we all in this Detail are pledged to bring every murderer to justice, that we possibly can. That includes somebody carrying a damn hatchet around, in their backpack, or even stuffed down the front of their pants, as Art says it could be carried."

She grinned at me as she said that, clearly indicating she had no faith in my idea.

It occurred to me that I should bring in a hatchet to show how it could be done, with the shirt tail hanging out to hide the head of it, in the waist band... but I didn't own a hatchet. I had a few tools in my garage, but no hatchet. I just let that remark slide.

Martin Garcia was by far the tallest Detective on our Team. He thought it was a real possibility, that the hatchet wielder was unusually tall and could therefore bring the blade of a hatchet down exactly as he wished.

"Fellows," the Lieutenant said, "I'm going over right now to the Crime Lab to find out what they've done, with the five victims' phones they should have analyzed by now. Sergeant Snyder, please come with me. We've gotta get some solutions to these mysteries."

The meeting broke up then and I went back to my desk to puzzle more and more, about the hatchet homicides. Without the perp slipping and leaving a fingerprint, I had not the foggiest idea what would lead us to the killer. We needed a lucky break. We needed a witness.

Just before time to shove off for our three days off, Sergeant Snyder came by to let me know, the phones we captured were devoid of any worthwhile numbers. The phones were used sparingly anyway, and mostly for ridiculously idle chit-chat which could be expected of those whose minds had been well scrambled with those awful poisons.

Every single one of the dealers whose phones we had, were wary of leaving information on their phones, that might be useful to the Narcos people or to any of "their enemy," the Police.

After parking my Mustang in my garage, I came in the back door to my house to see my Su standing in the hall, as though in shock. She had already changed to a flowery dress.

"Oh honey, Lu just phoned me to tell me our dad just died. She's calling the Police now. Would you mind if we go over there to be with her, please?" she asked.

"Of course, sweetheart," I said. "We knew this was coming. Poor Lu; we've gotta help your darling sister as much as we can."

We got in the Mustang and we pulled up to Lu Chi's house in pretty quick order.

Walking into the living room of that house, we saw Mr. Chi laying crumpled up on the floor, near their sofa, as though he was heading there but didn't make it. I thought it had to have been a heart attack. I checked and he had no pulse. His daughters, Lu and Su stood by a wall, embracing each other and sobbing as though they might never stop. I found myself with tears in my eyes, responding to their tears.

Feeling that I just had to give it a try, I immediately rolled the man over on his back. I began pumping his chest, as I had over the years, done for at least a dozen other men and women. And oh yes, for two little kids that I saved. Whether the girls were watching, I didn't know or care. I simply kept up the work on his chest, without actually expecting results.

Su and I had been there for probably ten minutes before a Patrol car pulled up out front. The two Officers knocked on their door and someone let them in. As I continued pumping, I told the Officers that both Su and I were also Officers.

"The Medical Examiner people will be here shortly," one of the Officers said to the girls. "What would you like to do with your dad's body?"

Lu tried to get control of herself but didn't do well. Su spoke up, then.

"My father, after our mother's death two years ago, got prepared for his passing. He pre-paid for cremation service, just as he did for our mom. Should we call them now?"

"No ma'am," the Officer said. "We must wait for the Medical Examiner's people to examine the body first. Then I would think, you should call the crematorium."

Having delivered CPR for well over ten minutes with not the slightest response, I stopped.

To my surprise, both of the girls seemed in control of themselves by then… perhaps because of the two Officer-strangers in the house.

In about another half hour, the Medical Examiner's van pulled up outside and a very tall woman and a tall man came in, pulling a gurney into the house.

None of us wanted to look to see what the examination consisted of, so we went into the dining room to sit down. I offered to bring the sisters each a glass of water and they acted grateful for that bit of thoughtfulness.

The tall woman examiner came into the room and, since someone told her I was a Detective, asked me if I had anything to do with trying to solve the mystery of the hatcheted people.

"Actually ma'am," I replied, "I'm on the Homicide Team looking into those mysteries."

"Well, I ain't gonna wish you good luck on solving it, because those sons-a-bitches, they deserve to be killed. I hope whoever hero is doing it, does all of them in!" she said and turned to go back to the dead body.

Before she got away, I asked her name and what she did in the MedEx lab.

"Oh me?" she asked, pointing to herself. "Hell, I'm Nancy

Monroe and I've been with the lab a lot of years. Just lately, I've begun to pick up bodies, like today."

"Thanks ma'am," I said. "I just hadn't seen you before."

Not only was she a big and tall woman, even with her wearing slacks, I could see she had what some guys call, "piano legs"; they were unusually big around.

"Detective Abrito," the other examiner came in and said to me, "it appears Mr. Chi had a heart attack. We must take him in to find out for sure. I can see the man was not in good shape."

"These ladies' father had Alzheimer's for about two years and for the last little while, he was practically a living-dead-man. He got so he could not remember how to eat or drink. It looks to me as though he simply stumbled; he stumbled, he fell and he died," I told him.

"I'm sure you're right, Detective," he said. "Even so, we've gotta take him in for further examination. Have you any objections to that?"

"Oh no; of course not," I said. "Then the daughters should notify their crematorium about where the body will be, eh?"

"Yes Detective; that is correct," the MedEx man said.

Then he and the Monroe woman with him, lifted Mr. Chi up and over onto the gurney, raised the gurney up and wheeled the body out to their van.

I went back into the dining room, to be with the sisters.

"For as long as I live," I said to them, "I shall never forget the great loving care you girls had for your dear father. I am so very much in awe of you, Lu, that you actually left your job to care for him so faithfully as you did. I shall sincerely be proud to be a part of your family, as soon as Su and I can tie the knot.

"Now then, why don't we go over to Su's and my house and whip up some bit of dinner?" I asked. "We have three kinds of ice cream for dessert!"

That brought a weak smile to Su, but not to sister Lu. In fact, Lu got up off her chair and dashed right over to me. She hugged me tightly.

"Art, you won't mind too much if I stay at your house for a

couple of days, will you?" she asked in a whisper by my ear… as though it could be a secret.

"Of course, you can stay with us, Lu," I said, looking at Su so she'd know.

"Well sis," Su spoke up at last, "we both know you've been through a terrible ordeal. Okay, a bit of time will get you relaxed like your old loving self. Our father, we both know, is infinitely better off now than he was, no matter how much we loved him. Okay, let's lock up the joint and get rolling," she said, trying to show good cheer.

Su decided to ride with Lu… and Lu asked her to drive. I saw Lu also had a Chevy Impala like Su's, but hers was blue while Su's was white. I later learned their dad had bought those cars for his daughters, because, he had said, they were the best-looking cars for the money.

Their hard-working and excellent father, had left Lu with a valuable house, all paid for and for Su, Amazon.com stock, worth some thousands of bucks.

The girls followed me, driving my Mustang. I felt badly that most adults have a miserable time sitting in my cramped back seat. Ford built the car as though for little kids back there. But then, without back doors, it would be difficult to put children in seats there and buckle them in safely. Right then, on the way home, I decided to sell my Mustang and only drive the huge Ford Expedition, which could haul eight adults comfortably.

There was a few grand in my bank account, but it would be good to have more in there. Mostly, my account was swelled from selling the tons of cardboard the old hermit had hoarded. I actually was paid $3,200 just for that recyclable cardboard. Other trash and junk that I got rid of, brought me less than a $1,000.

When I got to our garage, I got out, opened the third door and waved the blue Impala in. I parked the Mustang in the twelve-foot space between the garage and the bad wooden fence along the top of the canyon. I wanted to replace that fence with a chain-link fence that could be seen through.

To each side of the garage, there were double gates. They'd be replaced with carports. We could actually park five cars off the alley; three in the garage and two in the new carports.

Then, going up to the house, I told the girls I planned to sell the racy-looking Mustang because of the back-seat problem.

It was a good thing to see Lu helping Su get up some sandwiches for our dinner. Lu also opened a can of baked beans to go with them. We all went out into the hall and walked down to the door into the parlor. There, we spread out our dinner stuff and drinks on the coffee table, sat on the sofa and turned on the television mounted over the fireplace.

As we sat to eat, Lu began to talk for practically the first time since her dad collapsed.

"You two have gotta know," she said, "that our dad dying has got to be a tremendous big load off my shoulders. That disease he had, made him worse and worse, every damn day. I've gotta get myself back into living again. Art, maybe you and Su will please allow me to help out with your house here. I've got to be doing something useful until I get back working at Ralph's or I feel like I'll go crazy."

"Sis," Su said, "what Artie and I had planned for the next three days, was to make a really detailed list for an architect, for what we'd like to have done with the house and the yard. You could be helpful in suggesting things we might not think of. Right, Artie?"

"Hey Su," I said, "that's a very good idea. All of us ought to get our minds off the tragedy we've experienced and onto to something positive. Okay, let's begin right tonight."

We ate and more or less watched some of the news on television.

The first floor of this so-called Craftsman Style house, had an eight-foot ceiling while the second—no, I like "main" floor better —had a ten-foot ceiling. The first floor never had living space in it; it was mostly used as storage over the eighty-nine years of its existence. We would make it usable as guest rooms for visiting families and also put a pool table and other things for fun down there; both for kids and for grownups. I told them that sometime in the future, our situation might call for renting out the first floor.

"You've gotta have an old-fashioned juke box down there, for dancing," Lu surprised me by saying. "You can both count on it. I'll buy one for you to celebrate your beautiful new home!"

Wow! That sister was coming awake, at last. She was actually smiling.

"You are so very thoughtful, Lu," I said. "Thanks. I know those are expensive.

"Okay girls, let's clear away our supper stuff and I'll get a big pad to write on," I said. "Now Lu, I must admit, I probably never would have thought of a juke box. That's one very good idea. Smart gal and also, very, very nice!"

Walking down the steps at the rear of the house, and then stepping down the rest of the stairs to the first floor, presented a problem. I hadn't much troubled to think it could be done differently. I sure didn't want stairs between the two levels to take up space inside the house, on either floor. There wasn't any difficulty going up or down in fair weather; but what about during a rainstorm? You had to go outdoors now, to go between the areas.

"I know girls; we'll make a note for the architect to consider that problem. What about a laundry and cleaning items storage? There isn't one in the house now; I've just gone to a commercial laundry to wash and dry my laundry," I told them.

The concrete walls of the basement came up from the floor, only three-and-a-half-feet, inside. Outside, the concrete portion was only about half a foot above ground. For the four-and-a-half-feet yet to the ceiling inside, it was stucco over wood framing, with windows lined up with the windows above. When the house was built, they put in the framing for a hallway down the center of the first floor. But the studs were double-spaced and never covered with lath and plaster or doors. It had been like that for all of eighty-nine years.

We would have three bedrooms on the main floor, each with a bath and large, walk-in closet; it would be sensible to lay them out, exactly below. The truly beautiful mahogany hall doors to the parlor, dining room and kitchen, could be used on the bedrooms below. The lower ceiling should be insulated to reduce the transfer of noise between floors.

The first floor was not heated then. The house had no insulation in the walls or in the attic. It got cold inside the house in winter. Insulation could to be blown into the attic and the outside walls. That would have to be taken into consideration with a new and more modern gas furnace. All of the eighty-nine-years-old piping, and baseboard heaters, would have to be replaced. The floor-coverings would have to be decided and so would a great lot of lighting and ceiling fans; which were less costly than air conditioning. San Diego rarely got hot enough to warrant even such fans, let alone the great amount of expensive ducting necessary for air conditioning.

I had heard instead of big solar panels that were plopped down on roofs, solar generating shingles could be chosen in the near future. So, I hoped to wait to re-do the roofing until solar shingles were available.

There was only the one bed in my house so that night, sister Lu had to sleep on the sofa. She was up Saturday morning before Su and me and had the coffee pot happily at work.

She really did seem to be adjusting well to her new-found freedom.

Other than the girls going to get more clothing… and for Su to move everything of hers to our place… we three continued all Saturday and much of Sunday, making lists of things that we thought should be done to the house, and the yard… front, back and sides, too. I welcomed ideas for a swimming pool and a patio in back, since there was thirty feet between the house and the garage for that; and the lot was sixty feet wide. We also included questions about outdoors lighting, motion-sensing lighting and alarms.

Computers are no strangers to me, but I soon discovered my bride-to-be was a whiz at organizing and typing up our notes. Those six solid pages of notes would be printed with copies for us and for the architect we had an appointment with on Monday morning.

The roofs of the house and the garage, had a low pitch. So, the attic is low, merely six feet from the ceiling joists to the ridge board. I had rented a large vacuum with a long three-inch hose, to lay on my belly to clean the dust and animal droppings on and from between the redwood joists and even the rafters. That project alone, took fully four days, working full time.

Apparently, all of the framing of both the house and the garage, was of redwood. Redwood from those gigantic trees in northern California, would be prohibitively expensive to build with, these days. At the start of World War II however, I've heard hundreds of houses were built of redwood, for defense plant workers. That was done in San Diego's Linda Vista neighborhood.

It was in the attic that I discovered the original blueprints—covered with an inch of dust—for both the house and the surprisingly large, three-car garage. Automobiles, were in the 1920's, just then becoming widely owned. Possibly, the original owner of the house was a car dealer. He must also have come from the east, to think of having even a shallow basement under the house. Basements were rare in San Diego. I don't know why that is. Basements are a relatively inexpensive great addition to the living space and storage space for a house.

On Monday morning, February 10th, 2014, the architect showed up on schedule and I let him in to give him a tour of everything.

"My fiancé's and her sister's father died Saturday and they are right now arranging for his cremation and later, for a remembrance ceremony. But they and I have made this six-page list of what we think ought to be done. Also, I can loan you the original blueprints, if you wish," I told him. "Oh yes; we also have nearly a hundred photos of the place for you to use."

"Wow! You actually have the original blueprints of this Craftsman home? Those drawings and the photos could be an enormous help to me," he said.

"Believe it or not, I found the blueprints in the attic, between some ceiling joists, near the front gable. It was terribly dusty up there, so I spent four entire days vacuuming everything up there, including a ton of dust and getting rid of some old animal droppings," I said.

"Then there's no insulation up there?" he asked.

"Neither there nor in the walls, sir. It should be vented also. I'd like to have an exhaust fan at about the center of the ridge, including on the garage. Both buildings have louvered and screened, nicely wooden-rope-framed, circular vents, on all of the gables. You can give us an estimate of cost on certain parts of all of this. For example, we may have to put off having a swimming pool until years later," I said.

"May I ask what sort of budget you anticipate for all this, Officer Abrito?" he asked.

"When I bought the place, I happened to have a bit more than a hundred grand that I used as a down payment. My mortgage is a hundred-eighty-five-thousand and I expect to raise it by another three hundred thousand, tops. That would make the investment in the property of under six hundred grand which is, I would think, more than the value of many of the houses here in this South Park neighborhood," I told him.

"Officer Abrito, I happen to know that here in South Park, there are some few houses valued at more or less, a million bucks. You are fortunate that this old house is in such good shape. Being built of rot-proof redwood has helped with that. The roofs appear to be sound and so does the foundation and the basement floor. Well sir, I'd like to take your blueprints and your lists and make some proposals. You understand of course, I'll have to charge a fee for my efforts," he said.

"Why no sir," I said as though surprised. "I expected charity here! Come on; can you tell me your fee now and I can write out a check."

"Three thousand will cover it," he said, "and that will include inspection mid-way and on completion of the work. That will also include writing the various detailed specifications and contracts for you."

"Fair enough, I've gotta say," noting his fee was about ten percent of the work to be done.

The girls were just then coming into the first floor.

"Sir, here's my future wife and her sister. Girls, the architect and I have been going over the lists that you two and I have worked on," I said.

After introducing the women to him, we all went to the parlor. The man seemed amazed I would want to cover seven feet of the wall on each side of the fireplace, with shelves all the way to a seven-foot height, for perhaps a thousand books.

"Sir, this is an old house," I said. "I've seen pictures so very many times, of old mansions with a library full of books and that's what I want this room to be. The fireplace with that amazingly detailed mahogany work on it, is classic. Su and I will want a matching desk built for under that front window on the right there.

"We'll watch TV here and socialize here, but this room will also serve as our library. I'm a studious man and so's my Su here. I think it will be an improvement to remove the hall wall from along this room, the dining room and the kitchen, too. Eliminating that hall, will open the place on the south side here, to be five and a half feet roomier; to twenty-feet, wall to wall. The library will be the largest room; about twenty-feet-square."

"Ah yes, and that will give us a lot of mahogany to work with," the architect allowed.

Then I covered in detail, what I thought about adding long screws to the nails already in place, where two feet of 2" by 10" ceiling joists overlapped above us, and the same for floor joists below us. With the bedroom walls on both floors supporting everything above, the architect and I judged there would be more than sufficient strength. We could eliminate the halls on both floors and have much more living space.

He then added, "People, this is going to be a really fun project for me. We architects love challenges and this project sure gives me a lot of them. I can have the plans, specifications and contracts for you in a couple of weeks, I do believe."

We next went to the kitchen where Su told the man about some of the ideas she said she had to have. For one thing, she wanted a long enough kitchen island so at least six could sit at it, on one side and the ends, for breakfast and lunch. Dinners she insisted, must be eaten in the dining room.

Although it was included on the lists given him, she mentioned too, that the entire kitchen, pretty much as it was, would serve well enough, transferred to the basement. It would go exactly below, where it was then.

I suggested he might design something about the stairs going up and down and a laundry, with a broom closet in back.

The architect spent a couple of hours with us, going over the list we made and looking over everything inside and out. The only thing he missed was the attic, but I told him all he needed to know about that place.

Su accompanied her sister to Ralph's grocery store, to see if she could come back to work. Well, that sure didn't take any time; they gladly returned her to work as a trusted cashier, as she had been doing since high school, fourteen years before. She'd again be a union member and make pretty good money there. She'd also have plenty of chances to flirt with male customers there, she told us with a big smile. Wow! Lu Chi was about to be back in life again!

On Monday night, Su and I had dinner in a fine restaurant—the Hob Nob Hill—with Lu. That night, we slept in her house, too. We returned to our house and cleaned house part of the time and goofed off most of the day.

On Wednesday morning, February 12th, Sergeant Su Chi, dressed beautifully, and Detective me, dressed like a banker, were back to work.

Sergeant Snyder was interested to hear of Mr. Chi's passing. He was even more interested when I told him about the strange and quite tall woman who works in the Medical Examiner's Lab.

He was surprised that someone in that field, would be so clearly cheering for a killer.

"Very well Art," Snyder said, "what do you make of that Nancy Monroe?"

"She sure seems strange to me," I replied. "There are probably lots of people who feel the same, that killing those drug dealers is an okay thing. Damn; how the TV and the newspaper have given so much publicity to those homicides. But you know Sergeant, we have had zero clues as to who to look for in these five hatchet homicides. I wonder if we could find out more about that lab woman and maybe, just maybe, it might be a good idea to stake her out."

"Wow! That's sure as hell jumping to conclusions, Art," he said. "But hey, let's you and I go right now so you can tell the Lieutenants what you told me. They can decide what to do."

We did that very thing and both of our Commanders seemed only mildly interested.

"Tell you what, fellows," Lieutenant Brian Alan said, "I've got a secret contact in the MedEx lab. Over the years, she's been helpful to me, unofficially. With her help, I'll find out what the hell is going on. I'll call her at home tonight. By tomorrow night, we should have the scoop on that woman. It might turn out, she's an angel; she might be in fact, a wonderful person. Okay, leave it to me and I'll get the straight dope. Then we can know what to do or not."

That was it. We let it slide until the next night when the Lieutenant would meet with the woman and perhaps get some important information.

What the Lieutenant was told by a "person" supposedly knowledgeable about the Monroe woman, was that she was an especially nice woman and all of her co-workers liked her. No, she never married. She owned her own house and her mother lived with her. So, that was that.

Meanwhile, we were all glad the killings of drug dealers with a hatchet buried in their heads, had stopped at four males and one female.

Sergeant Snyder turned his four-Detective Team to fidgeting with old, cold, cases.

The case handed me was about the killing of a young wife, a couple of months before. She was shot in the back of her head and was made dead instantly. She was close to her rented house, returning from a nearby grocery store, with a bag of food, when shot.

A prime suspect by those who worked on the case, was her husband of merely a single year. She was six months pregnant when killed, and the Medical Examiner compared the DNA of the unborn child to the husband of the woman, and found the DNA matched.

The husband was most carefully watched while he was told about the matching DNA. He nodded his head and acted as though, of course, he knew he would have been the father.

It was understood then that since her husband had impregnated his wife, instead of some other man, her husband would not have that kind of motive to kill her. The woman had no insurance at all. So, getting a large life insurance payment, could not have been a motive. All he got from her death was her automobile, worth no more than three or four thousand dollars.

They knew everything, however, about the gun that killed the housewife. Whoever shot the gal, immediately dropped the gun on the sidewalk, and vanished. It was a popular .38 caliber, Ruger revolver. A single shot had been fired. The bullet was found in the front of her brain. The scoring lines on the bullet, matched the markings inside the barrel. Fingerprints on the revolver, and on the shot brass cup and the five cartridges left in the gun, had been wiped off.

The file on that case covered a large number of pages.

Checking to see who the other characters in the story were, I saw the husband was said to be, "close to his mother and his sister"; what the hell ever that meant. Neither of those two seemed to have been interviewed much. It seemed, all the previous investigators were zeroed in on the husband as the suspect, despite having not a shred of evidence against him show up.

Stepping over to my Sergeant's desk, I said, "Sir, the Marie Alexander case that I'm working on, needs to be brought up to date. I'd like permission to check on the former husband and others, to see what they're up to now."

"Ah yes; I remember the Alexander case fairly well. All of us were certain the husband killed Marie, but we could find no evidence. You've found something in the case that smells, Art? Well, go right on ahead friend, and let's see what you can add to that file," Snyder said.

As I left, I had to smile thinking the Sergeant thought, "I might add something to the file." He of course meant there was not the slightest chance, I could solve the case. But "solving the case" was what we Detectives are in fact, paid to do.

Having memorized most of the information in the Marie Alexander file, I drove up first to the Vons large grocery store on West Washington Street. I parked my Expedition there. Then I walked the two blocks south from there, to the little rented house where she and her husband had lived then.

The file gave an excellent description of where Marie Alexander was shot, a little after the sun went down. That was on Thursday, January 2nd, 2014. I found the yellow-painted fire hydrant which her bag of groceries hit as she fell. She had fallen face first, right there on that sidewalk.

As I stood there, looking at the sidewalk, almost as if the body was still there, I heard a woman say something to me. As I turned to my left, I could see her standing on the porch of a small house, staring at me. She was just a few steps away. She was dressed as a housewife of about sixty-some years, with her hair almost totally gray.

"You gotta be a Detective," she said. "You know 'bout the woman what got kilt there?"

"Yes ma'am, you are correct," I said and began stepping over to her, going up the stonework laid in her lawn. She had a definite southern accent.

"Tell me ma'am," I said, "do you know anything about that murder?"

She made a quick study of the badge I revealed to her, as I opened up my suitcoat.

"Onliest thing I knows, is a young woman was kilt there. Some said, it has got to be her damn fool husband, what dunnit," she said, squinting her eyes. "But the Cops, they didn't arrest him, so's I gotta think, twarn't him what dunnit."

"Did you happen to see the shooting or hear a shot fired that night?" I asked.

"Nope; didn't," she said. "I'd have to s'pose, the TV bein' on, it was too loud. Anyway, I don't know who saw the poor thing lyin' there, but they musta called the Cops, because what I heard was sirens comin' near an' stoppin' out front. That's when I shut off the TV an' went out to see what's what. Damn, there sure was lotsa blood on that there sidewalk."

"So, that was it for you, ma'am?" I asked.

"Yeah; guess so," she said. "I 'member the murdered gal's husband, moved outta that house they rented. I think that was jest a week later. A neighbor tol' me, the man moved in with his mama and his sis. Okay, nothin's wrong with that, I sez to him. But he said, he knows the house they got, and it's only got one bedroom. Seems strange to me, Detective… ah, Detective Abrito… two women 'n one man, with only one bedroom? 'Course, they could have a sofa or somethin' fer him to sleep on. Or, maybe the damn floor."

"Right you are, ma'am," I said. "Do you know his new address?"

"No, but I been by it," she said. "Next street over, you'll see three houses from University Street, west side, a tiny white house. That's where that mama an' her son an' her daughter's livin' now. That woman's husband, he up and died jest like my ol' man, year or so ago. I seen the girl there. She's knocked up. She's got a helluva belly on her now."

"Thanks for all that, ma'am," I said. "Well, I'd better get going. Goodbye."

As I walked back to University and then over one block, I recalled the murder took place less than two months before. So, if I understood the old woman's unspoken suspicions, the brother could not have "knocked up" his sister to have her with a very large belly in so short a time. With a very large belly, she must have gotten pregnant seven or more months before.

Chapter Four

Right where the old lady said it was, I found the tiny white house where presumably, David Alexander lived with his mother and sister. Just as I got within steps of being in front of it, I saw a young woman coming out of the house. Wow! She certainly had a very large belly! She had a pretty face and looked to be a teenager.

I continued walking south on the street. I looked back after a bit and saw the big-bellied one walking north, towards University Street. Then I walked to where I saw a very old man with pure white hair, on his knees, tending the flowers bordering his pristine lawn. That was next door to the tiny white house.

"Good morning, mister," I said to the old man.

"What? Oh, a good morning to you, too," he said.

"You sure do have a lovely front yard, what with all those flowers, even in the winter. I have a picket fence in my yard too, but I haven't planted any flowers there yet," I said.

He put his knuckles down on the grass to raise himself up, to stand.

"Where do you live, sir?" he asked.

"My house is in South Park. I got a great price on the house because it was so very dirty and filled up with hoarded cardboard, mostly. I've finally got all that junk and dirt out of there, so now I'll have a contractor bring the house up to date. By the way, speaking of houses, do you know the Alexander's in that house there?" I asked.

"Oh yeah; you know you can't pick your neighbors," he said.

Parting my suit coat a little, I let him see my badge. He glanced at it.

"Ah, so you're Homicide," he said. "I was on the Force for only three years. Damn, that was a long time ago. I got run into by a damn robber who tried to kill me with his car. Well, he got put away for a helluva long time and I was too disabled for a long time, to be on Patrol. So, since then, I've had some pretty good jobs that didn't require me to be chasing after bad guys. I've been retired four and half years now. Anyway, what's up with you here?"

"Sir, do you know anything about the Alexanders?" I asked.

"Well, you of course know about David's wife Marie getting shot down on the street, a while ago. David's back with his mom and sis. It's strange, I must say, that the brother and sister seem to be lovey-dovey a lot. I've seen them kissing and I've seen him playing with her tits. Hell, they don't draw their blinds much at night and you can see right in there. She's pregnant now, but I can't say he did that deed. Mrs. Alexander has got a pension from something and the boy works in a tire shop. Really Detective Abrito, I haven't had much to do with the Alexanders so that's about all I know of them," the long-ago old Cop said.

"Would you say there's no change in that house since the guy's wife was murdered?" I asked him.

"Change? Oh, you know David moved back with his mom and sis, I think a few days after his wife was killed," he said. "I do have the impression that since he moved back, his mother is rough on him. I've heard her screaming at him a lot. I don't remember she did that before. She maybe isn't crazy, but I gotta say, she's getting near that. She makes poor Jeannie cry a lot, too. I don't have any idea of why she's got so damned crotchety lately. I know she didn't change any when her old man died… oh, maybe a year ago now. So why would she be acting so strange, since her daughter-in-law, has died with a bullet in her brain?"

"Indeed sir… why in the world would Mrs. Alexander get rough on her children now?

I can tell you, my friend, I would very much like to know why. Something doesn't seem right in that house. Who would want to murder that pretty young bride, of David Alexander's?" I said almost to myself.

But the old man was paying attention.

"It seems odd, but I know Mrs. Alexander was licensed to own a gun. But I don't think she's licensed now. Why? Damned if I know," he said.

"Sir, how would you know she had a gun permit?" I asked.

"She told me she did. Oh, that was some years ago, when she was the cashier in some restaurant, and she had to take the money to the bank after work every night. So, I guess now she doesn't do that, she doesn't carry a gun," he said.

Having studied the file on that case that very day, I sure couldn't recall anything being said, about the mother-in-law of the murdered girl, having a gun permit.

Thanking the white-haired old ex-cop, I hurriedly walked to the Vons parking lot to retrieve my huge Ford.

Within fifteen minutes, I was back at my desk, staring at the computer.

From the file, I checked and made certain, no mention of a gun permit was in there. Okay, I checked the official records and found indeed, Mrs. Alexander had a gun permit for all of fourteen years. The permit was rescinded when she stopped working at that restaurant. Excitedly, I checked the serial number and description of the gun in the permit and the gun now in our storage, in the case of the murdered Marie Alexander… *and the numbers were identical.*

Jumping up, I dashed over to Sergeant Snyder's desk and asked him to come over to look at my computer.

He acted as though it was an odd request, but he come over to my cubicle anyway.

"Sergeant, do you see this? The gun the mother-in-law of Marie Alexander had a permit for years ago, is the same identical gun used to kill Marie," I told him.

"Well now; sonofabitch!" he exclaimed. "I would not have thought ever, that such a woman could have had a gun, let alone once have a permit for one! Let's you and I go talk to that woman. You know where she lives?"

"Yes sir. I was just there; right next door to her house," I said.

The two of us were quickly in the Expedition and on the way. We got there, to that little white house south of University Street, in a matter of minutes. I parked in front of the Alexander house and then we knocked on the door.

An older woman came to the door with a frown on her face.

"Oh shit; you two gotta be Coppers," she said. "What the fuck do you want now?"

"May we come in, ma'am? We'd like to talk to you," the Sergeant said.

"I s'pose you're gonna come in, one way or t'other," she said and opened her door wide.

We tried to act friendly, but she obviously sensed danger in us. She pointed to a sofa and we sat down. Damn, that house seemed awfully small to me, especially since I was used to going about in my roomy house with thirty-seven-hundred-forty-four square feet.

The woman pulled up a kitchen-type chair, right in front of us and sat down. She definitely had a worried look on her face.

"I'm Homicide Sergeant Ray Snyder, in case you don't remember me, Mrs. Alexander. This Police Officer is Detective Arturo Abrito; he's recording what we say on his cell phone. He just found out that you owned the very gun that killed your daughter-in-law, Marie Alexander, on January 2nd, of this year 2014," my boss said.

The change in the woman's face from mere worry to out-and-out horrified grief, was instant. She almost fell off the chair she was sitting on.

Neither the Sergeant nor I said anything further. We stared at her, waiting for her to stop crying and to speak up. But she didn't speak right away. She bawled her head off and shrieked again and again. Still, we said nothing.

After I had had more than enough of that wailing, I asked the woman, "Mrs. Alexander, would you like to confess to us right now to murdering your daughter-in-law or would you prefer to exercise your rights. You have the right, you know, to be represented by an attorney of your choice. If you cannot afford to pay for an attorney, the Court will appoint one for you and the State of California will pay him or her. You have a right to have an attorney present when you speak to us. Okay ma'am, what's it going to be?"

She began to stutter but then she took in a deep breath and spilled all of it out.

"Yeah, hell yes, I shot the little bitch," Mrs. Alexander said. "My boy, he's got no damn sense. No damn sense at all. First, he screws his sister. Been doing that for I don't know how the hell long. She's got the biggest damn belly around and he still's gotta screw her every damn night.

"Anyway, I told him not to marry that goddamn dumb Marie, but he does it anyway. A course, he knocks her up, too. So, he told me, damned if he could make up his mind, which baby he's gonna be the papa of. My boy is so damn dumb. Anyway, okay, I made up his mind for him. Okay, I shot that stupid Marie. I did it and I'm glad I did. But dammit, I some goddamn way dropped my gun and I was afraid someone would see me picking it up, so I just ran to hell away from there. That's the truth, goddammit, and now here I am, and I finally got that damn thing off my chest."

We of course stood her up and put the cuffs on her, telling her that she was under arrest and being charged with the murder of Marie Alexander. We didn't even wait for a Patrol car to come by; we loaded her into the middle seat of my Ford Expedition and hauled her off to Police Headquarters.

It became quite interesting in the office when not just my fellow Detectives on Team 3 came to congratulate me, but so did

Lieutenant Alan and Lieutenant Brightwell. The Detail Commanders were especially effusive in their praise for my solving of that puzzle.

Of course, I followed form. I almost as effusively insisted, it was just a little bit of luck, on my part, that the case got solved.

My darling Su had ridden with me to work and then, after our ten hours on the job, she was with me on the drive back home again. She told me she had heard of my success in the case. There were a few offices between mine and hers, so that was quite an accomplishment right there.

Su's sister Lu Chi phoned Su to say she was going out for dinner with some of the Ralph's employees, who wanted to celebrate her return to work. That seemed to be working out nicely… and I thought, if only now, she could get interested in a man again.

Lu had told me of her marriage, just after turning twenty years of age… twelve years before… to a really charming man of twenty-five. The marriage was a disaster because the guy did drugs… and she had no idea before, that he did. Anyway, the guy would "get high" and get rough with her. Within six months, he was actually using his fists on her. Of course, she left him and got a divorce. But that gave her the impression, unfortunately, that it was wise to be wary of men. The exception to that was her father, who the sisters admired, respected and adored… and rightly so.

Lu had been the one mainly to make arrangements for cremation and for a celebratory dinner to honor the lifelong carpenter. She had taken the very fancy, Chinese style, urn with their mom's ashes inside, to the crematorium to add their father's ashes. They were to mix them up good, since the parents had been so very close in life, so should it be in the forever after.

The dinner would be in Lu's house on Sunday, February 16, and she had a long list for the sisters to invite. That included relatives in San Francisco and of course, a number of Mr. Chi's co-workers and long-time friends.

With no luck at all to solve further homicide puzzles, I labored with the rest of Team 3 to unravel cases from our files. That was on Thursday and Friday. When Team 3 came in on Saturday norming, February 15th, we were told of a hatcheting of a drug dealer that happened a little after midnight, Saturday morning.

Of all places it could have been, that hatchet homicide occurred at the Navy Hospital gate, where people enter and leave, to and from Florida Street, in the very nearly pristine, Florida canyon.

The entire Team 3, of the Sergeant and us four Detectives, arrived at that gate in Florida Canyon. The Navy Hospital was far, far more than a single building. It was a sprawling complex of buildings and served not just active duty Sailors and Marines, but also retired service people, of all the service branches, and their families. That complex served a great many thousands of men, women and children in the San Diego area.

Long before we arrived, the murdered man's body had been removed by the Medical Examiner people. Even so, we all looked over the area thoroughly. But even though the Saturday morning sunshine shone brightly, none of us could discover any sort of clue to the murder.

We spent but a short time there and went back the little half mile to our office. That was where we got some useful information from the MedEx office.

On our computers, we could read that the dead man was Black and named Isaac Moya. He was six-feet-three-inches tall and weighed just over two-hundred pounds. He was thirty-eight years old. He was married with four children. His wife was a Navy Hospital nurse named Arlene Moya. The man was "unemployed" … if being a nasty drug peddler was not counted.

Detective Martin Garcia spoke up.

"Sergeant Snyder," he said, "I think I know Arlene Moya. I'm pretty sure she's a gal I went to school with… in the tenth grade. I'll try to get in touch with her and see if she'll be cooperative with us. Although I haven't seen her for a very long time, I remember she was one of the nicest gals around."

"Good, Marty, see what you can do with her," Snyder said. "Anybody else got something to say about this hatchet job?"

"I must mention, Sergeant," I offered, "that idea about someone being tall, and wielding that hatchet on six victims, so far, is simply screwy. To over-tower Mr. Moya, you'd have to be damn awful tall, that's for sure. I'm buffaloed. I cannot imagine how the hatcheteer gets the victims to lower their noggins to get struck like they do, after he gets his hatchet out."

"Well Art," Detective David Mann said, "it's gotta be that the hatcheteer must drop something… oh, like the money for the drugs… he must drop it on the floor, the dealer bends down to pick it up… the guy pulls out the hatchet and whammo! Another hatchet is down inside somebody's thinking spot."

"I do have to admit Dave, you're probably correct," I admitted. "But what about at that same time, the hatcheteer has to pull that instrument of death out of his pants or a backpack… or where-the-hell-ever. The guy bending over to pick up his payment, isn't going to make himself ultra-vulnerable like that, for any long time. So maybe there's some other idea on this?"

As I said that, I looked around to see if someone else on the Team had any ideas as to how the hatchet wielder managed to get the job done. No one else, other than Dave Mann, seemed to have an idea on that aspect.

"It seems to me to be an odd thing," Sergeant Snyder offered, "that the husband of a nurse who worked at that hospital, would be murdered at the entrance to it. That's really strange. And why in hell would a drug dealer make a date with someone, right there at that gate, at midnight, where his wife works? Anybody got an idea on that aspect of this sixth, in these dizzying cases?"

"Does anyone know whether that gate to the hospital is kept manned all night?" Detective Ray Mason asked.

"Good question, Ray," I spoke up and said. "Yes, of course they do have some one there all night, but also, at that hour, I suppose guards might fall asleep. Even so… hey guys, I get it. And since the drug dealer knew that, he figured that would be a safe place to sell his drugs. How about that? His wife worked there… we don't know what hours she kept, but we'll find out… so he was familiar with probably two guards, in Navy uniforms, being there to observe any such thing as murder. Aha, fellows. Perhaps the guards were bribed to not see what they saw; they might be addicts even and bribed with drugs.

"Sergeant, that makes that homicide even more suspicious," I offered. "Can any of us imagine two United States Navy Sailors standing on guard in that gate house, not paying attention to a couple of people making a deal? And at such a time of night? They each must have had a car; would guards ignore two men in two cars right there within what?... thirty feet of them?"

"Aha Art, you're saying those guards," David Mann said, "had to have been bribed by the drug dealer, to not report what they saw. That way, the dealer would be safe from the buyer. You make sense, Art."

"That has got to be why the guy would make a drug deal in such a place," I said. "Of course, at that hour of the night, there'd be virtually no traffic; no more than an occasional ambulance bringing in a woman for the delivery of her baby, or some such emergency.

"We all know from our experiences as Police Officers, that men and women in the Services, aren't necessarily immune to the false and tragic appeal of those "lots of fun and harmless" drugs," I added.

"Turns out Lieutenant Brightwell had something personal to take care of today, so she didn't come in," our Sergeant said. "I know Captain Morgan is here and I'll go ask him, right now, to go with me to the Navy Hospital and talk with their Master at Arms about this. That Navy Official would certainly want to know if one or two of their own were being corrupted and doing drugs."

The Sergeant left and we four Detectives turned to looking over unsolved homicide cases again.

Snyder returned and called the four of us to his cubicle. That was at almost eleven o'clock.

"Guess what, fellows?" our Sergeant began. "Captain Morgan had quite the talk with not just the Navy Hospital's Master at Arms, but with a pair of Seamen. The two who had been guards last night at the gate by Florida Street, it turned out, had indeed been bribed. Both of them. Both had been given heroin by Isaac Moya for several months, to look the other way when, after he got out of his car and a second car pulled up.

"That's all those two had to do. They both claimed they, in reality, did indeed see a car there by Isaac Moya's car, the deal going on and the hatchet hitting the guy as he bent over to pick something up. Those two young fellows have just ruined their lives, to get those goddamned illegal drugs, cheaply. They're in the brig right now, awaiting Court Martial."

"Well, well," I said, "those two young Sailors are in very big trouble now. But that doesn't lead us to a damn thing, except we can probably count on nobody doing drug deals at the Navy Hospital gate again."

Maybe that was a mistake, saying that. The Sergeant looked positively crest-fallen, as though he thought he had accomplished something for us… but he had not. Our sixth hatchet homicide was nowhere nearer to being solved. All we learned further, is that two young servicemen were now heading for a Navy brig for not reporting, they saw a hatchet homicide.

No one in our Team expressed gladness that it was, after all, criminal drug dealers being murdered, and therefore, it was sort of okay for them to get their heads split open. Homicide is homicide, and there never can be any excuse for that to be done.

All I accomplished by the end of that ten-hour workday and our Team's four-day work week, was to become more and more familiar with some old, cold cases.

Su and I spent nearly all of Sunday at her sister's house. The remembrances voiced by the many friends and relatives of Mr. Chi were quite touching. He had been a good man, a faithful husband and an attentive father. He had also been an especially good carpenter, as some of his customers over the years, told us.

Half a dozen of those attending, had flown down from San Francisco. So, I got to meet several of my future relatives. Su of course reminded them all that our wedding would take place the following Sunday, February 23rd, in Las Vegas. I had already told my family in Chicago and they had their plane and hotel reservations all set.

Su and I would also fly there, because there were times in the winter when snowfall screwed up road travel to Vegas. That was especially true in that engineering marvel called Cajon Pass, about halfway to Vegas, on Highway 15. It was amazing to see when climbing up that terrific grade, the mile distance that separated other lanes, going downhill.

All of us reserved rooms in the hotel-casino, Golden Nugget; it's in old, downtown Vegas, but it's been recently remodeled. It is near several wedding chapels. Su had already arranged for our wedding, too. She was wonderfully efficient; I was glad to find out.

On Monday evening, February 17th, Su and I finally took in the movie we had heard such good things about. It was called "Riders of the Purple Sage" and the late Chief Leslie's stepdaughter was the starring actress. San Diego girl Anne McCarty certainly "stole the show" in that movie. Her five minutes of bawling over having to shoot her injured horse, and then doing it, had to be a tear-jerker for anyone seeing it on the screen. Both Su and I were extremely impressed with the girl's acting ability... especially since, you are not supposed to know that the actress is "acting."

Su told me she was quite happy with her new job, of mostly helping to prevent, elder abuse. She said that so far, she appeared to have changed attitudes, of the young ones toward the old ones.

People see beautiful women celebrities all the time on television, in movies and in magazines. So, to see a strikingly beautiful woman like Su Chi, up really close, has got to affect people... and I told her so.

Old people sure could be ornery and could expect to be treated as such. But she said she had some pretty good success in calming situations so that no arrests had to be made... which an arrest could mean, there'd be no young ones to care for the old ones.

Both of us were very much looking forward to the next Sunday, which was "getting' hitched" time.

We spent some time boxing up, on Tuesday, some of the kitchen stuff. We would, after all, be without a kitchen for a while, until workmen had transferred that kitchen and done some other work in the basement. The plumbing and electrical work was going to be complicated, and I felt more and more happy that I would not be engaged in that sort of work.

Su and I also began haunting furniture stores to find out what was available. All six of the bedrooms planned for, would need to be completely furnished. Also, a dining table and a variety of chairs and a television would be needed in both places. Oh yes, and TV cable would have to be run everywhere.

For our upstairs, both Su and I wanted the fanciest furniture we could find. Neither of us liked Scandinavian modern, squared things. Su said we should not look at Chinese style pieces, nor at Mexican furniture. We were Americans. We should furnish our home with American furniture. And anyway, the house was very old and should be furnished as such, we thought.

We would fully furnish our main floor master bedroom, at the front of the house. The other two bedrooms would serve our children, eventually. In the meantime, we'd furnish those two rooms for adult guests.

Ah, come Wednesday morning, February 19th, both Su and I were back to work.

Sergeant Su Chi now wore her "business attire," with a knee-length, pleated pant-skirt, instead of her Police Uniform. She ordinarily would not need the belt of Police gear around her waist. She wore her pistol in a holster under her left arm; it was covered by a lovely jacket.

On this particular day… with temperatures not quite up to the 60's… she wore her blue wool suit. She also wore matching dark blue stockings that nearly covered her calves. To me, the "sneak-peek" bit of her flesh between the stockings and her knees, looked sexy; she had beautifully perfect legs.

Quite by coincidence, so did I wear a blue suit.

Su assured me she was beginning to truly love her job. Already, she had smoothed the relationships within several families, so the conflicts were settled. That was what she tried in each case of Elder Abuse to do. Mostly, she told me, either drugs or excess alcohol stirred up problems with seniors feeling knocked around, and the younger ones, feeling imposed on.

Happily, there were no more hatchet homicides reported. So, the number of those horrific homicides, stood at six. Not a single one of us had any such thing as any firm idea of who to suspect of hatcheting to death, dishonorable, indecent, uncouth, evil, poison-pushing salesmen and saleswomen.

Like the rest of Team 3, I dug into some old, cold cases. All of them had been reviewed time and again by very sharp minds, without a winnable court case, of whodunnit.

Although it was also true, that in some cases, Detectives and maybe the entire Homicide Detail, had been certain of who committed the murder… but, either the evidence necessary for a conviction in court was not there… or, in so many cases, the perpetrator had fled south of the border, down Mexico way.

Having sat down at my desk after lunch, I was surprised to hear my desk phone ring.

"Detective Abrito…" I started to say.

"Art, this is Commander Macias. I want you to meet Captain Morgan and me at my car in the parking lot. Right now!" he said and hung up.

Damn! What in hell is this all about?

"Sergeant, I've been ordered to go with Commander Macias," I said as I flew by Snyder.

I saw first the two-bars Captain and then the two-stars Commander, about to climb into a big, totally black, unmarked Ford Crown Victoria. I ran to the car; the rear door was held open, and so I jumped in.

"Abrito!" Captain Morgan said, as I slammed the door shut and the car roared away and headed, with siren blaring and lights flashing, toward Highway 163. "We've got bad news for you. Su Chi has had her left leg chopped off! No shit! It's gotta be that hatcheteer you guys have been hunting, who did it."

The Commander cut in. "Art, we just got word from a

Patrol there. Your fiancé is right now on the way to Sharps Hospital. That's where we're heading. She's not just lost a lot of her leg, she's lost a helluva lot of blood. According to Police right there, when they arrived in response to her phone call, she was lying on the floor of an apartment with her left leg actually chopped off. She and an old woman had managed to use the woman's robe's belt as a tourniquet, to slow the loss of blood. The woman who wielded the hatchet, was all shot to hell by Su."

"Art," the Captain said, "we knew you two lovers were engaged and that you'd want to be with her there in the hospital. You can forget coming back to your duties for a while. You'll want to care for your very precious fiancé."

"Thank you both with all of my heart, Commander Macias and Captain Morgan," I somehow managed to get out.

Of course, I was in shock. Impossible! How could it happen that Su actually had a leg chopped off? That's crazy! That is as insane as anything I've heard of in my whole life! Somebody chopped Su's leg off? That's nuts! That just could not possibly happen! But by God, it seems to be true! *Oh, my beautiful darling Su!*

Trying to calm myself, I realized that by the time we got to the hospital, she would already be in an operating room. The surgeons would be sewing up whatever remained of her leg. Hey! Maybe they brought the cut off part of the leg and they could sew it back on! That'd be great! They'd sew my Su back together!

As the siren wailed, I tried to reason with myself about what could be happening at the moment with her. Poor darling! To have someone actually chop at her with a hatchet! How grisly! How very painful and how very shocking for her, that had to be!

Closing my eyes, I tried to make myself relax. There was not a single thing I could do for my future bride right now. It would be up to the surgeons to perform their miracles on her.

Hey! We've got a date in only a few days, to get married! Then we're to let out a contract to get our house made beautiful! Su and me? We've got things to do!

Meanwhile, the Commander and the Captain were talking to

each other. I paid no attention to them. My mind was strictly on the love of my life, Su.

Still with lights flashing and the siren screaming, the Sergeant driver of the Commander's car pulled into the Sharp Hospital by the sign saying, "EMERGENCY."

Jumping out on my side of the car, I held the door open for my two superiors. They nodded thanks to me as they sped by, rushing to the Emergency door. I was right behind them.

Inside, the Commander asked about Sergeant Su Chin. Immediately, he and we were informed she was at the moment in surgery and of course, sedated.

"Nurse, do you have a prognosis yet?" Commander Macias asked the woman at the desk.

"Oh, no sir. But you can bet she's in the best of hands. She was conscious when they wheeled her by me here, so I have high hopes for her," the woman said.

Well now, that was encouraging to hear. She was conscious as she went by right where I was standing. Yes; that was encouraging.

Looking around, I found a place on a bench to sit. My superiors did the same and came over to sit to my left and right.

"Abrito," Commander Macias said, "you know I'm the one who wanted Su Chi to have that job in the Elder Abuse unit. I had a feeling about her sensitivities. She being Chinese, I know that culture calls for the old people to be cared for by their young people. She seemed to me, to be perfect for that role. She being so very beautiful, why, that calms people, too. So now, should I feel responsible for her being so grievously attacked doing what she does so well? No sir, I still think she's the best in town for that work."

"Commander, I can tell you truthfully sir, that Su has told me many times lately, that she loves the work, that she feels she's doing good things in it, and she is very happy that you insisted that she get into it," I told him.

"Thanks for that, Art," he told me. "An Officer on the spot said something about all of this happened at a Monroe residence. I guess it's an apartment. Does that ring a bell with you?"

"Monroe? Well sir, the only person with that name I've heard of for a very long time is an employee of the Medical Examiner's office. She helped take away the body of Su Chi's father just recently. Perhaps you've heard, her dad had Alzheimer's disease and he collapsed and died from it.

"While that Monroe woman was there, she ranted on something about how someone killing those drug dealers with a hatchet, was a very good thing. Damn! Could it have been her that did such an awful thing to my Su?" I asked.

"Sometimes Art, it seems to be a really small, small world," the Commander said.

"Lieutenant Alan told us," I said, "that according to someone at the MedEx, they had known Nancy Monroe for a long time, and she was a wonderful person. From what she said when in Mr. Chi's house, that didn't add up at all. Either she's a Doctor Jekyll —Mr. Hyde type, or… far more likely… she's a drug addict. Or I should say, *she was a drug addict.* That would answer how she knew drug dealers she wanted to kill. *And Commander, she has maybe killed six of those drug dealers with a hatchet!*"

"As the Commander said, Art," Captain Morgan cut in, "it really is a small world. It has to be no coincidence. It might very well be the same woman and as you said Art, she must… she would have to be a drug addict to do such insane things. Commander Macias, you and I can bet, Art, is going to make a big thing of what drugs can do to perfectly decent people. Right sir?"

"Well now, my good Captain," the Commander said, "you of course know of my urging people to stay to hell away from those awfully dangerous chemicals that broil people's brains to a very altered state. Absolutely. That Monroe woman, who the hell ever she is, got herself killed, and very rightly so. She also has greatly affected the life of a truly fine young woman whose goal in life was to help her neighbors here in America's Finest City."

For the first time, I began to feel overwhelmed when the Commander said such nice things about my darling Su. I laid my head down in my hands and cried. I just had to cry.

Those two gentlemen were in their splendiferous Police uniforms. I was glad to be in a business suit, and not to be seen crying, as a Cop.

Naturally, I regained my composure after a bit, because of the men, women and children also in the emergency waiting room, seeing this grown-up man, bawling like a baby.

In time, a nurse came to inform us that Su Chi would be out of surgery soon and would be taken to the Intensive Care Unit on the fourth floor. So, we took an elevator up there and again, found a seat to wait on.

Meantime, the Commander and the Captain were both on their phones, talking about the situation with those back at Head-quarters. The Commander also began calling TV stations and the Union-Tribune newspaper about some of the events. I heard him say, he would not hold a news conference until Sergeant Su Chi was awake and for certain, on the path back to good health.

The respect he obviously had for my darling, was cheering to me.

Also, I overheard Captain Morgan talking with someone at our Crime Laboratory—which I knew was a part of his Investigations II Command—about their efforts to gather samples of dried blood on the hatchet brought in. Of course, if my suspicions about the Monroe woman were correct, I knew if that hatchet had not been absolutely, and perfectly cleaned after each killing, some tiny molecules of blood would remain. Possibly, they could eventually identify blood from all six dead victims… and from my Su.

We had sat for perhaps ten minutes when here comes my Su, all covered up but her for her face, on a gurney. She was asleep. But I did get to see her darling face as she rolled by. She had an oxygen mask on, I supposed to aid her in regaining her healthy self.

A doctor came up to us, telling the Commander with the two brilliant gold stars on his collars, that she was going to be okay.

"Doctor, were you able to sew her leg on again?" Commander Macias asked.

"Oh, not at all sir. From about five or six inches below the knee joint, down for about four inches, there were almost countless chops delivered with some sort of hatchet. The bones in that stretch of her left leg, were in tiny pieces. All of that leg tissue there was shredded almost as though it had gone through a meat grinder," he said as the three of us raptly listened.

"I do believe though, she was very intelligent in getting a tourniquet tied tightly just below her knee, to almost stop-up the blood, and to save not just the rest of that leg, but probably her life. We've already given her lots of blood and she may need more. She's being fed and medicated, intravenously. But just now, she needs rest. She'll need a lot more rest too, but I have confidence Miss Chi will be alright," the Doctor said.

"Thank you very much, Doctor," the Commander said. "Let me introduce to you, Detective Arturo Abrito. He and Sergeant Chi are engaged to be married. When was that to be, Art?"

"Sir, that was to be this coming Sunday in Las Vegas, but such a happy ceremony will just have to wait a bit," I said.

"I'm pleased to meet all of you," the Doctor said. "Detective Abrito, your fiancé will be sleeping for some time yet. She will be monitored at all times, here in the ICU, of course. If you wish to wait until she wakes up, you are certainly welcome to do so."

"Thank you, Doctor," I said. "I'll wait right here."

Both Commander Macias and Captain Morgan left then. They would be conducting a news conference outside the hospital, to let the public know, what happened, and that Sergeant Chi would be okay.

The big shots left and as I was sitting there, I finally had the good sense to call Su's sister Lu. That was agonizing, giving Lu such bad news on top of all the trouble and strife she had been through lately. But she said, she would be right over here with me.

I thought it best to phone Sergeant Snyder then. I not only told him about the great misfortune that struck my Su, but about how it appeared that Monroe woman was quite possibly the monster who had hatcheted to death, those drug dealers. He wanted all the details and I did not have all the details. I told him what I knew, and that was that. He said he'd let the Lieutenants and the entire Homicide Detail know that Sergeant Su Chi was in the hospital but was expected to be okay eventually.

Although I was tempted to call my family in Chicago, I knew all of them would, at that hour, be fully occupied in their restaurant. I decided to call them after their 10 o'clock closing time, which would be 8 o'clock here. I'd ask Lu to phone her and Su's relatives about her lost leg and the delay of the marriage date.

Having the name and numbers of our reservations in Las Vegas, I called them to put off our wedding date, for probably a month or more. They told me, they understood and to pass on their best wishes to my fiancé.

Lu Chi came up to the fourth floor and waited with me. She naturally wanted me to tell her everything I knew about what happened to her sweet sister. I couldn't tell her how Su came to be in that apartment where her leg was chopped off. We would find out such details from Su, when she was awake… and especially, when she was better.

Chapter Five

It seemed Lu Chi and I were on our phones most of the rest of the day. We talked to people we hadn't talked to for quite a while. Even our architect called me, when he heard the news about Su, on television. I told him I would be in touch about when we could get together.

By 4 o'clock, both Lu and I were hungry, so we went to the hospital cafeteria and had a bit of grub. Then we hurried back to our waiting room, outside the Intensive Care Unit.

Our timing was perfect. A nurse informed us that Su was awake and wanted to see us.

Gosh, Su looked so dragged out. But her black eyes looked okay to me, although the usual sparkle wasn't in them. I held one hand and sister Lu held the other. I couldn't help but smile, just to be beside her; to touch her hand.

I spoke up while Lu seemed still too shocked to say anything.

Reaching down to pull her oxygen mask aside, I lightly kissed her lips.

"Darling Su, you have gone through such a terrible ordeal. I know you must have been brave to get through all that," I said.

She reached up with one hand to get that mask off further.

"Artie my sweet," she whispered with a weak smile, "you are always so nice. In fact, I was in that Monroe apartment for only seconds, when I was knocked flat on my back and out cold. That huge woman was a crazy monster! She was jealous of my pretty legs! She told me that! She was so jealous of them she wanted to chop them up! Her mother told me she had gone mad on meth! That's why I was there; the monster was slapping her mother, for no reason!"

"Take it easy, darling," I told Su. "You've had a terrific rough time."

"Damnedest thing;" she continued, "she was on her knees, and she held me down on the floor with her strong right hand, and she chopped me with that damned hatchet in her left hand. Dammit, that hurt. She chopped just as hard and fast as she could.

"I had one helluva time getting my pistol out. Some damn way I managed to get it out of the holster. She was fighting me the whole time, but she was having a happy time of it, chopping my leg. I shall never in my life forget her madly laughing, while she chopped, just as fast as she could.

"I don't know how I did it, but I finally… after what seemed a long time, I racked in a round in my pistol. So, I shot her. I think I got her in the chest. It seemed to only make her crazier! I then shot her again and again! Finally, those shots pushed her backwards and she was off of me.

"Honey, it was amazing. The monster's very old mother was right there, watching all of this. But she came right over to me when the mad woman was dead. She took a belt off her robe and she tied it really tight around my leg, just below the knee, as I asked her to do.

"Believe me, I wasn't at all surprised to see my left leg, lying all by itself in a pool of blood, on that floor. I hurried then to call 911 and got some help pretty quick. That old woman, there, she had a much-bruised face; she even had a black eye. Poor lady; now she's all alone, I guess," Su told me.

"Oh, but my darling wife-to-be is alive!" I exclaimed. "Commander Macias told me not to think about going back to work yet. He wants me to take care of my darling. That might give you an idea of how much you are respected there, honey. I'm not the only one who recognizes the best of things in my sweetheart."

Su's eyes closed and I don't know if she even heard what I had to say. I shut my mouth and simply stood there, holding her hand. Lu let go her other hand and sat in a chair near the bed. Then Lu looked up at me.

"Art, my little sister has sure had a shocking day," Lu whispered. "I knew that she being a Police Officer could be risky, but who in hell could imagine she'd have something like this happen? Poor Su. She's had a leg chopped off! What madness! Drugs do awful things to people, don't they Art? As a Cop yourself, you must have seen how that junk affects people."

"Lu, for many years, it was men and women who went bananas on us, with too much booze screwing up their minds. Now it's still alcohol and often very much worse, with those illegal drugs frying and altering people's brains.

"Commander Macias will surely use Su's example to again impress on the public, the very real dangers in putting those 'unknown chemicals' into one's body… chemicals which the blood flow takes right up to a human's head to go to work on fouling their brains," I said, keeping my voice low.

After I adjusted the oxygen mask to lay gently on her face, I just stood there, in wonder of what that beautiful woman had been through. There were two bottles held up on poles with tubes feeding both food and medicine into her arm.

Another was a bag of blood on a pole, also with a tube into her other arm. She was getting replaced in a transfusion, some of the great amount of blood she surely lost out of that hatcheted-off-leg.

I allowed myself to glance down toward the foot of her bed. Plain as anything, I saw the bulge in the covers stop near her left knee while on her right side, the bulge continued to her foot. That seemed to bring home to me, a realization of what had happened to her.

Yes, Su has perfectly tapered and long legs. And hell yes, they are sexy. I had admired those legs from the time I first met her, while a fellow Patrol Officer. Getting myself between those legs was to me, a truly fulfilling… and very much a loving, accomplishment.

These days, it looks as though the young women in the nation have finally realized, how attractive their legs are to men; so, they wear bikinis, skirts, shorts or dresses, to barely cover down, to where their legs begin.

Recalling that MedEx woman named Nancy Monroe, I knew she had the worst sort of legs. They looked more like fat posts, than legs. She was overweight all over, anyway. Those who knew her where she worked, had had a good opinion of her. But ah, when at home and full of methamphetamines or what-the-hell-ever, she became increasingly a mad woman… and she had aimed her rage at her old mother and especially, at my darling Su.

Captain Morgan came to the door of Su's room and whispering, asked to see me.

Putting her hand down gently, I stepped outside the room.

"Art, Commander Macias asked me to find out if your gal has told you anything yet," he said.

"Yes sir, she has," I said. "But then, she has gone back to sleep."

Then I related, as exactly as I could to him, what she had told me.

"Thanks for that, Detective," the Captain said. "Commander Macias has of course got word from all of those who were called to that scene where she lost her leg. That includes your Homicide Team 3. He's about to give a news conference to let the public know of another instance of those damn Sinaloa cartel's drugs causing such madness. Believe me, he'll have ample compliments for Sergeant Su Chi."

With that, the Captain left, and I went back into the Intensive Care Unit, which was bristling with mysterious equipment I hadn't noticed before. Ah, I saw a wide band was wrapped around

Su's arm to now and then take a reading, of the highs and lows of her blood pressure.

As I sat staring at my darling fiancé, a nurse came and stuck a glass thermometer into Su's mouth. That made Su stir a bit. But then with the thing out of her mouth, she went right back to sleep. That was good. Her body had been through great trauma. She needed rest.

After a bit, a Doctor came in and told me he was her surgeon. Without waking her, and standing between me and her legs, he lifted the covers to have a look at the bandages he had put on. He told me everything was looking okay.

"You must have heard about prosthetics, Detective Abrito," he said. "She'll be getting fitted with a new lower leg. They are more or less difficult to get used to. But if she's really determined, she'll get by just fine. She's a healthy young woman and she'll do well. How long have you two been married?"

"Doctor, we were to get married officially this Sunday. I've had to call and cancel our reservations in Las Vegas. Her and my families have had to do the same. So, we'll have the ceremonies in a few weeks. To me, we are already very much a married couple; we are most certainly, permanently in love," I told him.

"Hey, you; I heard that," came Su's voice quietly from the bed.

Standing up, I stepped over to her and said, "If I'd known you were eaves-dropping, Su, I'd have said it louder. How're you feeling, honey?"

She looked at the Doctor and said, "Sir, you must've given me something good, because I don't feel any pain right now at all."

"Young lady, I'll have to ease up on the dosage in a bit, because you sure don't want to get addicted to such stuff. It's oxycodone; that can be terribly addicting for most folks," the Doctor said.

At the same time, he was holding her wrist, to check her pulse. Then he walked out of the ICU, leaving sister Lu, a nurse, and me with the only patient there.

"Honey, what I'm trying to do, is to keep my mind on our

house, instead of my little problem here. I think that can be called, *positive thinking;* don't you agree?" she surprised me by saying.

"That seems like an excellent idea to me, if you can do it," I said.

"When is our architect due with the drawings and contracts?" she asked.

"That was to have been Tuesday, honey," I told her. "But you might still be in the hospital, so…"

"Oh no, Artie," she said with a smile showing her pearly white teeth, "Tuesday is almost a week away. I'll be home before then. We'll have to get a wheelchair for me, I suppose, until the time I can walk about on my own two feet again. See there, darling? There's some more positive thinking for you! I am definitely not going to mope about and feel sorry for myself. I know what has been done, is done. And that's that. I'll get a prosthetic, like those many, many Soldiers and Marines coming back from "playing in the sandbox," in the middle east, have to do."

"I should tell you darling," I said, "that Commander Macias has instructed me to not worry about going back to work for a while. He wants me to take care of my loving sweets."

"Yes, I heard him tell you that," she said. "But I want you to know, Artie, I'm a big girl now and you'll find, I'll shoo you off to work to bring home the bacon! Hey! Here's something! While we have some contractors remodeling our house, I can be there to be absolutely certain they do everything correctly. Won't that be a good thing, honey? I can be there every single day to make sure they do it all right!"

My darling Su then went on to begin thinking about the City of San Diego Police Department always taking care of their own. Both of us were, of course, in the Police Association union. She was sure the City would pay for a prosthetic leg for her. Their insurance would take care of her hospital bills. But could she ever be able to be a Police Officer again, wearing a phony leg? She hoped she could return, to the same work she had been doing.

"Oh-oh, sweets," she said, "we might be pregnant! Maybe

while I'm right here, that can be checked so we'll know for sure. I sure hope I am… ah, don't you, too?"

"Hey darling, I hope you're knocked up with quintuplets, so we can get it done!" I laughed. "Seriously, I hope we do have one on the way and if not, I'll just have to keep making love to you, night and day, day and night… like that old song says!"

"Sounds like the thing to do, I'd say," she said, actually laughing for the first time there.

She tired quickly and I helped adjust her pillow. I then gave her an easy smooch as she faded off to dreamland.

Wow! I had to say to myself as I sat back on a chair; I've got myself, quite the woman! She's so very positive. She seems to be refusing, to feel sorry for herself. Could I do that as well as she says she will? I had to doubt I could.

All of this had happened since I became a Homicide Detective on January 29th, merely three weeks before. She had moved in with me right away and we were boundlessly in love. Would her losing a leg… or rather, a part of a leg, change anything for us? Certainly, it was a terrific problem for her. She would have to heal first… that could take some time… and then struggle to get used to an "artificial leg." Well, I was certain I loved her so much that it changed nothing at all for me.

A different nurse came into the ICU. She suggested Lu and I should leave and let my Su get all the rest possible. As it was, she told us, her sleep would be interrupted all night in order to have her vitals checked and the needles feeding into her arms, changed.

Lu and I left and stopped at a Denny's restaurant for a light dinner. I suggested to Lu that she really ought to go back to work at Ralph's; especially so because she needed the money. I had already got permission from Commander Macias to stay home to help my bride-to-be recover. Lu agreed and said she would visit with her sister at every opportunity.

Wow! In the drive home, I realized I felt so very alone now. In three weeks, life had changed a lot for me, mostly because of that gal I left behind, in the hospital.

On Thursday morning, February 20th, I was back to see my

Su. She ate a pretty good breakfast. She was still groggy from the pain medication she was on.

While I was there, her surgeon came in to change the bandage on her leg. He said it would be a good idea for me to see her leg unwrapped. So, I braced myself as I watched the old bandages come off.

Well now, I had of course never in my life seen such a stump and I didn't know what to expect. But a stump it was, with the skin pulled over the leg bones, called tibia and fibula, and sewn together. The redness of inflammation was on that skin for a little way up the stump. But beyond a few inches up, and over her knee, her leg looked normal.

Watching as the Doctor applied an antibiotic salve and re-wrapped the wound, I learned how I could do that for her, myself.

Both the Doctor and I reassured Su that her leg looked alright; and was healing well.

When the Doc left, she closed her eyes and went back to sleep. I had bought the San Diego Union-Tribune newspaper, as I came in the hospital, so while she slept, I read.

Su Chi's encounter with the mad woman was reported on the first page. It repeated for all the readers, the horror of the crazy one chopping off the leg of a female Sergeant of Police. It told of Su's position of preventing and helping to prosecute Elder Abuse and the dedication it took for an Officer to accomplish that. They were quite complimentary to Su Chi, for her very good work. Also, it laid blame for the tragedy to the use of illegal drugs, by the now dead Nancy Monroe. Her mother was also given credit, for helping Su with the tourniquet.

Just as every Police Officer involved in shooting a "suspect," Su would eventually have to go to the District Attorney's office to explain the need for shooting a "suspect." I had done that myself; and more than once.

My staying at the hospital, part of the time holding Su's hand, didn't accomplish a lot. The beautiful lady in that bed needed her body to get all the rest possible. She sure did sleep a lot of the time.

But I did stay with her most of Thursday, Friday and Saturday.

On Saturday, Chief of Police Williams was gracious in visiting with Su. He talked with her for quite a while and pinned a pretty commendation on her gown. She also had friendly visits from Commander Macias, Captain Morgan and the two Homicide Detail Lieutenants. On Sunday, all of Homicide Team 3 came to visit with her before she was discharged from the hospital and I took her home.

A union representative came and handed over a brand-new wheelchair and a pair of crutches for her, from the union's health insurance. Her hospital bill would be paid for, also.

I managed to get up early Sunday morning and went to a laundry to get our stuff washed and dried. Then I went to bring my Su home. The Doctor didn't discharge her until almost noon, when I had the privilege of thrusting my right arm under her thighs, picking her up and sitting her in the hospital wheelchair. A nurse had helped her get dressed in slacks, etc. Her situation was obvious with her left pant leg, hanging limp a bit below her knee.

By hospital protocol, a nurse had to take her out to our car in their chair. When we got to my big Ford, I again picked her up out of the chair, and sat her in the car. She belted herself in.

On the way home, she suggested we have lunch at a Carl's Junior. So, we drove through the drive-through, and we each had a burger with fries and a soda, right there in the car. Su really enjoyed doing that, as though she had been confined for months, instead of days.

When we got home, I got the new wheelchair we had been given, out of the back seat. I loaded her into that and wheeled her and her new crutches out of the garage. That was when she finally learned how she could be taken in and out of the house. She acted thoroughly amazed that I had built a ramp on top of the back-porch stairs, for me to be able to push her up and down in her chair.

"Artie darling," she said, "this is really an amazing carpentry feat for you to accomplish. Hey, and you can re-use the plywood and those two by fours."

"Thanks, my sweets," I said, appreciating her compliments.

The angle of the ramp was rather steep, but I got her up to the porch and house level easily enough. We would be using that ramp until that whole area was re-built by a contractor. So, I had to paint it grey a couple of coats to weather-proof that lumber.

She acted delighted to be home again. As for me, I would have no more bouts of loneliness. But Su tired easily and she asked me to lay her down on the parlor sofa. I put a pillow under her head and covered her with a blanket. Soon, she was sound asleep again… and getting rest for healing, as she should.

Su's sister Lu came to visit, bless her. She insisted that she'd make dinner for the three of us, and she did very well at it. She told us she had to be to work at Ralph's early Monday morning, so she didn't stay late.

Both Su and I were all pins and needles, anticipating what the architect—due to visit Tuesday morning—what the architect would come up with. I was particularly curious about what sort of book shelving he would design, for the areas left and right of the fireplace. There were no windows there to account for. On that wall in the present dining room, there was a very large window. And to the right of the parlor, facing out onto the front porch, and beyond, there was another large window. Those two windows, as well as many others, would be replaced with vinyl-framed, and doubled, insulating glass.

We went to bed and although it "had been a long time," I didn't even hint at love making, because the remainder of her leg had still, to be really sore. We both slept well. Bright and early Monday morning, I was in the kitchen, making coffee.

Hearing something behind me, I turned around to see Su standing there, on her crutches, in her gown, with a smile on her face.

"Hell, yes honey, my leg hurts," she said, "but I've gotta get used to doing this until I'm finally able to get a prosthetic leg. The Doctor told me, it'd be maybe six or eight weeks before I can be fitted with one. After a while, I should be able to navigate stairs with the crutches, too. But I'll be patient; and not rush things too much."

"Well now, you are something else," I told her. "I supposed you'd use those crutches in two or three weeks from now. Oh, my Su, you are a wonder!"

I stepped over to give her a peck on the lips.

"Would you rather have your breakfast, my dear, here in the kitchen or on the coffee table? And, what would you like me to fix for you?" I asked.

She wanted to sit on a stool at our kitchen counter, as usual. I noticed she winced as she sat, so I knew lots of the movements she made, hurt. She had an excellent sense of balance and not once, did I notice her fumbling to stay straight up.

After we ate, I helped her dress in shorts and a short shirt. Then I wheeled her out to the backyard so she could get some sunshine on the rather warm, late February, morning. She loved the idea of soaking up the sun, to help herself recover.

After a simple lunch, we both went to the backyard again. This time, we each took a book to read. But I noticed she napped more than she read.

My Su actually seemed to improve by the hour. I was so proud of her determination, not to end up being a cripple, and dependent on others for many things.

Come bedtime again, she insisted there was more than one way to satisfy the man she loved, so she did. Wow! What a lover!

Ah, in the morning it was Tuesday, February 25th. We dressed decently and ate a fine breakfast, since the architect was due at 9 o'clock.

He was exactly on time and I welcomed him inside. He remarked right away, in greeting Su, that he had followed her story both on television and in the newspaper. But soon, he and we got down to business.

He had made new floor plans and elevations, plus many details, based on the original, 1925 blueprints. And he showed us a sheaf of papers with him; ah, the specifications and the contracts to be let out.

The first thing he brought up was Su's pride and joy, the kitchen. He had made a perspective sketch of it for us. Everything in it looked just the way Su wanted it.

The sketch of our fireplace wall in the parlor, showed full-inch-and-a-half thick, bookshelves. Beginning at the floor, shelves went up seven feet. They were nicely "boxed in" by cove molding up there. The shelving was fourteen inches deep at first and got shallower to seven inches, as they went up. The shelves and the uprights, were to be dressed by a router on the edges. Very nice.

Again, we spent about two hours with the architect. I got Su down the ramp in back and the architect and I carried her, in her chair, to the first floor. There he showed us where the old kitchen would be placed and where the new furnace would go, in a small room at the far end. Also, the electric panel would be in that locked room, out of the reach of children.

She asked us to stop on the way back upstairs. She said the drawing showed the potential pool to be on the south side of the lot. She said that was the best place for some sort of garden. So, the pool, if we were to have one, should be on the north side of the back yard. I had to agree.

Other than that, neither Su nor I could find a single fault with all the changes he had made on the drawings. He also gave us the names of half a dozen contractors we could call. He assured us, that he knew of satisfactory work done by all of them.

As soon as he left, Su called several of those contractor references. Each former customer said nice things about the men. Picking one of them at random, I called to make an appointment. He said he had heard of a Craftsman Style house being remodeled and he was anxious to look at it to see what was to be done. He said he lived and operated out of North Park, which was of course a short distance from where we were, in South Park.

"Then sir, why don't you come right over, and have a look at this project. We heard good things said about you, so right away, we should be able to trust you," I said.

"I can be there within minutes," he said.

And sure enough, he was.

Inviting him into the house, I showed him in the future library, the drawings, old and new. He looked those drawings over for a while. Then I took him first on a tour of the main floor, beginning with the kitchen. He checked the only existing bathroom, that was to become a half bath; the four bedrooms that were to become three bedrooms, each with their own bath and large, walk-in closet. Next, I showed him the dining room and parlor; that was where we wanted the walls gone.

I pointed out to him the chimney flues must be checked for safety, and the fireplace converted to burning gas instead of wood.

All the while as we walked about, he made shorthand notes and wrote dollar figures down on a big yellow-lined, paper pad. He told me he was estimating costs.

After showing him the front porch, and the picket fence that needed to be fixed, we went to the basement. All this time, he merely checked the drawings and the specs. But he asked questions, too, and made his notes. And I told him about the pool, if there was to be one, was to be on the north side of the lot in order to someday have a sunny garden for flowers or veggies, on the south side back there. Of course, that area might remain grass, for children to play on. She could watch the kids there from the kitchen window.

We returned to the parlor. While Su and I sat on the sofa watching, he sat on the floor in front of us, spreading out the drawings on the coffee table and figuring, plus making more notes. He did all of this while we could see exactly, what he was doing. That made us trust him. He took something like an hour on the floor there, before he looked at us and told us the news.

"This project is a beauty; I must tell you. I want very much to have the privilege of completing it for you. My price for every bit of it, including the carports, the pool and patio in the back, is just $284,500. I figure to complete it in thirty working days from next Monday, but I must put in the contract, another couple of weeks' extension, in case of something unforeseen. During this week, I will bring you samples you'll need to choose from, such as kitchen and bath counters granite and tile colors, paint, carpet and wood flooring, on both levels.

"I'm familiar with all the materials the architect has specified, including the green-plastic-coated chain link fence all along the south lot line, by that canyon. The insulating siding is a very good choice and so is the vinyl-coated picket fencing and the gate in front. Mr. Abrito, are you confident the roof is satisfactory for now?" he asked me.

"Yes sir, since I spent four whole days in the attic, vacuuming everything clean, even the rafters and between. I could find no sign of leakage," I said. "Someday we may want to replace the roofing there with solar electric shingles."

"You may have to wait a few years yet for those," he said. "Well folks, is next Monday, March 3rd, a satisfactory start day for you two?"

That was interesting. He didn't ask us if we wanted to sign the contract for him… cute, him asking about the start date.

The contractor picked up the contract the architect had made out, filled out his name, our names and address, dates and of course the price, and handed it to us with a pen laying atop the papers. Cute; that man with the silvery hair, had done all this before. But he very much gained our confidence in him; and since he had been recommended by the architect, we both signed.

"In my forty-three years as a carpenter and contractor," the man said as he put the signed papers down, "I don't think I've had more than six or seven projects quite like yours. I am very anxious to get started on it. We'll first have to re-run all the piping and wiring lines. A great variety of trucks, will be able to unload on both sides of your garage.

"That is, trucks can go there before we build the carports. We can do the pool and patio at the same time as we get started on your lower level. As it says to do, we'll move your furnishings and kitchen down there and then proceed to remodel this main floor.

"I want you both to know, I'll have the very best cabinetmaker in the business to do your kitchen and your library wall in here;

also, I'll have him do your desk fancily like the rest. But I want to point out, on the drawings, the architect has specified 'mahogany-like' wood.

"The cabinetmaker will use a tropical wood, with a grain much like mahogany, and then he'll stain it and finish it so's even an expert cannot tell the difference. That folks, has to be, since mahogany forests are mostly history now. But the genuine article we'll furnish him from the walls we take down, will be very useful to him also; especially on your desk.

"Mrs. Abrito, I read in the newspaper and saw your Commander Macias tell about the horror of that mad woman chopping off your leg, although he didn't mention your name. I want you to understand, all of my men and myself will hold you rather in awe, for being such a wonderful and caring Police Officer. Mr. Abrito, I should add that all of those I employ and sub-contract with, are very good people and they will exert themselves even more than usual, since you too, are a valued and caring Police Officer," the man said.

Wow! Neither of us had expected anything like that. But it did make us believe we had chosen a top-notch contractor to remodel out dream home, where we could live out our lives, and raise a bunch of happy children.

I was happy to make out to the contractor, a fifth of the price, a check for $56,900. Throughout the progress of the job, similar one-fifth checks, were to be made out and with one final check, within thirty days after completion.

When the contractor was gone, Su and I sat on the sofa, and gave each other a long hug and a juicy kiss. We were happy our project was underway.

Again, I fixed us a quick sandwich for lunch. As we began eating, the phone in my shirt pocket rang and I saw it was the office calling.

"Art, this is Lieutenant Alan, and I hope you and Su are doing alright," he said.

"Yes sir, thanks for asking. As a matter of fact, Su and I have, just minutes ago, signed a contract to have our remodeling done.

It's a big project and it will take six weeks or more to complete. We've decided to get married here, instead of in Las Vegas, because we can then have a large crowd of folks here to see our freshly remodeled house; and as well as witness, two happy people, committing themselves to a lifetime together," I told him.

"Art, that is truly wonderful. Congratulations," Alan said. "However, I'm asking you right now, to come to work as usual tomorrow morning. We just had another hatchet homicide. This one happened in the Logan Heights neighborhood. The victim had his head and even his face, chopped almost to nothing. I've never in my life before, seen such a thing. Also, we've got some personnel problems I'd like you to be involved in. But Art, we've gotta find the bastard that did this latest homicide and stop him. Very important, my friend; we've gotta get him quick."

"Sir, I had counted on being home with my Su. She's only just begun to use her crutches and it will be a long time yet before she can get a prosthetic leg and become used to it," I said.

"Yes Art, I think I understand," the Lieutenant came back with. "However, we both know your bride-to-be can lay down and sit all day until you get home to help her. I say this Art, because we really do need you here, very, very much."

"Very well Lieutenant Alan," I said. "I will be there in the morning."

"Thanks Art; I really do appreciate your loyalty to both Su and to the Department," said the Lieutenant.

"Hard to believe as it is, honey," I said to Su, "there's been another hatchet homicide. This one is apparently worse than the others. Anyway, Lieutenant Alan insists I should come back to work in the morning and I said I would. Darling, I hoped to be on hand for some time yet, to help you in any way I can."

"Artie, I don't think it will be any big deal," she said. "I'm learning every time I get on these crutches here. Hey, why don't we celebrate the contracting out, by calling for a pizza to be delivered?"

The occasion somehow made our pizza dinner, even tastier than before.

Su put an arm over my shoulder as we climbed into our tub shower. Mostly when in there, she hung onto a security bar while "I did all the work!" Some work! I loved bathing her and bathing together as we did. Of course, by the time I had both of us toweled off, "something began to rise" and we very much enjoyed ourselves in bed.

Chapter Six

With Su's assurance that she would be okay that Wednesday, February 26th, I drove off to work at Police Headquarters, at 14th and Broadway. Su also agreed to call all of those invited to our cancelled wedding in Las Vegas, to tell them we would get the hitchin'-up done when the house remodeling was finished. Then, we'd have the wedding in our home, where everyone could see how well or not, the work turned out.

As I came into the Homicide Detail area, our two Lieutenants called me into their office and asked me to shut the door behind me.

"First Art," Lieutenant Brightwell said, "I've gotta ask, how's your Su doing?"

"Thanks for asking, ma'am," I said. "You both know Su is a remarkable young woman. She's actually getting around the house pretty good, on her crutches. Believe it or not, she spends lots of time rubbing her left leg, to toughen it up for wearing a prosthetic. It hurts to do that, but she does it anyway. That's my Su.

"I should tell you both also, that yesterday we signed a contract to have our house extensively remodeled. The work will begin next Monday, we're told, and the job will require six weeks or more to complete. Naturally, I would very much like to be there not just to assist my Su, but to see that the work is done correctly.

"When that remodeling is done, we'll have our wedding done right there in our house so that you two, and all the others we invite, can share our happiness and see our new home," I told those two Lieutenants.

"Hey Art, that's all really great news," Lieutenant Brightwell said. "But right now, Lieutenant Alan and I have some questions for you. Sergeant Snyder is being promoted to Lieutenant and will transfer to the Robbery Detail immediately. So, we need to promote a Detective to Sergeant for Team 3. Of Detectives Ray Mason, Marty Garcia or yourself, which would you think to be most qualified for that job? Oh, and I should tell you David Mann is my brother. The Captain told us he hadn't known that and there's a rule about relatives serving together. So, David is promoted to Sergeant and replaces your Su, temporarily, in the Elder Abuse unit."

"Oh, no you don't!" I exclaimed. "Choosing someone to lead Team 3, is up to you two Lieutenants, absolutely. I've gotta tell you, that I met longtime Homicide Detective Charles Fredericks. That was about a year ago, and he gave me lots of scoop on this job of mine. You know he avoided being promoted all the years he served here. I intend to do exactly the same as Fredericks. My aim in life is to be a dedicated Homicide Detective, to bring some bit of justice to the murdered, for the rest of my working life. I hope you two will respect my lack of ambition, to ever being promoted."

"Damn! Art, you've made that plain enough, even for a couple of dumb Lieutenants," Alan said with a big smile. "Okay, now let us tell you about the latest hatchet homicide."

Kids on the way to school the day before, found a body, "in the bushes," in the Logan Heights neighborhood, with a terrifically mutilated head, they said.

He was a short Black man of no reputation other than having been homeless for several years. Selling illegal narcotics got him enough income to rent an apartment and more than that. He owned a three-years-old, shiny black, used Cadillac SRX; it's a mid-size SUV. He was prosperous enough to bring home a woman to live with him.

Whoever wielded that hatchet, went bananas and chopped at his head and face, to make it impossible to identify the man by sight.

"Can I guess; the murder weapon was not recovered?" I asked.

"Yes Art, that's true," Lieutenant Brightwell said. "We sure had our hopes up that Sergeant Su Chi had finished off the culprit in these cases. But those six previous hatchet homicides were given more than plenty of publicity, on TV and in the papers, by Commander Macias, in his fight against the chemical warfare business. We have to suppose, another person, thinking to be a do-gooder, wants to destroy more drug pushers in that horrible way."

"I'll add to that," Lieutenant Alan said, "the Narcotics Section reports a great drop in observed selling, of those goddamned drugs. Some addicts are amazingly reported to turn themselves in for treatment. But with six dealers hatcheted before, and now just one more, those numbers are as nothing, compared to the number of dealers, all around town, peddling that junk. But we can be glad the fear of a hatchet in the head, is holding back some of them."

"Yes sir, but murder is never justified," I said, "so I should get right over to my computer and begin work on this latest case."

They both seemed surprised I would say that. But they simply nodded, and I left.

Opening up the computer to that newest hatchet homicide, I was astounded to see how badly the man's head and face had been—literally—butchered. There had to have been quite a bit of noise, and great splattering of blood and tissue, while that hatchet was chopping his skull, and slicing away at flesh. That fellow's face was absolutely gone, eyeballs and all.

The hatcheting was obviously done where the kids found the body. Crime Scene Investigators had taken many high-definition photos that showed blood splatters all around the man's head, on the grass, and behind a bush in that little playground park.

Another difference in this case from the previous six, was that the victim's pockets had all been turned inside out. Whatever money and drugs he had had on him, was all gone. His wallet was left behind, with no money in it. But there was a driver's license, his car registration and even his automobile insurance papers, remaining in the wallet. That was important information to Police. There were no photos of kids or other relatives in there. His car was found parked on the street, half a block away.

Of course, the Crime Lab would be struggling to find a fingerprint of the perp somewhere among those things. But they reported the perp had worn latex gloves, thus leaving no prints. The TV news had pointed out about latex gloves, in the previous hatchet homicides. Thus, future hatcheteers were well informed, and would be wary.

Pondering this particular mystery, I called the Crime Lab and asked them to try to determine the size and shape of the hatchet blade, from the many cuts, for the record. Also, they and the Medical Examiner's people might try to find whether the hatchet had a wooden or a steel handle, in case we should see one sometime. Even a wood splinter found on the wounds, could be evidence at a later date.

"Have you been to the crime scene in this latest hatchet homicide?" I asked Detective Ray Mason.

"Yes Art, I have but Marty hasn't," Mason said. "He's going right away, so, why don't you go with him?"

"Thanks," I said. "I'll do that."

Stepping over to Detective Martin Garcia's cubicle, I told him I'd like to go with him to look the crime scene over. We immediately went out to his car and he drove the short distance to the small playground in Logan Heights.

Standing next to the Black man Garcia, was an experience. At five-feet-eight-inches tall, I was a full nine inches shorter than him. He was a good looking, and a strong man, too.

Someone had cleaned away the blood on the grass, so there

was no sign a murder had been committed there. That was good, for several mothers or grandmothers, with their pre-school-age babes, were playing there.

No matter how intensely Garcia and I looked at the ground and the bushes there, we could see no sign that anything had occurred there at all. So, we returned to Headquarters.

On the way, Garcia remarked that Team 3 had had a terrific number of people, coming and going. Su Chin, David Mann and Sergeant Snyder were gone, leaving only Mason, Garcia and myself. The Lieutenants would have to find three more Detectives, once Garcia or Mason had been made the Sergeant and Leader of the Team.

"The Lieutenants have talked to me about becoming a Sergeant," Garcia said. "They didn't actually say I was the one to make it. But I'm not sure it's a good thing, for a Black man to be the leader of Whities. What do you think, Art?"

"Oh now; come on Marty," I said. "As Police Officers, we're all pretty much grown-ups now. I cannot imagine anyone resenting your promotion. No sir, you'll do just fine as Sergeant and Team 3 Leader, I've gotta believe."

"Really? Well now, that's good to hear," he said. "But I had best not count my chickens, before the eggs are even laid, eh? We'll see."

Late that Wednesday afternoon, we got a report that the hatchet used to kill the latest victim was a model found like it, at the Home Depot store. And yes, this one had a steel handle, with leather rings around the steel, for the hatcheteer to grip. The length of that handle would give the hatcheteer plenty of leverage power. The blade appeared to be rather standard; it was sharp and slightly curved. *And I noted to myself, it would be probably the most expensive hatchet available.* It would be costlier than any ash wood or hickory-handled hatchet.

It had a rectangular steel hammer head for pounding. I studied that photo of the hatchet from the Home Depot. The thick leather rings, which had probably been cut from thick harness-making scraps, were colored fancifully. Once glued onto the handle, the leather rings had been sanded down, so they were all even and smooth; and then most likely, it was polyurethaned.

The two Lieutenants were conferring about something when I knocked on their door.

Being waved at to come in, I entered and asked them whether the Narcotics Section had been questioned about the latest hatchet homicide.

"Art, what do you mean, have we questioned them?" Lieutenant Brightwell asked me.

"Ma'am, the Narcos surely have lists of known drug addicts," I answered. "I believe we can be fairly certain it was a drug addict, as before, who has hatcheted the latest victim. Or it could be someone getting to hell off of those poisons. It isn't likely that they or anyone can simply pick the perp out of their list, but even so, their list of addicts, could be a start."

"Dammit Art; that could be one helluva good idea," Lieutenant Alan said. "I'll go over there right this minute and see if I can get such a list for you."

"May I go with you, sir?" I asked. "I'd like to talk to someone there, who could be familiar with the persons on their list."

"Come on along, my friend," Alan said, and we were quickly up to our necks with Narcotic Section Detectives. But Our Lieutenant wanted to speak with Their Lieutenant.

I walked into the Narcotic Section Commander's office with Alan, and the man acted reluctant to lend us such a list.

"This list is maintained of drug addicts who are," the Lieutenant said, "we suppose, trying very hard to overcome their addiction and are succumbing to treatment with methadone and other things. There is a lot of relapse, as you might have guessed. We don't want to do anything to dissuade them from their proper goal, to get to hell off those poisons. So, the list is strictly confidential."

"Well now, we're in the same business are you Narcos are, in a sense," Lieutenant Alan said to the other Lieutenant. "But Detective Abrito here, is convinced the hatchet homicider is a drug addict or an addict who is trying to get off of those poisons.

Abrito is sharp. I very much agree with him and he shall of course maintain the secrecy of your list."

"Very well; I don't think the list will do you any good," the head Narco said. "I'll tell Sergeant Ross over there, (he pointed) to go over it with Abrito."

Lieutenant Alan returned to his office in the Homicide Detail area.

I stayed behind to talk to Sergeant Ross, who turned out to be well-seasoned in his narcotics work. He was in his forties and told me he had no intention of retiring for a long time.

"Having only glanced at this list of addicts trying to get away from using dangerous drugs, Sergeant… well, to me they're just names, addresses and phone numbers. I sure don't intend to call them and ask them if they could be the latest hatchet murderer. Can you point out any of them who you know to be especially violent?" I asked him.

"Oh boy; that would be most of them," he said. "There are a hundred-thirty-three men and women on here and some of them are mousy, but most get crack cocaine or meth or heroin in them, and they can become really strong and strong-minded in their deviltry."

"What about those that are recently out of jail or prison and full of resentment at being locked up for the use of drugs?" I asked.

"Oh, hey! There's a possible link to murder," Sergeant Ross said. "I've known men especially, who come out of the clink thinking it's their drug provider who's to blame for him being locked up. You and I know, it's their own damn fault for fooling with drugs at all. But so many guys and gals, well, they'd prefer finding fault with someone, other than where it belongs, with themselves."

The Sergeant went over that long list with me. Of course, he could hardly know personally, each of the hundred-thirty-three men and women shown. He took out a yellow highlighter pen and marked about six of them that he knew to be violent men. That was surprising; that he'd only known so few to be that way.

He added, "Detective Abrito, I can't believe it makes any difference whether some of these people have been long-time or short-time users. Or what their normal personalities might be. They sure do change once they've got that crud in their blood and up to their brains. I hope this list might be of some help in solving your homicide case or cases. Okay? Give it a try."

As I walked back to my place at Headquarters, I reckoned there were to be perhaps, *lots more of those hatchet homicides.*

During my lunch break, I had managed to phone Su, to find out how she was doing. Well, she sure was doing alright because the contractor was there. He came with a whole box full of samples for she and I to go over, and select what colors, etc., we wanted.

Of course, that helped to make me hurry to get home so that I, too, could help with picking out the countertop granite in the kitchen, the baths and lots of other things.

I supposed Su might be getting a bit of "cabin fever" so I asked her where she'd like to go for dinner. Her answer was immediate: her sister Lu's. She had already arranged to do that, since it was Lu's day off and had spent the day, largely cleaning her house.

We knew we would probably be "eating out" a lot, while the remodeling was going on. However, since the first part of the project, was to be the plumbing and wiring, when that was done we could go back to using our original kitchen. When the job was complete, we'd be using our new kitchen, and eating our breakfast and lunch off our kitchen island, and then dinners on our newly furnished, and very beautiful, dining room.

We intended to choose the dining table and chairs to pretty much match the mahogany look of both the very elaborate kitchen cabinets and the library bookshelves.

Since I work ten-hour days, I was really hungry by the time we drove over to her sister's house. But her pot roast dinner was practically on the table when we walked in, so I was happy. I like Lu a lot.

Oh, and she had some news for us; she had begun dating a

baker at the Ralph's where she was a cashier. She would bring him over to introduce him to us some time, she said.

Lu followed us home in her blue Chevy Impala, to help us select some of the many options for colors, we had. By nine o'clock, we had accomplished quite a lot. Lu went home and Su and I "hit the sack."

As I crawled into bed, it hit me that no one had mentioned window blinds. I got out of bed right away and looked at the drawings. Ah, there it was: a note simply said all windows would be equipped with new bamboo blinds. Ah, those could have added up to be expensive items for us. I could sleep well that night, after all.

On Thursday morning, Su beat me in her gown and robe, to the kitchen. On her crutches, she made a fine breakfast of scrambled eggs, ham, toast, taters and coffee. I relished that meal like none I'd had for a long time. What a gal, that Su!

When I got to the office that morning, I was told another hatchet homicide had occurred. This time, the murder had occurred in City Heights.

After a short ceremony when Detective Martin Garcia was promoted to Sergeant of Detectives, we high-tailed it out to the City Heights neighborhood. Ray Mason had taken the day off. At the site, one of our Police Patrol Officers stood by a body whose head was mutilated about as badly as the one killed on Tuesday.

The White man victim was laid across the front seat of a brand new and shiny red, Ford F-150 pickup truck. I think they call it a "king cab"; it had four doors. I thought to myself, that Ford pickup has been the largest selling vehicle for several decades, in the United States. This had to be one very rare instance, of a murder in one of them.

The truck was parked at the curb, in front of a small apartment house. It was a residential street with no businesses on it.

All four doors of the truck were closed then and had been when the dead man inside was discovered, and reported to a 911 operator at 6:33 o'clock, that morning.

Someone had done a beastly thing to the man's head in that

truck. The body was laying on his back, across the front seat. His feet were dangling toward the pedals on the floor, and the remains of his head, was almost against the front passenger door.

Trying to imagine how it was done as he opened the passenger side front door, I spoke out loud to the brand-new Sergeant Garcia.

"Sergeant, looking at this dreadful scene, I'd have to guess the hatcheteer was sitting behind the victim. I suppose, in such a confined space as this, he might have held his hatchet's handle close to the blade. Chances are, he snagged the victim around the throat or head, with a tie of some sort.

"Then, with his head held in place and the guy silenced, the perp proceeded to whack the guy's head repeatedly with his hatchet. With him dead and laid down on the front seat, the guy then proceeded to chop up the rest of his head and face. Damn! What a thing that would be to witness!" I said.

"Hell Abrito, it's one helluva thing to witness even now!" the Sergeant said.

Again, the dead man's pants pockets were turned inside out. He wore a now terribly bloodied, grey tee shirt, so he had no shirt pockets. A large leather wallet, held to his pants belt by a chain, was on the floor near where a hand dangled. I put on latex gloves and picked up the wallet. There was no money in it. There was only his driver's license, the truck's registration and insurance papers in it.

Ah, I saw a slip of paper, also in his wallet, with perhaps twenty names and phone numbers on it. Oh boy; that list could be gold… unless the drug dealer was wary enough to use a kind of code for the numbers. I had seen that done by a burglary suspect, when I was a Patrol Officer.

It turned out every digit of those numbers the burglar put down, was one number higher that the real number. That was pretty smart, I thought, but a Burglary Detective then, easily figured it out, because of the area code. The true numbers were of homes which the burglar would call from his car, with his cell phone, to find out if anyone was home, or not. If not, he was out of his car and into that house in seconds.

Sergeant Garcia had the Crime Scene Investigators and a Crime Lab guy there to help with the investigation. I asked them to be sure to try for fingerprints in both front and back seats. It being still in the month of February, a few people were wearing gloves for warmth. So, this perp may not have attracted much attention from the victim, for wearing gloves.

But where would a guy carry his hatchet? That question bugged me from the first. We could not ask the previous perp about that, as she was much too dead to answer. But a man with pants or a woman with slacks—or even a skirt—I thought, could have it hanging on a belt or garment top, by its hatchet head, with the handle down and inside the middle-front of one's garment. Or maybe it could be hidden in one's backpack, if the pack was long enough.

However, it was hidden while carried, any hatchet, dull or sharp, could be a monstrous instrument of death.

Sergeant Garcia and I stayed on scene, waiting for the Medical Examiner's people to come and take away the body. When that had been done, the pickup would be hauled off to the Police Impound lot.

The MedEx guys came and looked over the chopped-to-hell head. One of them observed, to no one in particular, that it looked as though the same hatchet had been used as on Tuesday's victim.

"Hey, I heard that," I told the man. "What makes you suppose it's the same hatchet as used on the other one?"

"Ah, you're Detective Abrito, the handsome Mexican with the beautiful, wavy hair I heard about," he said.

"Anyway Detective, if you look closely, you can see on some of those isolated cuts, the blade curves a little. Why a hatchet blade wouldn't be straight across, I can't guess. I think most hatchet blades are straight. Damn, somebody practically made mincemeat of this guy's head," the man observed.

"Okay; thanks for that," I said and hurried to catch up with my Sergeant, who was to drive us back to Headquarters.

On the way, I put in, "Well sir, at least we can be pretty sure our perp is listed on this note we just took from the guy's wallet or, on that list the Narcos gave us."

"Damn, Art; do you really think so? Even if you're right, how in hell can we find out about those prospective bad guys?" Garcia asked me.

"Well sir, I'll begin with calling those numbers we got from the victim today. I'll see what reaction I get when they understand it's a Cop calling them. Someone who's just committed a tremendously bloody homicide with a hatchet, might tend to be a little shook up to have the law on the line," I said.

"Well Art," Sergeant Garcia said, "I'm supposed to be the Leader here, but I'll be damned if I can think what else we might do in this damn case. We've gotta remind ourselves, that we didn't solve those previous six cases. Your gal Su did that. Did she ever tell you how many times she shot that mad woman?"

"She told me she shot her a bunch of times," I answered. "I hardly think she would take the time to actually count those trigger pulls."

"According to the Medical Examiner, they found nine of Su's bullets inside that body. Nine times, she shot that woman! Right at point blank range, too. Anyway, that many shots got that crazy thing off of her and made her awfully dead. I've gotta ask, Art: has she talked about that in such a way that it bothers her to have killed that woman?" he asked.

"Sergeant, you and I know most women are much more sensitive than men, when it comes to shooting someone. I've had to return fire on bad guys on a few occasions, and it has never troubled me in the least. I believe I can say the same, for my Su.

"Indeed, I'm amazed at her pluckiness in regard to her chopped-off leg. She accepts that it is what it is, and she even works to make that leg stub tough. It'll be some time yet before she can bear to try out a prosthetic leg, but her mind is getting ready for that day," I told him.

Immediately, when I got back to my cubicle, I began phoning those numbers on the small paper I took from the dead guy's wallet.

There was no answer to my call to either of the first two numbers. I didn't know if they were land line phones or cell phones, of course.

The third called party, did answer.

"Hello; who's this," a woman answered.

"This is Detective Abrito of the San Diego Police, ma'am.," I said. "Can we talk?"

"You're Police?" she said nervously. "What the shit does you wanna talk to me about?"

"Before I give you some news ma'am, I'd like you to verify your name and address for me, please," I said.

"Why the shit should I do that?" was her answer.

"Come on lady, you know very well you should cooperate with law enforcement, what with an investigation going on," I said.

"Investigation?" she asked. "What in hell investigation you talkin' 'bout?"

"I thought you might know, ma'am. We're investigating the homicide of Mr. Walter Adams. He was killed with a hatchet this morning," I said.

"He was kilt with a… ah, I don't know no goddamn Walter Adams," she lied.

"Of course, you knew him, ma'am. He's the fellow that sold you your drugs," I said.

"Click!" the old-sounding woman hung up her phone.

That was that. Okay, I knew then for sure, she used illegal drugs. Narcotics could of course easily find out her name and address, from the phone number. We of Homicide would naturally turn over the twenty-name list found on the dead man, when we were through with it.

Sergeant Garcia came over to me. He had a big smile on his face.

"Art, I went back to where that Ford pickup was. I found out the one who called it in this morning, lived on the third floor there. So, I had a little talk with him. He's in his fifties. He lost his left arm in an accident, so he's on disability and doesn't work. Anyway, he told me he just happened to look out his bathroom window this morning. He saw that pickup truck there, he noticed blood, and called 911.

"I went to his bathroom to see for myself and was surprised to see a telescope on a tripod there, by the window. I asked him about that. He said he and a woman about his age in the next block—who he said he'd never met—did naughty things naked, as each watched the other with their scopes! I never heard of such a thing, but I guess it's harmless good fun for them. People sure can find ways to keep themselves entertained, eh Art?" the Sergeant said.

"Yes sir; we human beings are a laugh-a-minute," I said coolly. "I've called three of those numbers on the twenty-name list. I only talked to one of them and I found out she definitely is a druggie but hardly likely to be running around with a hatchet up her skirt. I'll keep calling those numbers, Sergeant Garcia."

By the end of the workday, I had actually talked to fifteen people on the twenty-name list. Only that first one, was a woman. Every one of them were obviously illegal drug users. Seven of them did, sheepishly, give me their names and addresses. Several were a bit belligerent. None gave any reaction—what I could surmise to be a positive reaction—to my announcing the homicide-by-hatchet of Adams.

In each case, I made notes on my computer about the talks I had or did not have.

Vowing to continue calling those five yet on that list and tackling the very long list from the Narcotics Section tomorrow, I drove home.

Since I always lock the back door of our house as I leave for work, I was surprised when I got home, to find it not locked.

In the parlor, laying down on the sofa, was where I found my Su.

"Honey, are you alright?" I asked.

"Guess I am now," she said. "I was going to go down the stairs to the first floor. I merely wanted to look it over again. My crutch slipped and I fell down. I had a helluva time, getting up and getting to here. Damn; I bumped my 'rub-a-nub-stub' pretty hard and the thing is sore as hell now. I did take a pain pill so I don't feel the hurt so much now. How was your day, darling?" she asked me as she always did.

She actually made up that term, rub-a-nub-stub for her chopped leg; she laughed beautifully, the first time she came up with it. She had to at least smile, when she said it again.

"Okay, my sweets," I said. "So, you took some pain-killer. Now, is there anything I can do for you besides love you to pieces?"

We had a little session of smooching and hugging.

Then I lifted the bandage on her shortened leg and kissed it tenderly. Oh yes, I could see the skin was red with being bruised. I got out the antibiotic salve and applied a fresh coat of that to her stub. Then I applied a fresh bandage, too.

"Shall I fix us a supper, or would you like to have a pizza delivered?" I asked and she readily assented to pizza. She liked it with all the goodies on it. I forked up the green and red peppers from my side and put them over on her side. She transferred most of the Italian sausage from her side and put those delicious bits on my side. As usual, we had fun with that meal.

She almost always got her wishes when it came to picking out colors for interior paint, the granite countertops and backsplash tile.

She wanted insulated white vinyl siding to be put on all over outside. I agreed to that since the house had originally been painted white with a dark blue on all of the trim. She suggested a medium light blue for all the trim would be best and I had to agree with that, too. The garage would be treated the same except there was no need for that dense—and supposedly very efficient—foam plastic insulation as was to be applied to the house walls.

Blown-in insulation couldn't be used in the walls, the architect told us, because the house had hundreds of horizontal boards between the studs as "fire stops." That was a very good feature as it slowed any fire from spreading and made the walls stronger. The architect told me thick insulating batts were best between the attic joists, instead of the blown-in kind.

We agreed on the light tan carpeting for the bedrooms and their closets, on both floors. All six-bathroom floors and two half-bath floors would be tiled. All floors not tiled, would be in oak plank, waterproof, laminate. Carpeting would cover the laminate in the bedrooms. The original—but now well-worn in places— floors in our Craftsman house, were maple.

By bedtime, we had together decided on all the sample choices the contractor had brought to us. Su would call him the next day with the results. We were both anxious for Monday and the contractor's people to begin the remodeling. Oh; come to think of it, they would begin by trenching in the yard for a variety of wiring and plumbing.

Anyway, that night I couldn't sleep very well. I tossed and turned practically the whole night, fearing we would see more chopped-to-hell human heads and faces.

The first thing I did Friday morning in the office, was to find out the names and addresses of every one of those phone numbers we had. That took up the entire morning since there were over a hundred on those lists. It turned out, nine of them were on both lists; supposed addicts trying to get off drugs, had been obviously, still customers of the chopped-up Adams.

The 911 operator actually referred a call to me, in the Homicide Detail, just as I got back from the lunch I had with Sergeant Garcia and Detective Mason in the cafeteria.

The caller said, "Youse wanna know 'bout someone wid a hatchet? He be Big Bob, a Navy guy. His name is Bob Benson, an' he's at 3881 Wightman."

"Click" went the phone so I got right back to the 911 operator to get the number of the guy who called.

"I'm sorry Detective," she said, "but the man told me he knew who was killing drug dealers, but he didn't want any Detectives to know who he was. He said he'd tell a Detective if I didn't say his phone number. He also said, if there was a reward for such information, he didn't want it. I told him, fair enough, and I'd switch him to one of you, sir."

"Okay miss; and thanks very much," I said.

Right away, I went to tell the Sergeant what the guy told me.

"Hey! This could be a good lead," Sergeant Garcia said.

Right then, he told Lieutenant Brightwell about the lead. Then our Sergeant, Ray Mason and I all got in a Cop car and headed to the City Heights neighborhood and Wightman Street. The address proved to be a small cottage on a tiny lot. The picket fence around it was not in bad shape but it could use some paint as the house itself, could.

Mason took one side of the front door and I hugged the wall on the other side. Naturally, I had my pistol out, but Mason merely had his hand inside his coat, ready to draw his gun out.

To my surprise, the towering Sergeant Garcia brought his right hand up and knocked loudly on the door and did not reach for his gun. Also, he stood right in front of the door.

There was no response from inside the house. There was a peephole on the door, but I couldn't see if an eye came up to it inside. If someone did peek out of that door, he could see a black Ford sedan in front, with unlit lights on the roof of it; anyone would know, it was definitely a Cop car.

Again, the Sergeant knocked loudly, and this time added, "Police here! We want to talk to you!"

I could see the doorknob turning slowly. So, I racked in a round in the chamber of my pistol. Suddenly the door swung open and somebody fired. BANG! I could barely see a man with a pistol in his hand, through a few inches of opening, and I fired at him. He fell backwards! I had hit him!

Right before my eyes, Sergeant Garcia melted onto the porch floor. Mason grabbed for him. I pushed the door open to see the man's pistol on the floor and him lying on his back, groaning. I held my pistol at the ready, in case there were other shooters inside or if the groaning guy was ready to shoot again. I picked up the pistol on the floor, put it in my pocket and looked around. A

Black woman stood in an inside doorway with her hands straight up in the air. She appeared to be terrified.

Dropping down on one knee, and still holding my pistol at the ready in my right hand, I used my left hand to check for a pulse on the neck of the now-not-groaning Black man. He had no pulse. My bullet had hit him in the chest where blood was pouring out onto his white shirt. It looked like I had accidentally struck his heart.

Detective Mason was saying something to me. Oh; he said Garcia was wounded.

Turning to the outside of the door, I then saw the Sergeant sitting on the porch with his back against a porch post. Mason was down on one knee, trying to assist him. He had his phone up to an ear, calling for an ambulance. Then I saw blood spilling out of Garcia's shirt, just above his belt.

I whirled around to the inside of the house again. The fortyish Black woman still stood in the same place, seemingly frozen, with her hands in the air. And now, she was crying loudly.

Hurrying across the room toward the woman, I still held my pistol at the ready.

"Ma'am? Anyone else here?" I asked her.

With my left hand, I opened my suit coat so she could see my badge.

She shook her head and said, "No. Is he daid?"

"Yes ma'am, I am so very sorry to say, he has expired. Who is he?" I asked her.

"He be my boy. He jus' got outta the Navy; three months. He be Bob Benson. He's jus' twenty-two an' he cain't no how leave heroin alone. He jus' cain't. An' now, he be daid."

She resumed her crying as I held her hand and led her to a sofa where she could sit.

"Ma'am, we're Police Detectives and we've been looking for the person who has been chopping up people with a hatchet. Did your Bob own a hatchet?" I asked.

"I don't know nothin' 'bout no hatchet," she said, and I guessed she was lying.

"Okay ma'am, we'll see," I said and told her I had to take care of business.

Glancing out the door, I could see Mason was nicely attentive to Garcia and had him then lying on his back on the porch floor. In another instant, Mason dashed to the Cop car to get a first aid kit out of the trunk for our Sergeant. Of course, Mason would know what to do; he had been trained in first aid as every Police Officer was.

I called Lieutenant Brightwell to let her know what happened and that we needed CSI, the Crime Lab and the MedEx to come to 3881 Wightman Street.

Sitting down on the sofa next to Mrs. Benson, I tried to calm her down.

She told me she only had the one child and had brought him up to be a good boy. She swore to me that her Bob had been very good in school, had never been in trouble with the law or anybody. He had served his country for four years in the Navy and she was proud of him.

But, when he got out of the Navy, someone urged him to try heroin and he could not stop using it. She said that drug completely changed him. He hated it that he could not stop using the stuff. He was angry all of the time, day and night, and had not even tried to get a job, she said. Sometimes, she told me, when he had shot the junk into his veins, she thought he was going to die right then.

"Ma'am, where did he get that pistol?" I asked.

"I'm sorry he had it, for what he did to your other Detective. But I know for shore it warn't licensed to him. I suppose he bought it from what they call, the black market," she said.

An ambulance was the first vehicle to arrive. While they tended to the Sergeant, I told them of the dead man on the floor inside. They were quickly on the way to a hospital with Garcia, while Detective Mason and I stayed in place.

Pretty soon a crowd of investigators were in that small house. I set them to searching primarily for a hatchet... or anything like one. Within minutes, they found a steel-handled hatchet in a dresser drawer in the young man's bedroom. It had not been cleaned. Dried blood was not only all over that hatchet, but on the drawer, itself. So, they did not touch that instrument of horrible homicide, but took the drawer with the hatchet untouched, for the Crime Lab to check everything.

The woman began crying again over her son's death and went into her bedroom. She shut her door, and I ordered everyone else there, to leave her alone.

Detective Mason and I were the last officials to leave the house. Before we left, I told Mrs. Benson she could call the San Diego County Medical Examiner's office the next day, to find out when she could have someone pickup her son's body for burial.

Mason and I got in the Cop car and drove back to Headquarters. Mason seemed still a little shook up over the two shootings. He had been a Police Officer a bit longer than I had. But I could find no way to think about it, other than it's what a Cop has to be prepared for, every day on the job.

When we called on Lieutenant Brightwell in her office, to tell her of what happened, she questioned us almost exclusively about Sergeant Garcia getting shot.

"Ma'am," I said, "I have not the slightest idea of why our Sergeant became so careless as to stand right in front of that door when he knocked. Standard Police procedure, as he well knows, is to stand to one side of such a door, just for the possibility that occurred today.

"Ray was to the left of the door and I was to the right. I was intent on watching the doorknob, of course, and when it began turning, there wasn't but a split second before the perp shot the Sergeant and another split second when I shot back. Luckily, the Sergeant wasn't killed although the perp was."

"That was it, then?" she asked. "What did you two do next?"

"Ma'am," I hurried to say as Mason seemed still bothered by it all, "while Ray dutifully assisted Sergeant Garcia, I pushed the door open fully and, with my pistol of course at the ready, hollered to ask who else was there. The dead man's mother answered, she was the only one present. Still, I was wary as I talked to her and she explained to me that her son was not long out of the Navy when he began using heroin. She told me it changed him to become a different person. He seemed to be angry, most of the time, because of that drug making him a slave to it."

"Thanks for that, Art," the Lieutenant said. "I'll call Commander Macias right now and ask him if he'd like to hear from you, the stuff you just told me."

She called and the Commander asked her to send me right up to him.

He asked the same questions the Lieutenant did, and I gave him the same replies.

"Abrito, you're one sharp Detective," Commander Macias said. "I want you to know, I'll have a news conference about this. Without mentioning any names, I'll repeat the story you told me about the young man becoming hooked on those damn drugs. He got so angry... maybe angry with himself... that he not only murdered a couple of drug peddlers but shot a Police Officer.

"Now, his faithful mother is all alone in the world. All the great effort and love of hers to raise her boy to be a successful man, was for nothing at all, because of those poisonous chemicals he became addicted to.

"Thanks, Abrito. You're a very good man to have on our side," the big man said as he shook my hand. He then added, "Abrito, I sure hope this is the last of the hatchet homicides."

"I hope so too, sir, and I thank you, but you know I was just doing my job," I said as I grasped his hand and then left his office for mine.

"A thing ain't done until the paperwork's done," some wiseacre told me. But it's true; I spent the rest of the day "Filling out the file."

Of course, I would have to explain to a committee, at the District Attorney's office, of the reasons for, and reasonableness, of my shooting the ex-Navy guy, Bob Benson.

Ah; it was such a pleasure that Friday evening to get home to my darling Su. After a few kisses, she told me she had heard on

TV about the shootings on Wightman Street and wondered if I had been involved.

Telling her about the anonymous phone call to me and the subsequent action, she voiced great pride in me for being a good Cop.

"Honey, we won't have a kitchen to use pretty soon, so I got up a nice dinner for us," she said.

Wow! Smelling those broiled pork chops made me even hungrier. I hauled all the dinner and so forth to the coffee table in the parlor, while she supervised, on her crutches. She was getting adept at the use of those sticks and could easily keep up with me as we walked.

As we ate, we got to see Commander Macias, at his usual friendliness, smoothly telling the TV cameras of the day's shoot-ings, and the reasons for all that. He was particularly convincing in mentioning, in his caring way, about the mother's terrible loss, because of those "infernally dangerous poisons" her son had got hooked on.

"Why would any reasonably intelligent person take those extremely dangerous poisons, into their precious body? We all have to wonder about that. Maybe they like the idea of sending their money to support those murdering Drug Cartels in Mexico," he said. "Who hasn't heard about the extreme murder rate in Mexico these days?"

Of course, the Commander mentioned no names, nor did he mention the anonymous phone call giving us the suspect's name and address on Wightman Street.

Team 3's Black Mexican Sergeant Martin Garcia was confined to the UCSD hospital, in Hillcrest—or as some called that neigh-borhood, "Pill Hill." I stopped to buy him a little bouquet of flowers and surprised him greatly that I did. His obviously Mexican Indian wife and two little kids were there with him. She found a vase for the flowers and fluffed them up nicely.

Garcia didn't show me his wound. He told me though that the bullet had plowed right on through him, and had done no favors on the way, to some of his innards. He told me a doctor had said he could probably go home in a few days. But they had in the meantime to be certain, that no sepsis would hit him… that it would not literally, "hit him in the gut."

I repeated the visit to our Sergeant, on each of the five nights he was in the hospital. On that final night, he had quite a crowd of well-wishers visiting him, including many fellows from the Homicide Detail. He would still be off duty for probably another ten days.

So far as I knew, no one asked him why in hell he stood squarely in front of that door where he got shot. It was but a temporary lapse of carelessness that cost him a lot of pain.

Chapter Seven

Since this Friday was the last day of the short month of February 2014, we felt like relaxing. Something in the air seemed to predict a great sunset to watch. So, I dragged a couple of chairs out to our front porch. The timing could not have been better. As we watched, Old Sol lowered himself in blazing glory, first into the end of the little canyon next to us, and he then sunk himself into the skyscrapers of our downtown and finally, he at last dove into the big blue Pacific Ocean. The few stringy clouds over our coast, were all set on fire for a dazzling while.

"Honey, when we get old, I'll bet we'll do this again and again," my Su said.

"Well, we can do this in our youth, too," I said and hauled the chairs back into the house.

Someday, after all the contracted work was done, I'd hang a porch swing there, near the left side of the porch, for future swinging as we watched other glorious sunsets. Our future children would love to swing there too, I reckoned. So, I'd put up a swing on each side of our front door, for balance.

Inspecting Su's knee, it seemed to me to be improving. The redness wasn't quite so bad as the day before. In the morning, after our shower, I'd change her bandage again. How I loved to do such little things for the girl I loved deeply. So far, she had not once complained about her misfortune in getting part of her left leg chopped off. She was one positive young lady.

On Saturday, March 1st, I had to bear up under questioning about my shooting… and killing… Bob Benson. It is, of course, California state law and policy to make certain any death caused by Police Officers is justified… or not. The District Attorney's people would agree, that my shooting of that man was perfectly justified. I was asked if taking his life made me sad, and I had to say, "No." I would much prefer that the man would have survived… but, the split-second in which I had to shoot, did not allow choosing a spot on him for wounding, instead of killing.

Happy that my four-day, forty-hour work week was over, I hurried my Ford Expedition home to my Su that evening.

I still had not advertised that my Mustang was for sale. Su and I would use the money we got from that sale, to buy furniture. I listed it for sale that day with a photo of it, on Craig's list, with the non-negotiable price. It was nothing special, not being souped-up at all. But it was a pleasure to drive and the previous owner and I had not quite driven 12,000 miles with it.

Su said she wanted to go see the movie, "Riders of the Purple Sage" again. So, to get her out of our house and "back in circulation," we went out for dinner at the Hob Nob Hill on First Avenue, and then to that very popular movie. To me, it was the riotous horse races in the movie that made it fun. For Su, it was the late Police Chief's stepdaughter, Anne McCarty's acting, that got to her. Her performance in the "gotta shoot my horse" scene, was truly amazing.

When the actress supposedly had to shoot her horse, the outstandingly beautiful McCarty bawled her head off and I suppose, so did most of the people in the theater. Even so, it was a darn good show, and we loved to see a gorgeous San Diego girl, making it big in Hollywood.

On Sunday, March 2nd, Su and I spent several hours going over the contract we had signed. We also studied every single detail on the drawings and the notes there. We went out to the front porch again, to see if we could spot the logical places to drill for large bolts to hold the chains of two swings. I'd put them close to the ends of the porch so they could not be swung against… and break… the two large front windows. One window was for the parlor and the other was for our master bedroom. Two swings should balance the looks of our Craftsman Style house in front, I supposed.

We took the opportunity to visit with Su's sister Lu. She had a split shift that Sunday, with four hours of cashiering in the morning and then she had to go back in the evening for another four hours.

She told us that she and her baker-boyfriend, were getting along very well. She admitted to being in love with him and he told Lu, it was mutual with him.

Naturally, Su and I were on "pins and needles," waiting for Monday morning and the contractor's crews to begin work on our place.

She of course, had regular appointments with the surgeon who had sewed up her leg. She also had another test done, to verify that she was happily pregnant with a little Abrito. She drove her Chevy Impala as though she had not a problem in the world.

Su and I had just finished breakfast, at 7 o'clock sharp, Monday morning, March 3rd, when we heard machinery in our back yard. Wow! We looked out to see a ditch-digging tractor ready to dig up the old water and sewer pipes to the street. The same rig would also trench out to the alley, for various wiring to the house. Men were afoot there with instruments, to find the pipes underground as we watched.

There would be a lot of busting up of concrete in our basement floor, also to run pipes for the transferred kitchen sink and gas line to the stove, for the three and a half new bathrooms, and for the baseboard heating, to surround that space.

The contractor himself was there, telling the men what had to be done. He greeted us in the friendliest of terms. He also warned

Su, on crutches, to stay out of the way of the men and the machinery.

Su was just as enthusiastic about all that work going on, as I was. She also made some yummy muffins to give to all the men there, at lunch time.

Breaking up the concrete first floor was a terribly noisy thing; it was done with "jack hammers." Burley young men, Black, White and Mexican, wheel-barrowed out the concrete chunks to a dump truck parked in the alley. It took three men to get that barrow up those six steps. Later, a concrete mixer truck would pump concrete through a basement window and wheelbarrows would dump it into the floor where needed. But of course, that would only be done when the new pipes had been placed in those trenches.

More than ever, I was glad the steps to the first and second floors were outside of the house instead of wasting space on both floors, inside.

As excited Su and I watched all day Monday and Tuesday, a great deal of progress was being made. We were careful not to have our noses closely "inspecting" everything they did. We were not at all experts in such matters, but merely curious homeowners.

Even that soon in the work, men tore off the fence and gates on each side of the garage. Then a big truck dumped crushed rock to cover the twelve by twenty-two feet of space on each side. A large machine with big rollers, then went back and forth to pack and smoothen the rock bed of the carports.

The architect had told us, grass would no longer grow there, and the city code would not allow a concrete floor tight to the lot line. Also, rainwater would soak through the rocks.

Amazingly, the piping in the trenches, in the first floor, had been concreted over by Tuesday evening. To help with curing all of that quickly, four large fans were set to blowing air over the floor, and all the first-floor windows were opened. The fans were to run, day and night, until Friday at the workday's end. Outside, the lawn trenches had been filled in and the sod replaced rather quickly.

Obviously, those sub-contracting plumbers and electricians, were experts in their fields.

Another sub to show up on Monday was the cabinetmaker. He told Su and I that our existing cabinetry, was hardly original to our house, built in 1925. The existing kitchen had been done in the 1970's or as recently as 1980, he said.

While the cabinets looked like mahogany, it was actually another excellent tropical wood. It had an almost identical grain but was lighter in color. So, he would use the same wood to "custom-make" our new cabinets and stain the wood to match the wood from the virtually extinct mahogany forests. His crew would also transfer the existing, and almost satisfactory kitchen, to the basement, but with a new stove, a new refrigerator and sink.

Come Wednesday morning, March 5th, I had to leave watching the construction workers to my darling Su and haul myself off to Headquarters... a drive taking only about five minutes.

Thankfully, there were no more reports of someone hatcheting another victim. As usual then, Ray Mason and I delved into trying to make progress with cold cases. Our vaunted Homicide Team 3 had been reduced from a Sergeant with five Detectives, to only Ray and me.

Lieutenant Julie Brightwell told us that it was planned to add three more Detectives to the Team, but only after our Sergeant was back on duty.

Were the other four Homicide Teams filled up with their required personnel? I didn't know and I didn't care. I tried to keep my mind and my nose concentrated on my own business.

During those next three days, Wednesday through Friday, we had no new homicides committed, that we knew of. I'll admit I made zero progress in solving the cold—and seemingly impossible-to-solve homicides—I worked on.

When I came into the office on Saturday, a glum Lieutenant Brightwell told Detective Ray Mason and me that she had just got the word a woman, this time, had been bludgeoned, apparently, with a hatchet. This victim lived in the Encanto neighborhood and it was in her residence that the hatcheting occurred.

The Lieutenant, Mason and I all piled into a Cop car. I drove the small distance to the Encanto area and found the victim's house easily. Actually, the house looked to be almost new and was in very good shape. Even the lawn and flower gardens looked really nice. Two Patrol cars were parked in front.

I parked our Cop car and the three of us went inside the house. We had been warned so that we didn't step onto a body, which we otherwise might have done. The uncovered body, in a nightgown, was just inside the front door of the house.

Our Lieutenant was in uniform as usual, and we Detectives were in business suits.

A young Black man and a young Black woman were sitting on a sofa and sobbing.

The inside of the house was just as nice as the outside was.

The Lieutenant went right over to them. Ray and I followed her.

"Young people," she said, "I know this has got to be a terrible shock for you. But we Police have to have all the information we can gather, in our investigation over her death. Would you please answer some of our questions?"

The young fellow didn't say anything, but he nodded, yes, he would cooperate.

"Is that your mother? The mother of both of you?" the Lieutenant asked.

The lad said nothing; he just nodded, yes.

"When was she discovered like that?" she asked the boy.

"I think it was about 6 o'clock," the lad finally spoke. "It took us a while, to think, that you Police should be called about it. You can see for yourselves; our mom has been chopped a few times. It must be another hatchet homicide because we heard, two of those murderers were already found out, and were now dead. We knew our mom sold drugs to people that wanted them really bad, but we never dreamed someone would murder her for doing it."

"Do you know how long your mom sold drugs?" the Lieutenant asked him.

"No ma'am, I don't know," he answered. "But I know for sure by the time I started high school, she was doing it. I'm in the eleventh grade now, so I have to say, she's been selling drugs to a few people, for some years."

"You said to a few people; do you know who they are?" she asked the lad.

"No; no, I have no idea who they could be. My mom knew them personally; she told me that and she said she would only sell to those people she knew quite well," he said.

"Okay; did she give anyone credit?" the Lieutenant asked.

"Oh, yes ma'am," he said. "She did that and I know she kept notes of who they were. Oh! Do you think it might be someone in her notes that might have killed her?"

The young fellow stiffened right up, at that thought. So, did the girl next to him. They were both good-looking Black youngsters.

"Lieutenant, would you like to have her notebook, to possibly find her killer?" the young lady asked.

"Yes; oh yes, her notes could very well be vitally important in this case," Brightwell said.

While the girl stepped away to get her mom's notebook, the boy spoke up.

"We knew mom sold drugs. She made some pretty good money doing it. She told us again and again, to always keep it secret. She said the people she sold drugs to, needed them desperately or they could die. Those folks could actually die from not having the drugs she sold them, she told us, and that's why we had to keep it secret," the lad said.

The girl came back and handed the Lieutenant a small—purse size—notebook.

"Thanks, young lady," the Lieutenant said and put the thing in her pocket without looking into it. "Surely, this will be helpful in our investigation."

"Our Crime Scene Investigators will be here very shortly," the

Lieutenant told them. "Also, the County Medical Examiner's people will be here soon, to take your mother's body for laboratory examination. They must do this with every crime, in order to hopefully trace the murder to a particular person. After that, an adult relative can arrange for a funeral, and all that."

The two youngsters and the Lieutenant went on talking about wills, funerals, and such.

For myself, I wanted to see up close, those hatchet marks. But I sure didn't feel like doing that in front of those kids. Well, I'd have to depend on the MedEx report for that.

Indeed, just as I was thinking about them, the MedEx people came and in short order, had the woman's body in their big white van. They were then on the way to their Kearney Mesa laboratory.

When the three Crime Scene Investigators came, the Lieutenant briefed them on what was what, and I drove us back to Headquarters.

Detective Mason and I followed Lieutenant Brightwell to her office, since she beckoned us to do so. She sat behind her desk and we sat on her sofa. She took the dead woman's notebook out of her pocket for the first time and opened it.

"Wow!" she said. "This is filled with names. She used codes, and dates. 'C' could mean credit, or it could mean cocaine. 'P' could be for paid. 'H' is surely for heroin. Wow! Look at all those names and their addresses! Fellows, it's obvious that woman didn't think anyone else would be reading her notes. Here, you two take it and thoroughly examine it to find out all you can. Who wants it first?"

"Ma'am," I said, "let me take it and I'll make copies, page by page, with our printer, for you, for Ray, and about a dozen copies for the Narcotics Section. That way, all those names and phone numbers can be checked out properly."

"Hey Art, that's good thinking," she said. "Go right on ahead with it."

After making those copies and distributing them, I got to look through that little book itself. I counted but eighteen customers.

Here and there, the amount of a sale was noted, because it was on credit. That was usually for $50 and most often, a check mark would be on it; that surely meant it had been paid for. Several figures showed instead of a check mark, a 'd' which had to mean, the money hadn't been repaid, because the illegal drug-using customer died.

The drug seller had made the addresses explicit, such as "343 Such and such Street, knock on back door"; that would mean, she delivered the stuff. Customer phone numbers were also shown. Our Narcotics people would have all the evidence needed, I'd think, to go to those addresses and do some quick arresting after a search showed drugs in the place.

But none of that information actually led us to the perpetrator of that hatchet homicide.

By the time quitting time came to me that Saturday, I felt weary, and glad to get to hell out of the office and go home.

Each time I came home, I inspected Su's remaining left leg, massaged it, salved it and put on a new bandage. Her lower left leg had been chopped off twenty-two days before and I must say, she healed nicely. The end of the stub was well-rounded. She also seemed to have her former vigor, since by now, she had replenished all of the blood she had lost.

She had called the surgeon involved and made an appointment for the next Tuesday to have it examined. If the doctor said the knee was well enough, she could then go to get fitted for an artificial leg. It would be custom made for her and paid for by the insurance.

My Su was such a wonderful human being. I loved her with everything I had in me.

By the end of my ten-hour workday, four days a week, all of the workers on our project were gone. They worked eight hours, usually, and for five days. It was a pleasure for me to look over what they had done each day. On Mondays and Tuesdays, I could watch the crew in action. Every worker seemed to be a specialist. Most of the work was done for a fixed dollar amount, sub-contracted, so there was no clowning around; there was no dawdling whatever. They each got their jobs done professionally.

Just as I completed my little duty with Su's shortened leg, she told me something about a man coming, even though it was Saturday, to climb up on our roof, to put up the non-electric cooling fan on the center of the ridge of the house. He put up one like that on the center of the ridge of the garage, also. The architect had told us merely warm air coming up from the attic would make such fans turn; as would any breeze at that height.

"Hey, my sweetheart is on the ball!" I said with a big grin. "I'm glad you saw what was going on. What would you like to do this evening? I am at your command, your Highness."

"Well, my sis came over today for a nice visit," Su said. "She's working again this evening so we can't visit her. If you don't mind too much, how about going out to look at more furniture, that we'll be buying pretty soon. And we can eat out, too."

So that is what we did. After a really nice meal at the good old Hob Nob Hill on First Avenue in Banker's Hill, we found a store still open that sold antique furniture. We both liked some of what we saw. But we had to be aware, we'll have children to contend with, so we had to be careful not to buy anything that seemed too fragile or finished in fabrics too dainty and easily stained.

That was an interesting evening for both of us. Su got around very easily now that she had plenty of experience with the crutches. She was a determined young lady... and oh! So very beautiful!

We again sent out wedding invitations, expecting to have the ceremony on our new patio, on a Sunday, April 20th, nine days after the remodeling was scheduled to be completed. The contractor had said he needed thirty working days, or six weeks, to complete the job. April weather in San Diego was often especially beautiful.

That would give all of our invited guests plenty of time to plan for that rescheduled day. Su and I should have all the new furniture in place by that time. By then, we'd be able to temporarily house my parents, two brothers and two sisters, on the first floor. Some of her relatives could bed down in the two future kid's rooms, on the main floor.

Sunday, March 9th, was a very nice day. I set up a couple of folding chairs and a table in the backyard. Su and I were almost topless as we soaked up some sun and read the Sunday Union-Tribune.

Being pretty much housebound was no fun for her. So, I suggested we go for a drive… "and Su, you can do the driving."

That was a really fun day. Su got behind the wheel in her lovely Chevy Impala, I got in the passenger seat and she drove straight for Mission Beach. She parked and we walked over to watch the waves slamming the shore. She then drove us up through Pacific Beach to La Jolla. There we spent a while watching the seals occupying the beach and waters of the Children's Pool… where children—and adult people—were forbidden to be.

"Damn it all," Su said, "all the city would have to do is anchor a sizeable raft offshore some ways, for the seals. The seaward side of it could be pointed to repel waves. The other three sides could be slanted for ease of the seals climbing up to rest and sun themselves. People would never bother those creatures then, but they could watch them. The seal poop would never be fouling the kid's swimming place, or their playground on the beach. There must be lots of men and women in La Jolla, who are smart enough to think of the raft solution to the problem, that simply goes on and on."

"Well Su, you type on your computer very well," I put in, "so you should write to the mayor or somebody… or even, everybody, to get some attention for your solution."

She did type a single page letter to the mayor, with copies to a lot of other politicians and animal rights groups, too. I thought her suggestion was excellent, for both those wild animals called seals and for everyone's blessed children.

We stopped for yummy ice cream cones; that was another nice pleasure together.

Each time we stopped, Su got out of her Impala with no problems and walked around on her crutches expertly.

Su surprised me when she said she would like to see the "Riders of the Purple Sage" movie again. She had met the now-famous actress Anne McCarty once and had been impressed with her beauty, her poise and her self-confidence. Okay, I'd enjoy that movie again, too. Once more, I had to marvel at the fabulous occasion, that superb actress made of "putting down" her supposedly, "very badly injured horse."

Su and I were up, showered, dressed and breakfasted by the time men began arriving to continue with the remodeling, on Monday morning, March 10th. It happened that electricians were there to do lots of "pre-wiring," in the attic and in the first-floor ceiling. Plumbers came also, and ran their piping for the six full baths, the two half baths, and for both kitchens.

In the outer walls, all of the windows had to be replaced with double-glazed, white vinyl-framed windows. Some of them had to be relocated, allowing for three bedrooms and baths, instead of four bedrooms and no bathroom windows. That took a five-man crew the entire Monday, to get all of those windows done. The garage windows would be unchanged.

Again, on Tuesday, I enjoyed seeing things getting done. The solid mahogany doors, door frames and the trim were taken down from both sides of our main level hallway.

Then the hallway walls and the two dining room walls came down. The workmen were careful not to destroy any of the precious mahogany moldings and paneling. That wood could be re-installed and re-finished, since I had cleaned it all so thoroughly.

Wow! That really opened up our space on the main floor, just as I had envisioned. Even Su was amazed at the great space difference that was made. From now on, our Great Room, encompassing the kitchen, dining area and library, would total 1,020 square feet! That was more space than a lot of small houses had, total!

Work was begun in building all those walls on the first floor. A concrete foundation was poured to hold up the stairs-laundry room in the back of the house.

Both Su and I were very pleased with the progress being made, to remodel this eighty-nine-year-old Craftsman Style house, in South Park, into our dream home.

Now and then I pitched in to help, where mere brawn and not know-how was required. My help seemed to be appreciated.

Back in 1925 when our house was built, interior walls were finished with lath and plaster, not drywall. The plaster always took a long time to dry and that nuisance was overcome and done more cheaply, by using modern drywall. That material is still plaster, of course, but it is dried in a factory efficiently, between two sheets of really tough paper.

Tearing off that lath and plaster was a very messy occupation. My help in gathering up that stuff off the floors and wheelbarrowing the debris to an outside dumpster, was appreciated by the crews. But heck, I'd done that sort of thing for months before, so I was used to it.

Well, so much for that fun. On Wednesday morning, March 12th, I was back on the job and facing bad news. I was quickly informed that on both Monday and Tuesday, there had been hatchet homicides.

Since Team 3—all two of us—had those days off, Team 4 had taken on the investigation. Lieutenant Brightwell, Detective Ray Mason and I got the scoop from them and from Lieutenant Brian Alan.

Team 3's Sergeant Martin Garcia, was still home and off duty. He was yet recovering his health after being wounded by the crazy guy I shot and accidentally killed, February 27th.

We were told the hatchet homicide on Monday, had happened in Barrio Logan, right next to downtown San Diego. This time it was a young and very illegal Mexican, who had his head and face chopped up. It was in that wonderfully decorated park, under the bridge to Coronado. The color photos of that man on our computer monitors, were terribly grisly. The man was absolutely unrecognizable, as being human. He was found next to his souped-up Mustang GT. Well, that very fast vehicle may have helped him elude Cops, but it didn't hold off his killer.

Thus far, no progress at all had been made in discovering a suspect in that homicide.

The Tuesday hatchet homicide was discovered in the Golden Hill neighborhood; again, close to downtown San Diego, but east of it. That mutilated body was in the parking lot of a Mexican fast food restaurant, next to a sun-faded black Honda car registered to the dead man. The murder had happened in the wee hours of Tuesday morning and discovered and called in to 911, by a passerby, just after ol' sunny Sol rose up to light another day.

This time too, it was an illegal alien Mexican. He was a known drug dealer and had been both imprisoned here in California for drug dealing and had also been deported numerous times. It seems that deportation for some of those people, is merely a kind of entertainment. Many of those deportees know how to easily get back north across the border, from dear old Mexico.

Neither victim had on him any money whatever. Whatever drugs they had in their pockets, also was missing. Neither man had anything like notes on him. But they did have phony driver's licenses and equally imitation passports, as their identities.

Homicide Team 4's preliminary investigations paved the way for Mason and I to continue to try and find the perp or perps, of those two horrible homicides.

The Medical Examiner report said in each of those last three homicides, *the same hatchet had done the butchering.* Thus, there was a single hatcheteer responsible for killing a Black woman and two illegal-alien Mexican men, each of whom had been actively peddling illegal drugs.

A report from the Narcotics Section said they had responded to the notes made by the Black woman drug seller, by arresting— so far—fourteen of those eighteen mentioned in her notebook. They said not one of those men and women arrested, seemed in the least capable of hatcheting someone to death. Oddly, most of them were elderly and had been using illegal drugs in considerable moderation, for some years.

But many people, when they become addicted to one drug or another, keep increasing their dosages and thus end up dying young by over-dosing. Often, because the scrambled eggs in their heads, are so mixed up, they have no idea of how much of that dangerous stuff they've already taken in, so they take in some more to feel even better... or even dead.

The quest for a suspect in any or all three of these hatchet homicides was very exasperating. But then, that is often the way with murder. So many men and women, eager to end the lives of others, think of their own alibis, first, last and foremost. Often, that's well in advance of committing the homicide, to throw off really dumb Homicide Detectives, like myself.

We had no more hatchet homicides reported on Thursday, Friday or Saturday. That was good news. But the bad news was, we had made no progress at all, even remotely, of discovering a suspect in those three prior hatchet homicides.

By Saturday evening, I felt extremely frustrated and told Lieutenant Brightwell so.

She said to me, "Art, don't you worry none about that. Something will turn up; I just know it. The news about these homicides has been reported loud and clear by all the stations and the newspaper. Somebody has just got to squeal, like somebody did on that guy on Wightman Street. In the meantime, I know you're having a grand time with the remodeling of your and Su's beautiful home. Have a great three days off, my friend."

Ah, I sure did like Lieutenant Brightwell. She gave me plenty of reason to enjoy my time off and away from horrible homicides for a few days.

On Monday, Su had the stub of her left leg examined by her surgeon and he insisted she was ready for a prosthetic. She was fussed with for some time for the fitting and matching to her undamaged right leg. She was to come back in only two days, to have it put on her and adjusted, if necessary. I had to be at work on Wednesday, but she of course could drive herself there.

On Wednesday evening, when I drove my big Ford Expedition into our garageshe was standing there to greet me... and without crutches. It was such a joy to get a cheerful hug and (HELP! I CANNOT CORRECT THIS AREA!) kiss from my Su… and then to have her walk along to our house, arm and arm with me. Yes, she limped, but we knew she would become accustomed to that "new leg." The ramp up to the main floor was long gone. Even so, she climbed up those nine steps, if slowly. She would, with practice, soon be able to possibly run with that prosthetic on, just like those wounded warriors, we see so often on television lately. And she smiled when she said she was anxious to wear a feminine dress and skirts again,

instead of the slacks she had worn consistently, with the left leg of them limp and half empty.

We had a nice dinner at sister Lu's house and had a grand time with Lu's "boy-friend." He, like Lu, had been married before. They were divorced and he had dual custody of their two little boys. Lu was looking forward, she said, to having kids of her own and also, to caring part time for those two young kids.

Both Su and I liked Lu's guy a lot. He seemed a pretty good catch for her. And she was, don't you know, a very good catch for him.

That always had seemed strange, that men and women, no matter how in hell old they were, called their sweetheart a "boy-friend" or a "girl-friend." I had no right to call my Su, "wife," but that is what I thought of her, from the very day she moved in with me. Well, tying the knot with Su wasn't so far off anymore.

We got almost half an inch of rain on Sunday; that's a large rainfall for our paradise. We in San Diego never have to worry about really cold weather or very hot weather. There's never any snow here, or tornadoes or hurricanes. This paradise called San Diego, has about the best climate in the world.

Su and I stayed home, and she watched me with interest as I swept and mopped the floors again. I knew they'd be messy again on Monday, but I felt like doing *something*.

Other than that, we both read our novels. She adored Romance Novels and I loved adventure stories. I could not bear to read Detective/Mystery Novels, as I live that scene, day by day.

Of all things, I was most anxious to have that fireplace wall covered with bookshelves and primarily non-fiction books that I could learn from. Ah, the look of an old-fashioned estate library! That would make me feel really wealthy.

Looking around the room again, I marveled at the difference made, by taking that fifty-one-foot-long hall wall out.

There was work yet to be done there, particularly with the cove molding around the ceiling. Also, there were gaps in the flooring where the walls had been. But all of the flooring was to be sanded where rough and then covered over anyway. All of the original maple flooring was to be covered over with tongue and grooved, waterproof, oak-like, laminate planks. The new, pre-finished planks, were to be glued in place.

As soon as the existing kitchen was moved to the first floor, all of the flooring work could begin on the entire main floor. There was yet work to be done on that first floor, before Su and I could move to living down there for a while.

Both Su and I enjoyed seeing the progress made by professional carpenters, electricians, plumbers, painters, etc. The contractor provided a carpenter to be superintendent on the job, and he kept everyone busy and out of the way of others. He also contributed to the work.

We inspected the work in the first floor Tuesday evening, April 1st. It appeared to be, almost ready for occupancy. The "super" told us he thought we could almost certainly move down there after Friday's work was done. That included a crew moving our old kitchen down there, exactly below where it had been. It would have a new stove, fridge and sink.

Where the windows had been moved, stucco on the outside and plaster on the inside of the house had to be patched. Only then could the white insulating vinyl siding go on, with nails driven through the stucco and the tarpaper, into the board sheathing. When the siding had been installed and caulked, the window, door and corner trim could be painted a medium blue. Of course, that work included siding the garage, including inside the carports.

Rather than using scaffolding, the siding carpenters and painters, used big-wheeled "cherry pickers." Inside the "basket" of each machine, two men constantly changed positions to apply the siding, caulking and later, the painting. They used air-powered nail guns.

It seemed that every day, Su got more accustomed to walking again. She limped less and less. She was happy to be wearing *two shoes again*. The match of her two legs looked perfect. I could visualize her playing hide and seek with our future kids. She was one determined lady.

Well, another Wednesday, April 2nd, 2014, came and I had to go to my job of being a Homicide Detective. Bad news greeted me as one more victim of a hatcheteer was found that morning. This time, the victim was found in his alley garage, behind his house. The overhead door of the garage had not come down all the way. A passerby had spotted blood flowing out of the mutilated head of the victim.

Lieutenant Brightwell, Detective Ray Mason and I were about to leave for that address to investigate the murder, when the phone in my shirt pocket rang.

I saw it was a 911 operator calling and I answered.

"Detective Abrito, here's that same citizen who wants no reward or to give his name. Like before, he wants to tell you something. Go ahead, sir," she said, and the other voice began to talk rapidly.

"Detective, I knows who 'twas, what kilt that drug peddler this mornin'. It was Samshu Schaefer. He be a Black man what lives at 3874 Wightman Street, sorta across from Mrs. Benson. Be careful. That damn Samshu, he be dangerous."

"Click" went his phone and I immediately told the Lieutenant and Mason what the man told me.

"Art, do you think it was the same man who called about Benson?" she asked me.

"Ma'am, it sure sounded like the same guy," I answered. "If you want my opinion, I think we should head there now instead of to the new homicide case."

"Really? Okay Art, let's go see what 3874 Wightman looks like," she said. "It seems quite the coincidence that it's across the street from that Benson house."

Again, I got behind the wheel of a Cop car to drive us out to the City Heights neighborhood. On the way, I thought a lot of what the guy said about, "That damn Samshu, he be dangerous." Okay, the man gave us a warning.

Chapter Eight

Parking directly in front of 3874 Wightman Street, we could see it was a pretty common bungalow for that area. It was way overdue for painting. There was a porch reached by a single step up. The house had a front door centered on the porch. A small window flanked to the left and right. As we approached, I could see in both windows, that pull-down shades were drawn.

Instead of a mailbox as many houses had, it had a brass mail slot in the center of the front door. That way, mail could be dumped inside of the house. Samshu Schaefer then would not have to worry about others touching his mail. Packages, however, would never fit through such a mail slot.

As Lieutenant Brightwell went over rather far to the right of the door, I remembered she had been shot gunned in the leg in a similar case. Ah, she was right to be cautious.

Mason went beyond her a step and I hugged the wall to the left of the door. Then I knocked hard on the door with my left hand, since all three of us had our pistols out, and a round racked into the chambers, because of the warning we got.

"That damn Samshu, he be dangerous."

There was a glass peephole in the door, but without standing in front of the door, one couldn't see if someone looked out of it.

Banging on the door again, I shouted out, "Police here! Mr. Schaefer! We need to talk to you!"

To my astonishment, the brass cover of the mail slot popped up, and the barrel of a gun was shoved out a few inches!

With my left hand, I grabbed the barrel just behind the gunsight. I shoved it down with all my might. And the damn thing fired! It fired a burst of many shots into the porch floor!

In the meantime, I of course still held onto that barrel which had become extremely hot. And then the gun was yanked back inside. Damn! That really hurt my heated hand with the front sight ripping across it!

My reaction was to fire at the door. I did it not once, but maybe five or more times! The Lieutenant did exactly the same as I did! Mason stepped out beside the Lieutenant and he fired through the door, too!

Looking quickly at my left hand, I could see the tough flesh on the palm had been sliced. Wow! Damn! It really did hurt! Blood was pouring out of that ugly, four-inch-long cut.

Each of us stepped back away from that door. Did we hit someone inside that door who was firing that automatic weapon?

Banging the door with my right hand this time, and bloodying my pistol gingerly with my left hand, I roared again at the door.

"Are you wounded? We Police are here to help! Open the door! We can help you!"

Absolutely nothing happened as we stared at that damn door. It was terribly splintered, what with more than a dozen, 9-millimeter bullets, blasting through it.

My hand hurt like blazes and I grew impatient. Brightwell and Mason stood cautiously to the right of the door. Again, I shifted my bloody pistol to be held by a finger on my left hand as the blood poured out. Then I turned the doorknob. I pushed a little. The door swung open. I got that pistol back in my right hand and ready to shoot. Peeking in carefully into a living room, I saw a bright ceiling light was on.

I could see a man on the floor, three feet away from the door. Then I noticed his submachinegun laying away from him on the floor; it had been flung beyond his reach, as he flopped down.

Lieutenant Brightwell then jumped over to open the door wide and she walked in.

The man on the floor was bleeding profusely. He had been shot several times; I could see. One of the shots hit his left eye; that eye was gone, and blood was coming out of the socket, all over his Black face. The Lieutenant touched his neck and shook her head; no pulse. The guy had croaked.

She hollered, "Anyone else here in this house?"

There was no answer. Mason, holding his pistol at the ready, proceeded to check further into the house, to make sure it was not occupied.

As for my miserable self, I put my pistol back in its shoulder holster and grabbed a hankie from my rear pocket. Damn! That rip in the palm of my left hand really hurt! And it was pouring out blood! I wrapped it with the hankie, remembering that I had just laundered that one and a dozen more.

Not so dumb me, I called and asked for an ambulance for myself and the Medical Examiner for the dead guy. I even got blood on my phone.

The Lieutenant wanted to see it up close, so I unwrapped it.

"Damn! Your hand is really cut awfully, Art," she said. "Could it be burned, also?"

"Yes Lieutenant, I think it could be. I only held that gun barrel for seconds, but when it fired, it sure did get hot quick," I said. "I've got an ambulance coming for my hand. I've gotta tell you ma'am, it's hurting like a sonofabitch!"

She called for the Crime Scene Investigators, which I had failed to do. Hell, I was thinking mostly of my hurt hand.

Ray Mason offered to get some Tylenols from the first aid kit in the car for me, but I said no, a doctor would give me something really effective.

Gratefully, an ambulance was there in short order. To hell with the business at hand; I'd let the Lieutenant and Mason take care of that. I was on my way to a hospital emergency room.

The first thing they did in the E.R. was to ask how in hell I got my hand cut. I told them it was from a sight on a gun barrel muzzle being jerked out of my hand and the doctor and nurse there, looked at me as though I was goofy. But they needled some sort of pain killer into my hand and that pricking with the needle hurt, too. Within a few minutes, I suppose, that anesthetic was one wonderful relief.

Refusing to look while it was being stitched up, through that tough palm-of-the-hand skin, I spent that quarter hour concentrating my mind, on the remodeling of our beautiful home. That is what my Su would have done; I got to do a little positive thinking, too.

There was no need for me to be admitted to the hospital. So, I called for a taxicab and took that back to Headquarters. I waited a while for Lieutenant Brightwell to return. When she did —although my left hand was numb and no longer pained—I told her I didn't feel so doggone hot and I'd like to get to hell home.

Bless her, she told me I certainly deserved some time off—with pay—and she told me to take an entire week off. After that week, she would re-assess my situation. She said she'd notify the Payroll Department of her permission for that, and I was okay to leave right then for home.

That left only Detective Mason in Team 3, instead of a Sergeant and five Detectives!

With my left hand swelled with bandage, I got in my big Expedition and drove home.

Su happened to be outside watching crews of men, tiling our swimming pool and patio, when I walked out of our garage. She was surprised to see me and immediately concerned about my hand. I told her what had happened, that there was no pain just now, and that I had got a week off from work.

She pointed out the blood on my suit coat, pants and even on my shoes! I hadn't noticed any of that.

Su was "wearing" her prosthetic and walking around, with a bit of a limp yet.

Instead of going right into the house, I watched the patio tiling work, thirty-six feet wide—when including the pool—from the garage to the house. Damn! We sure had picked out beautiful tiles. They were being laid on in pretty patterns. By Friday that pool was supposedly to be ready for anyone to begin swimming. It had a maximum depth of four feet, so there would be no diving allowed. We were thinking of our future kids fooling around in the water, when we decided that.

All of the house windows had been replaced. The siding work had been completed on both the house and the garage. Painters were just then up in their "cherry pickers" putting on shiny blue paint on all the trim. They brushed on white paint, on the rafters that stuck out, uncovered. Those bared rafters were a characteristic of the Craftsman Style.

The painters could even reach our four identical gables in those machines.

The back porch-stairs-laundry room was done beautifully. The rounded design was lovely, with windows only on the upper half. The upper stairs curved down to a back-door landing and then curved again, to the first-floor entrance.

Su and I had moved our clothing and bit of furniture to the first floor, and we "lived there" for a few days. We expected by Friday night everything would be done and we could get much of the furniture delivered that we had ordered and paid for.

A large TV had been installed over our fireplace and that wall was everything I could have wished for—except many more books were needed to fill up those shelves. The shelves were made of inch-and-a-half thick "mahogany-like" wood and were graduated from fourteen inches deep at the lowest to seven inches deep for the highest shelf.

We found pool tables for the first floor, was too expensive to buy just now. But furniture for the three bedrooms and for TV viewing there, had been bought. Lu had promised us a juke box for music and that was also to be delivered in the next week.

It appeared the remodeling of our house and grounds was to be completed on time. The end of the thirty days of work time would be Friday, April 11th. The place was actually crowded with workmen, to get the job done in the remaining three days. The kitchen was almost completed. The bamboo window blinds were not yet all installed.

The green chain link fencing along the hundred-twenty-feet on the south of our lot was in place, but some of the white picket fencing in front was not. The north side of our lot, had a six-foot-high wooden fence, nicely done, by our privacy-loving neighbor. The north carport was tight against that fence, but of course, only to the six-foot height of it.

We had not yet bought a barbeque grill for the patio. We'd get one sometime, but not just then.

We'd store the wheeled propane grill in the garage, when we got it. That was where the lawnmower, shovels, rakes and the pool pump, heater, filter and chlorinator was also. I had room there too, to the right of the back-garage door, to build a workbench and house tools.

I had intended to buy and install myself, two old-fashioned front porch swings, when the contractor's job was done. But with my left hand in a mess, those swings would have to wait.

Su almost cried, because her L-shaped kitchen—not quite done—was so very perfect. She was especially enthusiastic about the twenty-seven-inch wide oven cabinet, ending the right leg of the L-shaped kitchen. In that lovely cabinet, she had for her use, a microwave oven at the top, then a baking oven, a broiler oven and below all that, a warming oven to keep things ready for a meal.

To the left of that cabinet, a window showed her the south side of our yard and the little canyon beyond the new green-plastic covered chain-link fence.

The beautifully built-in refrigerator terminating the left wing of the kitchen, was gigantic, and well beyond our present needs. It even had an ice and water dispenser, on the door of it. That was a convenience we'd surely use, as we both loved to drink water.

She looked forward to arranging her new pots and pans, in the big island cabinet under her six-burner, countertop gas range. The gorgeous range hood hanging from the ceiling over it, vented out the roof.

The granite counter tops on the kitchen and all of the eight-bathroom vanities, sure looked great. We had a two-inch-thick, solid "hard rock" maple countertop on the island. You could cut on it, without hurting the wood or a knife. Also, leaning on it while eating was a whole lot more comfortable than ice-cold granite. In addition, things didn't "clang" when dropped on that truly beautiful hardwood. It over-hung the cabinetry below, by eighteen inches, one three sides.

The stools for it, already bought, were of moderate height, since the island top was thirty-six inches from the floor instead of the too-high, ordinary forty-two inches usually specified.

Over her elaborate new sink, she had a large window from which she could see the entire back yard. She could watch our children at play around the pool, someday. Also, important to her, she could look over her future flower garden, through that big window. In the mornings, the dawn sun would pour through that glass, to cheer us as we began each new day.

For myself, I was most thrilled by the beauty of the elaborately paneled cabinetry. All of it looked as though it really was made of genuine mahogany wood. The cabinet maker even assured us, that the finish was especially durable. All of the insides and the adjustable shelves, were finished with easy to clean, light tan laminate. The very fancy handles and self-closing hinges were in gold-like brass. The brass was sealed in a clear finish, so as never to tarnish.

The kitchen island had room for four stools along one side and another stool on each end.

In the kitchen and in every room, including the laundry, the thirteen-ceiling fan/lights were already installed and working. All six bathrooms and the two half-baths, were vented. And each of the six bathrooms had an appropriate, obscured glass, window.

We had ordered beautiful furniture, including for the dining room. The table and chairs for there, had a capacity for twelve diners. Six of those chairs folded and were to be stored in our master bedroom closet. Because of that, I told Su we could have at most, ten darling kids.

To that she said, "You should have started breeding them when you were eighteen!"

There was a bit of advantage for me, to have the time off when the remodeling was winding down. That evening, I read for the umpteenth time, our contract and scoured the drawings with the numerous notes on them. The architect had inspected the work accomplished, up to three weeks ago. He was to inspect everything when it was complete, also.

That evening, Su and I went out for dinner… again. But I had no appetite at all. Without dampening her evening, I told her I was eager to lay down for a while when we got home. The painkiller pumped into my left hand was wearing off, so I took some pills the doctor gave me. I laid down in our first-floor bedroom and had a short nap.

She was so looking forward to using her new kitchen to make beautiful meals for us.

She had baked cupcakes for the workmen on our job, nearly every day, in the old oven.

Oh boy; Su was beginning to have "morning sickness" from her pregnancy.

Finally, I got an offer on my "fixed price" sale of my Mustang. I cashed the check for it and whew! it went through.

That money would pay for much of the new furniture, including in all six bedrooms. I hated the idea of getting high-interest loans for that purpose. We felt we had to furnish every single room on both levels, because of the needs of guests. Furniture for our children, was some time in the future. For the present and no doubt, a few years to come, adult furniture would furnish, the two-main-floor, kids' rooms.

Again, I felt it was fortunate we were able to get the cost covered by an increased mortgage, instead of putting her Amazon stock out to back up the deal.

The next morning, Su taped on a plastic baggie on my

bandaged left hand so I could shower with her. Then she replaced the bandage. Wow! It looked truly awful to me with those ugly stitches across the center of my palm. There was a lot of redness, too. And it sure as hell did hurt like blazes, even after taking the pain pills. She made up a sling to hold that hand up, and it did help make it less painful.

After breakfast, I called Detective Ray Mason, to ask him about the details of yesterday's death of the hatchet homicides murderer and so forth.

"Thought you had some time off, Art," he answered.

"Well, hell yes, Ray, but I'm still a Detective and I'm naturally curious about yesterday's shootings, and all that."

"Okay Art," Mason said. "That blast of submachinegun fire into the porch floor, put a dandy hole in it… which everyone seemed to step in. CSI counted seventeen of our shots through the front door. Of those seventeen shots, eight of them struck Samshu Schaefer. Most of those hits were in his upper body. One of them, with the bullet much flattened from going through the wood of the door, struck his heart and stayed there.

"CSI guys found the guy's hatchet, hidden way back in a bottom kitchen drawer. As before, it still had some blood on it. That will make it possible for the Crime Lab to verify that hatchet was the one to hack the hell out of the last two victims," he told me.

"Ray, I thank you very much for all that. I hope to hell there won't be any more hatchet homicides for either of us to wrestle with. And have a good day, my friend," I said.

In a few minutes, Lieutenant Brightwell phoned me, and I answered.

"Art, Ray told me he didn't think to ask you about your hand, so I will," she said.

"Ma'am, I wouldn't wish my left hand right now on anybody," I told her. "The cut is about four inches across the palm, as you saw when you re-wrapped it. The stitches look awful and there's a lot of redness and frankly Lieutenant, it's hurting a lot. I thank you, for asking."

"Okay Art Abrito," she said. "You are under my strict orders to take it easy and get that hand well again. Understand?"

(I CANNOT GET RID OF THIS STUFF TO THE RIGHT!!! >>>>>>>>>>>>>>>>)

"Yes ma'am. I shall obey you to the letter!" I said and that was that.

As I stepped out our back door, I could see a crew of men working on the carports, on both sides of the garage. I walked over to them to see them installing the mechanisms to open and close the overhead doors. That would allow someone in a vehicle, to open and close them, to park there, just as the three garage doors could be opened and closed. The distinct remote controls, numbered one through five, would have one button, to operate any one of the two carports or the three garage doors.

The tiling inside the pool had been finished the day before. Now they were filling the pool with filtered, warmed, chlorinated water. Men were also finishing the tiles all over the concrete patio. Someday, we would put up some kind of fence barrier, around the pool, to keep our kids from going into the pool, without an adult there to supervise.

Painters were just then finishing their work on the front porch railings.

Our now truly beautiful 1925 Craftsman Style home faced a dead-end street—as did the garage and carports, a dead-end alley. That was because of the little canyon to our south, getting bigger as it went west. Across the street to our front, the lot had very large boulders, so, there was no house. Other houses began to the north of us and across the street from them. So, we sure wouldn't expect much foot or automobile traffic.

We had two motion-detecting cameras now, at the front of the house, and two more on the alley side of the garage. A four-view monitor for them was in our kitchen. Even when we were asleep or not home, people appearing in those views would be recorded. Su was fascinated with that monitor as she watched trucks and workmen's activities, "fore and aft."

The painters were nearly done and so were the tile workers on that patio. It looked to me that they would complete the entire contract a day earlier than the scheduled tomorrow, a Friday.

Phoning the architect to tell him that, he told me the contractor had already notified him. Both of them would be at our job site Friday morning, for a final inspection. He told me the contractor would doubtless be here, this Thursday afternoon, to make sure the place was left in a clean and responsible manner.

Su said she was kind of sorry she would have no one to bake cupcakes for every day! She sure didn't want me devouring too many of them and getting paunchy.

The contractor showed up and looked around for a short time. Then he jumped back in his truck and left. But just to be sure, I ignored the hurt in my hand and toured our house and grounds once more. Sure enough, everything had been done and done well.

Ah, this time Su could finally make a really nice meal in her brand-new kitchen. We had no dining table or even a coffee table yet, so we had our dinner on the kitchen island. We sat on the two old stools we had kept for now. We'd replace them shortly with six new stools. We were anxious to have the many furniture items we ordered, delivered. But we were to wait until the final inspection, tomorrow.

Unable to contain my curiosity about the hatchet homicides, I called Ray Mason at the office Friday morning to asked what, if anything, further had happened with them. Ray told me; they had no word at all of any more hatchet homicides. I thanked him and he said, "Have a great day!"

That was a relief. I had also kept in touch with Sergeant Garcia, whose lower belly still bothered him, from the shot he received. He hoped to be back to work soon, he told me.

About 10 o'clock, both the contractor and the architect came to inspect. Su and I toured the place with them, as they scanned drawings and notes to check every item of the contract, which included the drawings and the specifications. None of us four could find anything contracted, not done. And none of us four could see any flaw in the workmanship.

Su and I thus agreed, we would pay the final $56,900, the fifth payment, within thirty days from today. Holding the final payment back, assured us we'd get attention if we found something wrong. We shook hands, told both of the visitors they had done very, very well, and they drove off.

Su and I each then got on our phones to call the stores where our furniture was waiting to be delivered, to do so. Only a small number of items would be delivered today and tomorrow. All the rest of our furniture, and a ton of mattresses and bedding, would be delivered next week. I felt it was a good thing that I could be home, to help make certain everything delivered, was in good shape, and placed where it should be.

Then we called everyone invited to our wedding the next Sunday, to assure them that we were still very much in love. Oh yes, and that the remodeling was complete. All of the furnishings would be in place by then, also. Those invitations had gone out not just to our relatives, but to our friends and mutual friends, on the San Diego Police Force.

We promised them not only a wedding to attend, but a newly remodeled house, a pool/patio to look over and a lunch with plenty of drinks to choose from.

They could bring swimming suits, if the weather proved to be warm enough. The pool water would be warm, whether the air was comfortable or not.

Su would not have people seeing her shortened leg, so she wouldn't use the pool with company here. Neither would I swim, because my hand would not be fully healed by then.

We couldn't be certain everyone invited would attend, but we assumed they would.

The first delivery Saturday morning, was of the six stools—with arm rests—we bought for the kitchen island. The wood on them was finished in burgundy color, so they went well with the cabinetry. They were covered in contrasting light tan leather, on the seats and backs. We thought them grand when in place.

Su's sister Lu promised to help make up the many beds, on both floors. She would also help, during the days she had time off, to arrange things here and there. There was at least one vase in every room, filled with—of present necessity—artificial flowers.

Lu had found for us, on the internet, two sets of chinaware, for the kitchen and the dining table. The grander, one-hundred-piece dining set, was "Made in China"; of chinaware called "Blue Willow." That pattern had been copied before by the English, but this was to be the genuine, perfect design from ancient China. Every item varied a little in the pictures on it. The paintings, by hand, were done solely in blue… even the willow trees, painted on every dish.

The Chinese-designed, eight-place set of dinnerware for daily use, was to be flowery, "nearly unbreakable," melamine.

The really grand sofa facing the fireplace and TV in the "Library," was made in Mexico in an elaborate style. It fitted in nicely with all the mahogany work, being in a richly done, burgundy leather. The sprawling coffee table in front of that sofa, was also a really fancy style. There were a zillion small brass tacks pounded into that furniture.

By Saturday, April 19th, our house was in tip-top shape. Su and I had worked every day, for long hours, to make everything ready for the "really big day." Sister Lu was a big help, too.

There are countless kinds of food fit for such a midday party out of doors. But Su and I hit on Dominoes' Pizza, which was our favorite "one dish meal." We bought seventy large paper plates, plastic forks and knives, napkins, Styrofoam cups, and filled ice-water tubs with sodas and beers. Then we ordered ten pizzas from Dominoes, each with different toppings. Those pizzas produced eighty slices. They were to be delivered hot, at exactly 11:10 Sunday morning.

We rented folding tables and fifty chairs, to spread out on the patio, for the joyous occasion.

After all, this was to be a patio party. And with our families as guests, they were hardly expected to have to do any cooking for the occasion.

Every last piece of those delicious pizzas was devoured; so, we had done right.

Even the weather looked to be decent, if not quite perfect. The high for Sunday was to be only 68 degrees, but it would at least be partly sunny and not windy at all.

Su and I picked up my dad, mom, two sisters and two brothers, at practically 11 o'clock at night at the airport, in—what else?—my huge Ford Expedition. It was 1a.m. then in Chicago. They would have to leave Monday night to fly back to Chicago and reopen their restaurant to get to work on Tuesday.

But my dad told me they were forming plans to open a first of perhaps many branch restaurants, and their five-days-open-each week was going to become open every day, eventually. They would be hiring lots of managers, cooks and waiters-singers, in the future.

We picked up from the airport, Sunday morning, Su's and Lu's relatives from San Francisco. The San Franciscans—who could stay until Tuesday—would get two bedrooms topside, and the Chicago crowd would bed-down in three first floor bedrooms.

When I told my dad about my plans to put up two swings on the front porch when my hand was fully healed, he became as excited as I've seen him. He insisted he and his two other sons would do it immediately, while they were here. Amazingly, we piled into the Expedition, went to a store I never heard of, and he bought the swings.

But the swings he chose were self-sufficient. They were to be screwed to the porch floor, with no ropes or chains required. And they were safer and there was no danger of swinging too far and breaking anything at all. They were already fired-on-painted in the factory.

With screwdrivers in hand, those three soon had those two large swings secured and a-swinging, on each side of our porch.

That was truly nice of them to do that, and naturally, Su and I were really grateful to them for buying and installing those swings as well.

Not to be outdone by the Chicago crowd, the San Francisco relatives bought and put up an umbrella-covered, really nice, six-foot-long, pre-painted, table with benches, for the patio.

Come 11 o'clock sharp Sunday morning, April 20, 2014, Su Chi and I stood in front of an acquaintance of mine, a San Diego Judge, to vow our love and fidelity to each other forever, etc.

Su seemed even more beautiful than before, in the flowing white wedding gown, handed down from her sister and her mother. I was as though ready for work, in a business suit.

Before a bit of important-to-the-occasion-words, however, the Judge bellowed out:

"Ladies and gentlemen, I want all present to know, this wavy-haired man in his fine Detective suit, and this beautiful woman in her wedding finery, are both truly excellent San Diego Police Officers. They can be expected to serve us honorably for many years to come. I say that, because although Sergeant Su—in a moment, Sergeant Su Chi Abrito—is getting used to her new apparatus, I do believe she will be back in service, preventing Elder Abuse and finding prosecution evidence when it does occur. Now, let's get these two-beautiful people, MARRIED!" he hollered with a huge smile.

And that he did, followed with the sweetest of kisses for me, from Mrs. Su Chi Abrito. After that, I had my hand shook almost off of my right arm. I got plenty of kisses too, from the charming females present. It seemed a long time since I had kisses from my little sisters.

My two brothers and two sisters had brought their guitar, banjo, violin and accordion. They sang for us all, I think, five times that day. Damn! My kin were really talented!

It wasn't too surprising that Detective Ray Mason and many other Homicide Detectives showed up, but so did Sergeant Garcia, who stayed for only a while, because of his sore belly. Also, Lieutenants Alan and Brightwell were there with their congratulations on the wedding and the remodeling.

Most surprising, was that Captain Morgan and even Commander Macias attended; each of them brought along a beautiful wife. I knew those two had an ulterior motive, as they talked for some time with my own brand-new wife.

They of course hoped she would return to the Elder Abuse

unit. It was testimony to her talent, that they did. I noticed those two high ranking Cops watching Mrs. Su Chi Abrito, to see how well, or not, she walked with her new prosthetic leg.

It was almost 5 o'clock before all the guests had gone, except for our relatives. Then all of us took happy turns in the porch swings. Oddly, that seemed to be the favorite improvement to our old-fashioned, and now spectacularly pretty, home!

Us "newly-weds" cuddled in the south swing as a spectacular, clouds-on-fire-sunset, settled across our little canyon, and our downtown, before finally making a swan dive into the Pacific Ocean. We could believe we'd be doing that for many years to come.

With darkness upon us, we lit up the back yard. But it was chilly out there, so we all headed for the first floor where we enjoyed Lu's gift of a juke box belting out mostly old-time music from the days of… well, from the days of juke boxes. Once more, my sisters and brothers played and sang for us. They were so very good.

Su would not dance. She was still not agile enough on that left leg. So, I didn't dance either. But my mom and dad did. My sisters and brothers danced with each other, too.

Two of Su's cousins worked in a Chinese restaurant in San Francisco. They and my folks had a good time comparing notes between the two culture's foods. Su's people were especially curious, about the "singing waiters," three-minute act the Abritos had, every half hour.

By 10 o'clock that wedding night, we were all pooped enough to try out the new bedroom furniture. As I shut our master bedroom door, Su gave me a wondrous big smile and said, "Hey husband; this is our wedding night and I expect a very hot screw!"

"My darling wife," I said, "that's exactly what you're going to get!" And get it, she did.

Su and Lu had spent a lot of time and energy, fixing up every bedroom and the accompanying bathrooms nicely.

There was soap and shampoo dispensers in all of them. They also put in powder with the powder puffs. Toothpaste was also there, and even still-wrapped toothbrushes—in quantity, they were very inexpensive. Towels and washcloths, plus of course that ultimate necessity of toilet tissue and Kleenex was in all eight of them. Su commented that they seemed to be working in a hotel!

When my hand was okay, I would put up a solar-lighted flagpole and a proud American flag, in both the front and the back yards. After all, both of us Abritos were no longer Mexican or Chinese… we were absolutely, one hundred percent, *Americans.*

Also, over time, I'd put up bird houses, bird feeders, hummingbird feeders and a bird bath. Both Su and I looked forward to planting flowers of several kinds. I was especially keen on making flower boxes with real posies in them, for the windows, the front porch railings and for the front picket fence.

We had both heard how those damnable black crows moving into some San Diego neighborhoods had devastated their songbird populations. That was because the crows raided nests and fed their own young with the babies of other birds. Well, the law says you can't shoot crows in the city, but it doesn't say you can't harass them away, whenever you see them in your yard.

I figured to get firecrackers and throw them at those intelligent black flyers, to frighten them away.

A surprise was that Captain Morgan phoned us Monday morning, the day after the wedding. He asked if he could visit and naturally, we said of course he could. He must have been calling from close by, because he was at our front door within minutes.

Su's and my folks and us newlyweds were still eating our breakfasts, at our new, beautiful dining table. I bid him to come in and enjoy something with us. He agreed to a cup of coffee and sat down at that splendiferous table with us as I poured him a cup.

"Su and Art and you relatives of the happy couple," the Captain said, "I have a fairly simple proposition to offer these beautiful newlyweds. Commander Macias and Chief Williams have agreed to what I'm suggesting, to you two Police Officers. What I propose, is that Sergeant Su Chi Abrito continue with her splendid and greatly important work of preventing and obviating Elder Abuse. What I want you to do, Detective Abrito, is to be her backup every time she goes to investigate an incident of elder abuse.

"Every Police Officer in San Diego and beyond were horrified to learn what had happened to our Sergeant Su Chi. We are all aware how those damnable illegal drugs destroy the minds of decent people. Much too often, either alcohol or drugs madden people and they do things unthinkable to them otherwise.

"Every Police Officer knows they cannot ever know in advance, what confronts them on a day to day basis, on the job. Sergeant Su Abrito, you are hereby forbidden to ever go on such a call as you did that last time, alone. Your loving new husband, dressed beautifully in his Police uniform, must be with you on every such occasion.

"Detective Arturo Abrito, you are hereafter to be known as a Detective-at-Large. A small increase in pay comes with that very rare title. That is, you will accompany your wife on her calls outside of her office and yet, your very real talents are needed in the Homicide Detail. Therefore, when not in fact backing her up, you should be as before, helping to brilliantly solve Homicide cases.

"I should mention, Mrs. Abrito, that one reason you can continue to be so successful in the Elder Abuse unit, is because you are—as everyone here is aware—you are stunningly beautiful. Every person in the world has seen beautiful women celebrities often on television, in movies and in magazines. But like nearly all of us ordinary people, they have got to be immensely impressed to see such a beauty as you, up close and in person. That isn't in the least flattery; it is just plain fact. Your perfect good looks, Mrs. Abrito, will help you greatly in your work.

"Chief Williams," Captain Morgan continued, "has suggested, Sergeant Abrito, that you dress in the finest clothing you can, every day at work. Also, Art, you are to wear your Police uniform always, even in Detective work. That handsome face of yours and that obviously powerful body, has also got to impress the hell out of anyone you meet, including bad guys."

He paused to catch his breath and then went on.

"Well, that was a rather long speech, my friends, but the good you two can do is extremely important. Can I tell my bosses you two agree to all that when you're both fit to go back to work?" he asked.

I didn't want to answer first, because it seemed to me, Su would be most important in this. She didn't hesitate but a short minute when she saw I didn't answer.

"Captain Morgan, as for myself, I can only agree to get back on the job, as soon as I can stop limping when I walk. I should be well conditioned to my prosthetic soon. Artie honey, what about you? Can you agree to handle both jobs, as the Captain suggests?" she asked.

"Captain Morgan; yes, I do agree. You know very well sir, I would be honored to accompany my darling wife, instead of having some other good-looking Officer drooling over her every day at work. Yes sir, you've got yourself a deal here!" I told him.

"Aha! Bravo to you two!" the Captain said. "Also, the Chief suggests that, since you have a three-car garage, that you can be assigned one of our Crown Vic Cop cars. You can go to and from Headquarters with it, as well on calls and keep it garaged when off duty."

Sipping some of his coffee, Captain Morgan offered that we should have a little time for a "Honeymoon" before going back to work. We agreed and settled on returning Wednesday, April 30th, when we should both be ready for work. We would have the same four-day work week as before.

The Captain shook hands all around and drove off.

Su and I hadn't thought much about a honeymoon to somewhere, because of her limping leg and my bad hand. Suddenly, she got an idea.

"Artie my sweet, why don't we toss a coin to see whether to visit San Francisco or Chicago for a week. Some other time, we can visit the other," she said with a big smile for her perfect suggestion.

The last place on earth we would have chosen to honeymoon, was to the south, with all those drug-boss killings going on… and maybe especially, since we were the dire enemies of those cartel people down there, south of the border, down Mexico way.

"Very well," I said. "Heads it's Frisco and tails it's gonna be Chicago."

I gave her a quarter from my pocket. She flipped it through the air, onto the floor. She squatted down, picked it up and pronounced the winner.

"Ah, 'tis Chicago we're heading for," she smiled.

But I noticed, she didn't actually let me see that it was tails on that coin.

We talked to my folks, right there at the table, about our coming honeymoon trip to see them. We got a recommendation for a hotel within walking distance of their home and restaurant. We soon had a room reserved there.

And just to be on the safe side regarding our brand-new-old-house, we hired a protective agency to monitor the place while we were gone. In the future, with both of us working, we'd never be leaving the house unguarded.

Chapter Nine

Bright and early on Tuesday morning, April 22nd, our Southwest Airlines flight had Su and me on the way to see my family in Chicago, the day after they made the same flight.

While there, we of course had several dinners at the Café Abrito and enjoyed, very much, the singing and music from my brothers and sisters. We spent an entire day at the fabulous Chicago Art Institute and the Shedd Aquarium. With the family restaurant closed on Sunday, we and the whole family took in a baseball game at Wrigley field. That was only a few blocks walk from their house. Neither Su nor I were big baseball fans; but we were that day, as the San Diego Padres beat the Chicago Cubbies!

My dad and mom were particularly excited to tell us they were then negotiating to open up a branch restaurant. It would be further north in the city. My dad, especially, was enthusiastic to open up more and more such Café's. He'd insist on the same pattern as then in use, with singing waiters and the very best Mexican style food…plus top-notch American burgers.

My Su took advantage of our time there, to shop for a few new dresses; dresses that she thought not just gorgeous on her, but somewhat appropriate to a female Cop.

The days zipped by and too soon, we found ourselves flying back to San Diego. We got to our house at our bedtime—10 o'clock—on the night of Monday, April 28th.

We would take all of Tuesday to reorganize ourselves and get ready to go back to work. Su only occasionally limped slightly and my left hand was pretty nearly okay again.

Su had a great idea. She suggested altering the right pockets, of my uniform shirts, where I habitually carried my smart phone. She got out her small, electric sewing machine that she kept in her closet. She adjusted the shape of those pockets so that the camera lens was just above the cloth. Without removing my smart phone, I could poke the video camera "on" whenever I was to confront a possible bad guy or gal. At the same time, it would record sound, and I would have a fairly accurate record of who said and did what.

Su and I took her Chevy to Headquarters Wednesday morning, as we were to be assigned a "Black and White" Cop car. I took along the left-hand garage door remote to use, when I drove the Police car home.

She was "dressed to the nines" and I wore my splendiferous Police uniform, fresh from the shirt pocket work. While she went directly to her office, I checked out the Cop car, Commander Macias said was to be ours to use, back and forth to work, and while working. San Diego had a shortage of Police Officers, and therefore had a small surplus of Police cars.

It was the usual Ford Crown Victoria Police Interceptor model. It was not new, but I was told it was in top condition. It was fully equipped with a siren, lights on top, spotlights, computer between the front seats, and an angry-suspect-proof screen between the front and back compartments. The odometer showed 80,000 miles; not bad for a well-maintained auto. It even had a shot gun, stood up by the front passenger seat. It was spotlessly clean, inside and out.

Naturally, in the previous years, Su and I had each driven a great many miles, patrolling San Diego's streets, in the exact same vehicles.

I was assigned also, to a specific parking place at Headquarters, so that in a hurry, I could always know where to find our Ford Police Interceptor.

After locking the car, I then dashed inside and reported to Sergeant Martin Garcia, freshly back leading Homicide Team 3. I told him my primary duty was to drive for and guard Sergeant Su Chi Abrito and I was headed there to find out if she needed me. Her office was actually but a short walk from the Homicide Detail area.

"Detective Abrito," she said, sober-faced as I came up to her, "we've got a case of an older man beating up his younger brother. Their apartment is just north of Adams Avenue, on 30th Street."

We were already heading for the parking lot as she told me about a neighbor calling to report the screams to Police again. She said she was told, that an abusive brother had been at it, bullying his younger sibling, for quite a long time.

My wife was at her most gorgeous. She had been a fashion model during her high school and college years, so she knew very well how to apply her make-up, to best accentuate her natural beauty. Her dress was fashionable, without being too sexy. She was careful not to have half of her boobs showing, as was so common these days.

Her dresses made her pregnancy not noticeable.

She carried a small and pretty purse, slung from her shoulder. In her purse was her 9-millimeter Glock pistol and her Police Sergeant badge, besides her wallet, keys, cosmetics, etc.

We had agreed, she would refer to me—on the job—as "Officer Abrito." There was no need for the public to know, I now had the exalted rank of "Detective at Large" Art Abrito… oh, and that we were husband and wife.

Without bothering to flash our lights or blare the siren, we were pretty quickly on 30th Street and in front of the apartment house we wanted. Purposely, I hurried around to the passenger side of the car and opened the door for her. That was so that anyone watching our little act, would understand, "that beautiful woman was a Very Important Person."

We entered the building and I knocked hard on Apartment 2-D. The sobbing noise from inside the place, stopped.

A male's voice inside said, "Who the fuck is it?"

"We're the Police. Open the door, please," I shouted in a gruff voice.

The door opened a little, to peek out. I pushed the door open further to see a gray-haired dude standing there with a dirty white shirt hanging over grey pants and bare feet.

"Police Sergeant Su Chi wishes to speak to the brothers Henkel," I said as I barged inside ahead of her. I had, as I entered, my right hand on my pistol handle, so whoever was there, could understand I meant business.

Another man was seated on a regular chair. He was fully dressed as though ready to go somewhere.

"Okay, which of you is George and which is Henry," she said in matter of taking over the situation.

Immediately, I could see the two men had their eyes glued on the most beautiful creature they had ever seen up close.

Henry was the guy sitting down and George was standing up, with his mouth wide open, staring at my wife.

"Right now, I want you two men to sit right there, on that sofa," she said as she pointed.

Henry jumped up to obey her, but George just stood there, as though frozen.

"Come on George," Su said, taking the older of the two men by the arm, and actually leading him to the sofa.

"I've got a very good reason for you two brothers, sitting together," she said. "We Police have had a number of calls from your neighbors about the ruckus kicked up in this apartment. We Police don't like that. I especially, don't like that. I think brothers ought to practice some so-called brotherly love. You two guys… have you never heard of brotherly love?"

"Yeah; I have," George said. "I've heard that from queers."

Su snapped her head around to me. "Officer Abrito, we've got a wise-guy here. He doesn't yet see how serious we are here today."

Turning back to the wise guy on the sofa, she said, "George Henkel, I take it you're the bully here in this family. I've heard you are almost sixty and Henry here is five years younger. A neighbor confided to me that you have bullied your brother for years. Now then, I want you to tell me, right now, why the devil, do you pick on your brother?"

George's face reddened as though embarrassed.

"Well, I gotta tell ya, Henry is such a sorry ass… excuse me, ma'am… He just don't think right some o' the time an' I gotta straighten him out. Go ahead Henry," he said as he turned to the other man, "an' tell her that's true. You just don't use the damn brains give to you."

"Ma'am, he just doesn't think he's ever made a mistake. He thinks I'm the only one that makes a…" Henry began to say.

"Yeah; like this mornin', eh?" George said, cutting in. "Ma'am, this mornin', he takes a gallon jug a milk outta the fridge and drops it on the damn floor. Crissake! There's that damn expensive milk all over the damn kitchen floor… it was splashed on ever' thing! Made a helluva mess. See that? He does dumb stuff like that all the damn time! A course I get mad at him. Wouldn't anybody, ma'am?"

"Well, I don't think I've dropped any gallon jugs of milk lately," she said. "But just last Friday, I took a carton of eggs out of our refrigerator and swung it around. That carton accidentally hit the back of a stool. I must admit, there was raw egg splattered everywhere and my husband and I had to laugh at my clumsiness as he helped me clean up that awful mess.

"So, what I'm saying, such things can and do happen to people everywhere, all the time. You have to know that is absolutely true. Neither of you should be angry that the other one has an accident now and then. It's only normal."

"See there, George?" Henry burst out.

George said not a word then.

What was so revealing to me as a bystander, was the way she was able to quickly soothe the feelings of the two men. She didn't scold. She flashed her smile often. She somehow soon had the old bully almost apologizing to his brother.

Within, I'd guess, half an hour, we were heading out the door with the brothers seemingly on somewhat good terms for once. She however warned them, that if she had to return, she could bring down retribution on both of them from California law.

Driving back to Headquarters, she told me I had played my part well.

Then she added, "I don't think the good feelings between those two will last. They've been at odds, habitually, for a lot of years. I doubt they'll change very much."

Well, I was only an observer, so I reckoned she knew better than me.

She told me she'd call me the instant she had to make another house call.

Back to my desk in the Homicide Detail, I was informed we had another hatchet homicide and this time, it was in a tavern, in the Pacific Beach neighborhood. Drugs were being sold and consumed all over the city of San Diego, so that in Pacific Beach, with its countless bars, that was no surprise.

Before leaving with the other Detectives—they being in business suits while I was in my uniform—I called my Su to let her know where I was headed with our Cop Car, if she didn't need me just then. She said she would be on the phone almost the rest of the day, so I should go ahead on that case.

Lieutenant Brightwell, Sergeant Garcia, Ray Mason, three brand new Detectives and I, were pretty quickly at the Garnet Avenue bar. Two Cop Cars were already parked in front of the place, and our three "black-and-whites," had to stop in the street. A yellow tape was across the entrance. We walked in, to an especially gory sight behind the bar.

There on the floor was a human form, wearing a terribly bloodied white apron and formerly, a white but now mostly red, shirt. Above the apron, was a mass not at all recognizable as a man's head. Someone had chopped that head, that face and even that neck, into a remarkably bloody mess. If it proved that a hatchet was the instrument of death in this case, it had to have been almost countless times, that it was used, to make hamburger meat out of the victim's head.

Blood… and bits of flesh… were scattered about on the glass-washing sink, the floor and many of the bottles on shelves from the lowest shelf, to maybe five feet up.

Lieutenant Julie Brightwell—this time in uniform—was looking awfully pale as she asked a Patrol Officer, "Who called this one in?"

"It's that little man over there in the booth, ma'am," he told her, pointing to the fellow.

Anxious to hear what he had to say, I went along with the Lieutenant to the man.

"Hello," she said to him. "I'm Lieutenant Brightwell of the Homicide Detail in our Police Department. I understand you called 911 to report a murder here. Tell me sir, what did you see to report?"

The Mexican-appearing guy stood right up to his full height of about five feet.

"Ma'am, I comes here 'bout the same time ever day. I do janitor work in a restaurant, 'cross the street. I gets through work, an' I comes here on the way home, for to have a drink. I comes in today, and there ain't nobody here atall. I sat down on a stool, waitin' fer the bartender to come from the washroom, or where the hell ever he was. Couple a minutes, I smelt somethin'. It smelt bad.

"I lean forward a little an' I see a body on the floor behind that there bar," he continued. "Never in my life, has I seen any such thing as that. I felt like pukin', but instead, I hurry right over to where I am right now an' I take out my phone an' I calls 911, 'bout that chopped to hell body behind the bar. That's what I did ma'am, an' I sat right here till the Cops, they came in."

"Thanks for that, sir," she said. "Do you know who that man is back there?"

"Cain't tell by lookin' at him, but I gotta s'pose it's ol' Frank

Taylor. He's the usual barkeep, durin' the day, durin' the week, ma'am," he said.

"Okay sir, there was no one here when you came in," she said to him. "Did you happen to notice anyone coming out of the bar or like, going away down the street, or something?"

"No ma'am, I shore did not notice nobody like that," he said.

"Okay; thanks," she said. "Now, give your name and all that to Detective Mason here."

While the Lieutenant talked on the phone with someone, I went behind the bar. I leaned down to see close up, about those hatchet blows. The splintered skull showed they were done, it seemed, with great force. I judged it would require a strong man to deliver such blows… and so very many chops. A guy had to be a mad man—not just an angry man—a person absolutely gone bananas, to do such a thing to another human. Methamphetamines will do that to the brain. Others of those poisonous drugs will make a person go insane, also.

I saw the bartender's pockets were all turned out, too. So, he was also robbed.

Rising up from the butchered—literally, the butchered Frank Taylor, I went back over to talk to the little man in the booth. The Lieutenant and the rest of Team 3 had walked away from him and were talking to each other at the bar.

I was guessing that such a little fellow, a janitor, and getting on in years, would have few interests outside of a bar. He would be one to sit for perhaps hours and be curious about the other patrons. I've met men like that.

I poked my phone with my finger, making sure the man in the booth saw me do that.

"Sir, I must ask you a very important question, as I'm recording here," I said. "Do you know if Frank Taylor ever sold any drugs here?"

"Funny you should ask, Officer… ah Abrito," he said as he stared at the brass name plate on my right chest. He also looked at my face; he was seemingly fascinated by my looks. That was not the first time I had noticed men, as well as women, drinking in my countenance.

"I ain't no goddamn druggie myself, but I seen ol' Frank, he gets a twenty or somethin' from a guy now an' again, an' he slips 'em somethin' in a little plastic bag. Gotta be drugs, seems to me, but it ain't none o' my goddamn business," he told me.

"It would seem someone did not like him to sell drugs, sir. So, he chopped him up; he chopped him up really bad," I told the little man.

"Yeah, I saw that too, Officer Abrito," he said.

I sat down on the seat opposite him and leaned across the table.

"Sir, you're going to help us," I said, quite close to his face. "You liked Frank Taylor, didn't you?"

"Yeah; he was alright, I guess," he replied. "But he hardly never did give me a free drink. Ol' Frank was real stingy, with the boss's drinks."

The guy smiled at that, as though it was an excuse to be only mildly caring about the man behind the bar.

"Okay. You come here fairly often, and you've seen ol' Frank pass a little plastic over the bar for a twenty, now and then. I want you right now sir, to tell me who those drug-buying guys are. You and I can bet, one of them—some really strong man—we'll find was the one who chopped up ol' Frank."

"Oh shit. I think I know who the hell it's gotta be, to do such a goddamn thing. Never woulda thought of that, but you askin', well… Him? Hell, he's big as a damn house. He's been actin' real nuts lately, I'm thinkin'. That's gotta be Jose Salas. He's a real big Mexican guy. He's a concrete man. He don't have no concrete truck hisself, but he works at it, smoothin' concrete out, he told me onec't or twice."

The little guy didn't know where Jose Salas lived, only that he worked at concrete work. He didn't know where he did that either, but supposedly at such jobs throughout San Diego.

The important thing was, we had the name of a possible suspect. I told the Lieutenant and the rest of Team 3 what I'd been told. With the magic of those tiny computers in our hands called smart phones, some quick sleuthing through them, led us to a construction site just a little north of where we were, in La Jolla.

The Lieutenant and we of team 3 were soon at the building going up, up there. She talked to a supervisor there and was told the man had not come to work that day. But he gave her Jose Salas's home address. We were pretty quickly there, near where Garnet and Grand intersect, in Pacific Beach. We parked my Cop Car and the two other Cop Cars squarely in front of the Salas house, at the curb.

The address proved to be a pretty nice little house. Actually, it was a single-story cottage. The front yard had imitation grass on it. Also, there were well-faded, imitation flowers in two front window boxes.

As we piled out of our cars, the phone in my shirt rang. I grabbed it and saw it was my Su calling. So, I stopped on the side-walk, while the rest of the group hurried on to the house.

"Su! What's up?"

"Artie, where are you right now?" she asked.

"I'm right near the intersection of Grand and Garnet, in Pacific Beach. We've got a…"

"I've got a call that might be a homicide," she said. "It's on Clairemont Mesa, where I had been just before my leg was chopped. I'm on the way there in a squad and I'll meet you up there," she said, giving me the address.

"Sergeant Garcia, I've gotta go!" I shouted to our Leader and jumped back into my Cop car.

This time I put on the siren and the lights. The very last thing I wanted to do, was to get to where my darling Su was, too late!

In the meantime, on the way, she phoned me again to give me some details. She had been at that apartment, the very day and immediately before, as she said, that her left leg got chopped by the mad woman she soon shot to pieces.

That time she had to arrest a middle-aged woman who beat the hell out of her mother and was hauled off to the lock-up by a Patrol Officer. That woman had drugs both in her bedroom and in her body. The drugs in that apartment had of course, been confiscated. The malefactor had today just been released from jail and had gone home.

This time, a neighbor had phoned 911 to report gunshots coming from that mother-and- daughter apartment.

As I pulled up in front of the apartment house where the shots were heard, I spotted another Cop car coming on Clairemont Mesa Boulevard with lights blazing and its siren wailing. It turned out to be the Ford bringing Su.

She nodded to me and headed for the building. The other Officer and I followed her in.

I barked to the guy, that since shots had been fired there, we should have our pistols out; he followed my example, and brought his gun out, racking in a round, the same as I did. My Su also took her pistol out of her purse, as we got to the first-floor apartment, 1-G.

As we three stood to either side of the door, I knocked on the door and hollered, "Police! Please open the door!"

A gray-haired lady quickly did as I asked.

I remembered to poke my camera on, to record sights and sounds.

"I heard the sirens and I saw you Police out the window. Come on in," she said, seemingly full of calm.

"Mrs. Fleischman!" Su said, leading us in as she put a hand on the lady's shoulder. "Are you okay?"

"Oh yes, Officer Chi," she said. "It's my daughter Helen now, who isn't doing well."

Right in front of us was a small dining table, with two chairs next to it. I was startled to see, in plain view, a revolver—of .44 caliber—laying on that table. I hurried a single step, to pick it up gingerly and put it in my pocket.

"Come with me," the lady said. "She's in her bedroom."

We followed the woman and inside the room, was another female sprawled on the carpeted floor. Blood had flowed mightily over her rumpled pink dress and onto the carpet. Guessing, it looked to me like she had been shot in the chest, three or more times. Kneeling down on the floor, I checked for a pulse. She had no pulse. Her skin felt cool. That woman was dead.

"Oh Mrs. Fleischman," Su burst out. "What happened here?"

"Let's go back to the living room and I'll tell you," the gray-haired one said.

Practically calm, the lady pointed to a sofa for us to sit on, while she plunked down on a chair. Tension of course filled the air as we three Officers, waited for the woman to tell us what was what.

"Officer Chi," she said, "you've been here. You know how nuts my daughter became. You've been here before… what? Two times before? I worked hard for my daughter from the day she was born, and never once has she shown any appreciation for my efforts, in these thirty-six years. Never one time. Never!"

Suddenly, the old lady began to cry. We three Officers of the Law just sat there, not offering any comfort at all. We all supposed she had shot her daughter to death.

In only two or three minutes, the sobbing subsided, and the woman began again to talk.

"I'm sorry for that crying," she said. "I wasn't feeling sad for Helen; I was feeling sad for me, to have needed to shoot her."

"Mrs. Fleischman," Su said to her, "you told me once before that Helen hated you for not telling her who her father was. Was that truly the main problem between you two?"

"Officer Chi, that is exactly right; stupid as it was for her to think I lied to her about that," she answered. "I explained to her that when I was eighteen, and fresh out of high school, I was looking for a job. I applied in a restaurant in Chula Vista; but they weren't hiring just then, I was told. To this day, I'm rather confused about what happened after I walked out of that place. But a remarkably handsome young man followed me out, and said he overheard me, applying for a job.

"Well, he knew of a really great job as a waitress that would be perfect for me, he said. Anyway, he drove me, in an impressive new car, to Tijuana. First thing he did there, was to rape me… me, who was a virgin. He fed me booze; lots of it. He took me to what turned out to be a whore house. It took me I think about three months before an American customer managed to sneak me out of there and bring me back to San Diego.

"My shame was so intense, I never, ever wished to have sex again, with anyone whosoever. I've not dated any man since. I've never drank a drop of alcohol since, either… not until this morning, when I knew Helen was to be released from the jail.

"Since I found out back then that I was made pregnant by any one of dozens of men, I've worked, mostly as a waitress, for my baby. But for all the years after I told her about that, she always assumed I was lying. I cannot think though, why in hell she would not understand that I had no reason to lie to her."

"You said you've not drank…" Su said. "What about drinking?"

"Well, I knew that when Helen came home today, she'd be as always, completely disrespectful and mean to me. So, I stoked the furnace, so to speak, by getting me a bottle of vodka. I drank a whole glass of that awful stuff. I already, two weeks ago, bought me that gun your Officer put in his pocket. So quick as she walked in that door today, I was ready for her big mouth. Oh yes, she called me 'The old whore' again, and a 'liar' once more, and a 'rotten goddamned old woman', for the very last time.

"So, as you can see for yourselves," the old one went on, "I shot the shit out of that Helen, who I nurtured, and slaved for, all these years. She must have been crazy, I think, to be like that. She just had to be, absolutely insane, to be like that."

Without another moment's hesitation, my Su "read the woman her rights," despite her voluntary confession, to we three Police Officers.

We of course but the cuffs on the gray-haired one, and we called for the Medical Examiner to come and pick up the body.

Carefully taking the revolver out of my pocket, to avoid wiping off fingerprints, I showed it to Su and the other Officer. The chambers held six empty cartridges. So, Helen Fleischman had been shot by her aggravated mother, all of six times, in the chest.

As we waited for the body to be taken away, the lady mostly sat on a chair, crying, as well she might; for her life was now forever made ugly. She would be imprisoned, surely, for the rest of her life. She got vengeance, but at an awful price.

She had a cousin who we were to let know about events. That cousin was also the beneficiary of Mrs. Fleischman's Last Will.

She told us she had altered her Last Will that very morning, to allow her cousin to be both the Executor and the beneficiary of her small "estate," instead of her daughter.

So, the homicide was therefore, First Degree Murder, from being premeditated by Mrs. Fleischman.

Since this had become a homicide instead of elder abuse, I—as Homicide Detective at Large—was the one to take care of the details on the files, etc. I also got to take the prisoner to the lock-up at Headquarters and pleasurably, my Su back to her office.

Not until I got to my own office, did I learn what happened with Jose Salas. I had left the other Detectives at Salas' house, and sped off to assist my wife on her mission.

Sergeant Garcia told me the big and brawny Jose Salas answered his door and put on an air of innocence. He even gave permission to Lieutenant Brightwell to search his house. His wife was then at work, he told them, and his three kids were all in school.

Convinced as every one of the Detectives were, while the Lieutenant engaged the man's attention, Sergeant Garcia and four of his Detectives immediately began rummaging through the house. Two of them lifted a mattress on a bed in the master bedroom when, viola! There was a wad of money and half a dozen little packets of Meth! A further search, flipping the mattress right off the bed, showed a bloody hatchet lying there, making an awful mess, of the white coverings on both the box spring, and the mattress above it.

When Detectives began to put the cuffs on the powerful concrete worker Salas, it took all five of them and some help from the Lieutenant to get him correctly shackled. They had also, to put cuffs on his ankles, since he was kicking at them. Then, they had to have all of the Officers carry the man out to a Cop car for transport to the Headquarters lock-up.

When I got to our office, Salas was still in a holding cell at Headquarters. He was adamantly refusing to admit he had killed that bartender. He had "lawyered up" when the Lieutenant "read him his rights." But the entire Team 3 knew it was obvious, the blood on the hatchet found in Salas's own bed, would prove to belong to the drug-pushing bartender, Frank Taylor.

Everyone was fairly certain, that the construction worker who owned a hatchet, had used his weapon only on the one victim, ol' Frank. Another hatcheteer or hatcheteers, were still "out there" plotting again to strike.

Well now, that first day "back on the job" for both Su and I, had seemingly pointed to a future for me, that would be fairly easy to manage. So be it. Being usefully doing something at work, was far better than staring at those old, cold homicides on a computer, I'd have almost no hope of solving.

After filling the gas tank, I drove our assigned Ford Crown Vic Police Interceptor home, with Su there in the right front seat. Parking it in the far-left stall of our garage, was so quickly, to be a natural thing.

Walking out of the garage door onto our patio, we entered our own private, and perfect little world. Arm in arm, we lovers walked into our new/old Craftsman Style house, feeling good about our lives. It felt wonderful to be alone again with my gorgeous new wife.

We were both hungry after our ten-hour workday. Maybe I should say, our eleven-hour day, because we had two, fifteen-minute breaks during the day and a half hour for lunch.

Anyway, Su and I together got up a nice dinner which we both enjoyed. We enjoyed some TV news on our kitchen set and pretty soon, it was our bedtime.

We always left a bit earlier than necessary to get to our desks on time. The drive from our garage to Headquarters took only minutes.

On Thursday morning, May 1st, 2014, I drove the Cop car

and this time, headed south by way of 30th Street. But as we got to 30th, a bright red, Korean-made, KIA sedan roared right by in front of us, going south, at a terrific speed. I turned right, to get behind the KIA, and we were barely able to get the license number. While I turned on our lights and siren, and of course, sped after the dangerous speeder, Su called the license number in. A bit later, she called in to let those in our offices know, we'd be late.

We did as every Police Officer is obliged to do when a crime is seen being committed, an Officer is supposed to do all he can to apprehend the offender.

Aha, that KIA had just been carjacked, in Normal Heights! Over the radio, we got a description of the short, muscular, *and armed*, White man, wearing a black tee shirt and blue jeans. He had pistol-whipped the car's owner, knocked her down and roared away in the woman's car.

We followed the KIA south on 30th Street, where the man abruptly turned into the on-ramp, to highway 94-east. With no other Police in pursuit, I continued chasing the KIA on the freeway.

There was no way the man could not hear our blaring siren or see our flashing lights. And of course, our "dash-cam" camera was on, recording everything the bad man did. I had also turned on the recorder in my smart phone.

The KIA weaved nuttily all over the four lanes of the freeway, in order to pass cars and trucks in its way. That crazy criminal was exceeding a hundred miles an hour! He was not only endangering himself, but everyone else on the road. Lives were at stake here. Of course, being a Cop for over four years each, both Su and I had been involved in such chases. So far, no other Police had joined the pursuit.

In seemingly only seconds, we passed the off-ramp to Federal Boulevard.

Then, we were astonished to see the bright red KIA sideswipe a white Ford Fusion, in the number one lane. Both cars spun out.

The Ford very nearly tipped over onto the right shoulder. But it stopped there, banging itself against the guard rail.

The KIA bounced off the Ford crazily, over onto its left side and flipped, I think, three or four times, ending up on its right side. It slid along on the pavement on its right side, in the second lane, with the most amazing fireworks of sparks flying! Damn! What a mess flipping and sliding made of that car!

I screeched our brakes and barely managed to stop, almost ramming the KIA.

As I opened my door to go check up on the man in the car on its side, he suddenly pushed up and open, his driver-side door. The door had broken hinges, for it swung all the way forward against the front wheel of the car.

The KIA driver popped up out of the car with a pistol in his hand! As I screamed at him to drop that gun, he was aiming it at me with both hands! He fired! A bullet zipped by my ear! I returned fire! It hit him somewhere! I knew that, to see his reaction as he winced with pain! He again brought his pistol up to fire at me! But I got off another shot first! My shot hit him again and I could see blood gushing from a chest wound on him, as he screamed in pain.

His pistol dropped to the pavement. I dashed over to pick up his weapon and thrust it in my pocket.

Damn, how that banged, bruised and bleeding man cussed me! He surely did know, and use, every filthy word in "gutter language!"

But Police Officers get somewhat used to that dirt emanating from low-life criminal mouths; it's that filth shouted at Cops that you never, ever hear on TV. You might see on television, guys getting shot, but you'll never hear the nastiness, coming out of their mouths, directed at the Law Enforcement enemies of all crooks.

While Sergeant Su Chi Abrito ran over to check on the woman and two children crying while buckled in the back seat, I grabbed the shooter in the KIA. As I said, the KIA sedan was laying on its side in the number two lane, with its driver door swung up and all the way open.

Despite the lights flashing atop our Cop car, automobiles, slowing down, were still cruising by, but the drivers, a bit curious, were not terribly interested in other people's problems.

Grabbing the man, I tried to lift him out of the car. He was standing on the console between the two front seats. But his upper right arm had been grazed by my first shot and the second shot nailed him pretty good, high in his right chest, maybe four inches under his shoulder bones. He was moaning and bleeding badly onto his clothing, from both his right arm and his chest.

"What with your wounds," I shouted at the pale-faced man, "you'd probably best stay in the car until I can get some help to get you out. They're on the way."

"You goddamned mother fucker!" he screeched at me with his face distorted with not only pain, but also with hate and fear.

"One more filthy word out of you, mister, and you'll very much regret it!" I lied.

He of course saw that my pistol was still in my right hand, ready to fire. But shooting him now, would be a case of gross misconduct for an Officer. Even the dirtiest words can't wound; they can only hurt one's sensibilities.

In another minute or so, a Patrol car had pulled up behind ours, also with its lights flashing. There were two Officers in it, one being a rookie, learning the work, on the job.

The three of us men, were pretty quickly able to get the man out of the KIA. We laid him on the pavement, protected from traffic by the Cop cars. But surprisingly, the man's heart stopped beating right there. We three tried with CPR but could not get that crook's heart going again.

It would take a wrecker truck to get that KIA sedan righted.

Su had called for ambulances of course, and one was soon on the spot. They tended to the hurts of the family. The Medical Examiner's people would haul the deceased crook away.

The mother and her children in the Ford Fusion, were naturally quite shook up, but in fact not much injured except for some small cuts from flying window glass. Both sides of that lovely white Ford Fusion, however, were an auto body repair shop's nightmare. The side-swiped left side was a lot worse than the right side which had slammed against the guard rail.

The KIA sedan looked to me to be "totaled." However, maybe experts could make it viable. We could hope the victimized owner of it, had good insurance.

Lucky for me, the camera mounted on the dashboard of our Police car and the camera in my shirt pocket, would show the chase we made, the subsequent crashes and importantly to me, the sequence of shots being fired by the criminal and yours truly. The law and the public looks unapprovingly at Police Officers, who think they should be executioners.

Su and I didn't get to our offices until about 10 o'clock that Thursday morning.

Chapter Ten

Everything seemed to be quiet in our office at first. Then Sergeant Garcia hollered over to me to turn my computer on to see what he was looking at. There on the screen, was a picture relayed by a Patrol Sergeant's smart phone, of a head-chopped man in a little store near Costco's Morena warehouse store. Naturally, the victim and the floor by him, was a truly bloody mess.

That Costco was the original warehouse store established, I think about 1976, by Sol Price. The Price Club was bought out by former Price Club executives and merged with the Costco chain.

After telling Su what was happening—and getting her okay to leave—I jumped into our Cop car and sped off to Morena Boulevard.

Oddly, traffic on highway 5 north seemed unusually heavy for that time of day, so I was seemingly a long time getting to that little store. But at least, I arrived before Sergeant Garcia and the rest of his Team 3 did. There were two Patrol cars parked in front there.

Inside, I introduced myself to the Patrol Officers as "Detective at Large Abrito." I grinned to myself, since they pretended to understand the meaning of my title.

I stepped into the back of the store and looked over the deceased. This time, the butchery wasn't as extensive as on some other hatcheted ones I'd seen. But it was certainly bad enough.

It appeared that probably five or six blows with a hatchet, mostly to the top of the man's head, had been more than suffi-cient to send the guy off to eternity. He had been a good-looking Black dude, I supposed, despite the blood on his face. He seemed to have been in his thirties and of average height and weight. The shirt and slacks he wore were terribly bloodied.

Looking around, I could see but a few items hanging on the walls and possibly for sale. There wasn't even a cash register. My guess was that the dead man positioned his business where the many thousands of Costco customers, upon leaving that huge warehouse store, would soon find out, by word of mouth, about drugs being for sale in the little store.

They would park their car out front, dash inside, pay the man a small or large sum and go merrily on their way with "lots of fun and harmless drugs" in their pocket or purse.

But someone had become angry with his or her drug peddler. Perhaps they damn near died with an overdose or maybe their spouse died that way. That jilting experience might upset almost anyone. Maybe they had been told what they were taking, was not addicting... and found out, it most certainly was addicting, and *they seemed to be condemned to buying that crud for as long as they lived.* Who wouldn't get a trifle peeved at that realization?

A question for an addict could be: What to do about it? Well, the television news and the newspaper certainly seemed to enjoy relaying the ultimate goriness of the hatchet homicides. So, an addict could think, death by horrible hatchet, was most appro-priate for the people who sold him or her, those powders or pills that gained a lifetime stranglehold on him or her.

Or, it could be the hatcheteer had never used drugs himself. Maybe a loved one did and got sorrowfully hooked... so that appropriate revenge was in order.

Anyway, there was a guy on the floor in the back of that little store, a victim of homicide by hatchet. Ah next; *who dunnit?*

Sergeant Garcia, Detective Ray Mason and the three rookie Detectives, paraded into the store to look over the corpse. The Sergeant said he had Crime Scene Investigators coming, as well as a couple of fingerprint specialists from our Crime Lab. Also, the Medical Examiner's office would be sending a couple of people over to retrieve the body. That would be to examine the corpse in the lab, to professionally determine the cause of death, although it sure seemed obvious to anyone not vomiting at the sight.

As I was about to compare notes with Sergeant Garcia, my other Sergeant, my Su, rang the phone in my pocket.

"Yes ma'am?" I answered.

"Are you still on Morena Boulevard?" she asked.

"Yes, I am," I said.

"Art, about a minute ago, I got a call from a neighbor of a man and wife having a terrible spat. They live in a condo nearby, at 7th Avenue and Market Street. Tell you what; I'll walk there and wait for you before I go inside. If you should beat me there, please wait for me," Su said to me.

I agreed to hurry to the address.

After informing Sergeant Garcia why I had to leave, I got in the Ford Crown Vic and with lights and siren going, I hurried down highway 5, to the 10th Avenue exit and after a bit, turned three blocks to the right on Market Street. My Sergeant Su was right there on the sidewalk, talking to a man in a wheelchair, who owned two condos in that building.

Parking at the curb, I hurried to meet with Su. She filled me in about the situation as we headed up to the 17th floor. She said that an owner, wheel-chair-bound, lived on the 18th floor, directly above the one we were going to. Both condos he owned, had one bedroom. He had called the problem in to the Police, about the man and woman who rented his condo below him.

"I've also been on the phone with Mr. Snodgrass in the wheel-chair... yes, that really is his name... and he told me he at first thought, the guy and gal he rented to, were a nice young, newly married couple. But hearing their shouting matches, he learned they were not married. The guy is brutal to her, he says. He believes they use drugs, and something ought to be done about it. Well Art, that's what we're here for," my Su said.

When we got to the apartment in question, I put my ear to the door and heard nothing from inside. I knocked. There was no answer. I knocked very hard, a second time. I announced we were Police at the door, and they should please open it.

I punched the camera in my shirt, on.

Su and I carefully hugged the wall on either side of the door. Again, I banged on the door. This time, the door opened and was jerked open wide.

"What the fuck do you want?" a guy there about my size and age asked, as he looked Police Officer me, up and down disrespectfully.

The white guy only had pajama bottoms on and was barefooted. His eyes-gone-wild told me immediately, that he was surely on methamphetamines.

"Sir, we would like to talk with you and your wife," Su said and walked boldly forward.

It was obvious the guy was taken aback by Su's uncommon beauty. He backed up and allowed her to come in, with me following closely behind her.

Without mentioning that she was a Police Sergeant, my wife pulled her badge out of her purse and showed it to the man.

"Where is the lady of the house?" Su asked. "I'd like to speak with her."

"Oh, she ain't feelin' so awful good right now. She's asleep in bed," he said.

He surely was lying, I reckoned from the way he said it.

He had no sooner said that, when a young Asian woman in a flimsy, see-through nightie, walked out of what was obviously a bathroom, not a bedroom. She had a black eye and a bruise below that, on her cheek.

"Git your ass in there and git some goddamn clothes on!" the man shouted at the woman.

"Yes, go ahead, young lady," Su said. "We'll be glad to wait for you."

The gal turned around without a word and headed to what we could see, was a bedroom, what with the door being open.

That nightie she wore was about as though made of clear plastic. Wow! She was very well put together below her neck and it was obvious, she preferred not to be shaved.

The woman was back within seconds, wrapping as she came, a thin cloth robe around her near nakedness. But that robe wasn't a see-through garment.

"I've learned that you two are not actually married," Sergeant Su Chi Abrito said. "You sir, are Raymond Mentored, and you miss, are Rosie Ma. I understand you two raise a great lot of noise here. Also, sir, I've been told you beat up Rosie. It's obvious to me, that you have done that. Come now, why is there so much unhappiness in this house, instead of love?"

Both Ray and Rosie seemed to have become speechless.

"Hey people, let's sit a while and talk some; okay?" Su came up with.

Su acted as though she was in charge here. She waved at a sofa for the two to sit on, while she pulled up a chair to face them. I stood close beside my wife, as though ready to spring into action at any moment; which of course, I most certainly was mentally prepared to do.

"I asked you two, why was there so much unhappiness in your house," she said with a confident smile with her perfect, glistening white teeth.

"I do believe I know the reason for that," she said. "It's those doggone drugs. We Police see the results of good, loving people imbibing in those poisons… they really are poisons, you know. They're poisons because those infernal illegal drugs ruin lives. They mess up people's otherwise normal, loving, caring, clear-thinking, brains. Now tell me, you two, am I talking good sense, or not?"

Both the guy and the gal sat silent for a moment, but it was plain Su had set them to thinking. At last, Rose Ma (Ma being a Chinese sur name) broke the silence.

"Officer lady," she said to Su, "I've gotta tell you, I fell head over heels, madly in love with Raymond. But he's changed. Maybe me, I've changed some, too. We've both gotta leave those damn drugs alone. Isn't that right, Ray?"

Well now, it wasn't all quite that easy. It was a back-and-forth thing, between the two on the couch and the beautiful woman on the chair. Su promised them that if they would right then surrender every speck of drugs they had in the house, she would not arrest them. Again, and again, she put that magic word "LOVE" into the conversation.

After perhaps three quarters of an hour, Raymond was apologizing to Rosie for the black eye and she also apologized for calling him bad names.

The difficult part, was surrendering their cache of drugs. Raymond admitted he had a certain steady income from a Trust Fund, so that neither of them had to work for a living.

Su grabbed at that news and insisted they could do much good in their lives if they helped drug addicts recover. That was a very bold suggestion on her part, but they both seemed to be somewhat interested in doing something like that.

With that idea floating around, Su spent at least another half an hour, explaining to those two what they could do to help others. She wrote down names of men and women they could contact and organizations they could join.

By and by, I was surprised to hear Raymond actually tell "Rosie honey," to go in the bedroom and bring out all that damn meth! She brought out a gorgeous little music box. Then she turned it over to dump about a dozen or so little baggies of white powder, into Su's hand. Next came the paraphernalia they owned, to partake in that "fun and harmless" stuff.

It really did seem like a miracle, and as we were going out that condo door, I turned to see those two, arm in arm, hugging and kissing fervently!

As we piled into our Cop car to return to Headquarters, my

Su admitted to me that the case of Raymond and Rosie was an exception. She hoped the love between them stayed sparkling and that they did do something useful with their lives.

"We'll see," Su said. "We'll see."

"Hey Art; guess what?" Sergeant Garcia said as I arrived back in the Homicide Detail.

"We actually got a lead on the perp who hatcheted to death that guy on Morena Street. An employee of Costco saw all those Cop cars outside the business there, so he stopped to talk to us. He claimed he was taking a lunch break from work and was going to go see his insurance agent. Well, he said as he was getting close in his car to that little store, he saw a guy coming out of that store with what looked to him like a hatchet in his hand.

"He climbed into the right side of a pickup truck. He could see through the rear window that he slid over on the seat to drive it away. The guy said it looked like a really old pickup that had been restored. He said he didn't know whether it was a Ford or a Chevy or what, but it was painted a really pretty bright orange.

"So, I put out a notice for all Cops and Deputies to watch for such a vehicle. It's a possible clue, Art. It's a possible lead on a hatcheteer," Garcia told me.

"That's good news, Sergeant," I said. "Also, you might have all your Team visit with car and truck restoring garages. There must be some in San Diego, although of course, such restoring could have been done anywhere in the country. Also, he must be a wealthy man to afford such an expensive restoration, so he doubt-less keeps it garaged."

"Hey! Good point. That's a good idea, too," he said. "I don't personally know of any such places that do that sort of work, but some of my men might."

Garcia left to talk to his Detectives, and I got up the latest hatchet homicide case on my computer. I couldn't see that anything had been added to the file that I didn't already know— which sure wasn't much.

Driving home with my wife next to me that Thursday evening, I had to recall the remarkable calming effect she had on people.

Partly, that had to be because of her outstanding beauty. But it was also her self-confidence, and her obviously genuine interest in people. She had all of that, in spades. Hell, I had felt like slugging that fool Raymond, for putting the shiner on pretty Rose… who sure did show her perfect Chinese body off so well, that it reminded me of what I was privileged to see every night.

In none of the hatchet homicide cases, had the media been allowed to see the victim up close. But they did, in each case, get a scary version of the scene, to broadcast and scare the hell out of their readers and their audiences on television. That Thursday evening, the news on TV made the most of the "seven chops with a hatchet to the head, of Mr. Samuel Neal." I saw that Black noggin up close and I saw it was more like "merely" five chops. Oh well.

Parking the Ford in our garage that evening, I was reminded that I had intended to build a workbench to the left of the exit door onto our patio. I had visualized many tools hanging on the wall over a large bench. There was to be a very large assortment of bolts, screws, nails and that sort of thing. But since a bunch of professional workmen had done—and done beautifully—the work I had intended to do, there was but slight need for the workbench and other stuff on it that I had envisioned.

As it was, our new swimming pools heater, pump, chlorinator and filter almost filled up the space to the right of that door. But I had a gas-powered lawn mower there as well as a rake, two shovels and two ladders.

I grabbed my eight-foot-high step ladder while I was there, because it looked like rain coming. If rain came as I guessed it would, I'd check in the attic to see if there were any leaks in our roof. There were so very many new plumbing and air vents up there, a leak was possible.

Su's sister Lu called as we came in the house. She and her boyfriend were inviting us to dinner Saturday night, at that wonderful restaurant, Tom Ham's, on Harbor Island. It had been far too long since we had been there. Lu said her boyfriend, Jack Washburn, was paying.

Su and I had just about decided to rent out the first floor. We needed to buy a book on being "Landlords." Looking ahead though, we had the Contractor install separate heating-hot water furnaces, with the gas service on two meters. So too, were the electric and water meters separate. The television and telephone outlets were everywhere on both floors and were to have two billings.

That Thursday had been a tiring day for both of us. We were glad to be home by ourselves. The two of us together fixed a great dinner with a salad first, followed by peas, mashed potatoes, bread and broiled beef patties. We followed that with a desert of yummy ice cream. We even ate at the dining table, formally.

Then we tuned in the TV news. It was a big surprise to hear a reporter refer to the carjacked KIA sedan that rolled over and killed the criminal driver, as meaning "Killed In Action." Wow! That Korean auto company would surely get on that station for that!

It was exactly how my namesake, the Black Platoon Sergeant Benjamin Franklin, shot to death in the Iraq war, was referred to; he was said to have been K.I.A.; Killed In Action.

Sure enough, a hard-blowing rain came at us from the north that night. It beat against our bedroom window.

San Diego never has snow, bitter cold or even extremely hot weather. This place called "America's Finest City" never, ever has tornados, hurricanes and merely about ten inches of rain a year. That's why it is called, a "semi desert" technically, but "paradise" by most folks.

If only the City Council and the Mayor, would spend the money for fixing the streets and putting in "smart traffic lights" at every intersection, it would be even more perfect.

I got up a bit before dawn, and in my pajamas, went up to the attic to look for leaks. With a powerful flashlight, I looked at the underside of the roof the entire fifty-foot length. With so many possible places for water to sneak through, I found but one leak.

It was from around the pipe venting the sewer line, of the half baths, on both the first and main floors. Actually, that pipe had not been changed; it had only been moved a little on the roof, because it had previously vented the only bathroom in the house.

I called and left a message for the contractor, to please have someone get up there and caulk around that pipe better. They could do that whether we were home or not. I left the step ladder where it was, so I could check the attic again later.

The front porch floor was still completely wet from the rain having blown onto it. But it appeared the "waterproof" flooring overlaid on the original redwood planking, was okay. There were no leaks anywhere on the back porch nor at any window.

We had a good breakfast and I drove Su and I to a hopefully good Friday at work.

Sergeant Garcia had his entire Team 3 out checking "old car and truck restorers." There were probably some such outfits in San Diego. Around the nation, there were possibly hundreds of them, for restoring old American cars and even trucks, had become a popular thing to do.

If a guy had a really fat bank account, he could buy an old wreck of a vehicle, from maybe the 1950's, and get it made like it just rolled off the assembly line in Detroit City. However, that restoration could cost many, many times the original new car dealer selling price.

Unfortunately, the Crime Lab experts has found not a single fingerprint, of a possible suspect, in any of the hatchet homicides. These days, wrong doers are well acquainted with the necessity to wear latex gloves, when they go forth to bring to an end, to someone's life.

Team 3 had been lucky, to have that little guy in the Pacific Beach bar, tell us about Jose Salas. The pity is, Salas' wife will have no well-paid husband to support her and her kids. And those children will not only not have a father around for a long time but will have to shoulder the shame of having their old man being imprisoned, at the least, for Murder in the First Degree.

That has got to be a very great burden, on the minds of those kids.

It didn't seem likely that we would see many repeats of hatchet homicides, by the same perpetrators. But even so, what with the very considerable publicity about these goriest of gory homicides, the temptation was out there, for addicted folks, to grab a hatchet and get some "heady revenge."

They could get satisfaction by chopping on the heads of a drug dealer or dealers, who perhaps convinced them in the beginning, that after all, although the drugs they pedaled were made illegal by "some worthless politicians," those same drugs were truly "lots of fun and harmless." *And, they make you feel really great! However, in time, they could make you feel dead!*

We hadn't been at work long that Friday, when Su phoned me. She asked me to drive her to a bank downtown, where she had a case of elder abuse to discuss. When we were in the Cop car and on the way to the bank, she told me an elderly woman suspected her youngest daughter had stripped about a million bucks from her bank account. Wow! A million bucks!

Su told me the lady had noticed on her latest checking account statement that she had but a balance of three and a half millions. She then saw with alarm, that checks were made out that she had not signed. She immediately suspected her estranged daughter, who she knew was a drug user.

While we were still on the way, I asked my wife, "Honey, why in the world would anyone keep so much money in a checking account?"

"Oh, that's to have cash on hand for purchasing stocks and other investments," Su answered. "Guessing, I'd say that lady is worth many times, what's in that particular account."

"Well, that's an education for me, to know some people have such a great amount of money on hand, and easily available in a bank," I said.

Since I was driving a Police car, I could have parked at the curb by the bank. But being considerate of traffic there, I drove into their underground garage to park.

From there, we took an elevator to the first floor. We were soon led into a bank officer's office. As my wife pulled out her badge from her purse to display it, I merely stood to one side—literally, in my uniform, with my back against a wall—while Sergeant Su Chi discussed that case of elder abuse with the banker.

It was obvious that the banker was worried. Su had said it was the bank's sloppy practice to allow the daughter's checks to be cashed without verifying the signature and all that, with the lady whose account it was. Su had said, the bank could very well be liable to replace that loss. In addition, the bank could lose the business of a very wealthy customer.

Since I was merely Su's "backup" there, I paid almost no attention to what was said. The discussion lasted perhaps half an hour, with Su showing much enlarged photographs of the some of the checks involved in this case.

I did hear Su say, as she stood up to leave, "We both know this bank will not wish to have the great publicity, a trial would bring, in this case of the abused lady. You will very certainly be hearing a lot more about this, from myself and others."

With that, we left, and I drove her back to our 14th and Broadway Headquarters. She went to her office and I walked to mine.

Homicide Team 3 had no further hatchet homicides to investigate.

While the others on our Team were out and about, checking with auto restoration garages—if they found any—about who owned a brilliant orange old pickup truck, I sat at my desk. I pondered how in the world; we could possibly identify hatcheteers with no clues at all.

In every case of reporting another hatchet homicide, a reporter would almost always mention, that there were no finger-prints of the perpetrator to be found, because he wore latex gloves. That was as though possible hatcheteers—or shooters, or knifers, or clubbers, or chokers, etc.—were being instructed as to how to get away with murder!

Well, the main goal in my working life was to see to it, they did not get away with murder, never mind how the very bad deed was done.

That Friday at about noon, Detective Ray Mason visited a

garage, who had restored just the sort of pickup, as sped away from the Morena hatchet job. They gave Mason the name and the address of the wealthy businessman, and even his phone number.

Sergeant Martin Garcia led his entire Team, including myself, to the La Jolla address with haste. We rang the doorbell. No one came to the door. This time, the Sergeant poked the button for the doorbell. Although repeated several times, together with banging on the front door, no one came to the door. We phoned and no one answered those calls, either.

The seven of us walked around the house to the driveway. I banged on the garage door, with no results. Then I saw, higher than I was tall, there were small windows on that roll-up garage door.

I suggested to the nine-inches-taller-than-me, Sergeant Garcia, that I could boost him up, so he could see if there was an orange pickup in that garage. I backed up against the door and held my hands together for him to step on. He did that and peeked through a little window.

"By God, there's that orange painted old pickup we've been looking for!" he announced.

Immediately, the Sergeant called in for a Search Warrant for that address.

In the meantime, while we waited impatiently for the Warrant, a few of the Detectives looked around to the back of the house. There was a swimming pool there, a patio and lots of flowers, they reported to the rest of us. I supposed that property was worth some big bucks.

Just after 3 o'clock in the afternoon, the Search Warrant came. Ray Mason was able to pick the lock on the front door and we all entered that lovely, beautifully furnished house. With a peek in what seemed to be the master bedroom, we saw a terribly bloated and blackened corpse of a woman on a bed. Damn! The stink of rotting flesh was really awful!

We all got busy to open windows, as the Sergeant phoned Lieutenant Brightwell and the Medical Examiner to report that nasty find.

I was curious about the pickup in the garage, so I went through the kitchen and out there.

The bright orange truck was an old Ford and I supposed it was a 1950-or-60-something. There was a man inside. He was slumped over the steering wheel and obviously dead. Blood and brains were splattered on the glass of the door. I opened the passenger-side door. There on the seat, was a blood-covered hatchet. A big, .45 caliber revolver was on the truck floor, where it had apparently fell out of the guy's hand, after he blasted his brains to death. The San Diego County Medical Examiner would determine the causes of death of those two.

Using my imagination, I supposed the elderly woman had overdosed and died with some drugs or another, a day or two before. Her loving old husband knew where those drugs came from. Thus, he drove down to Morena Boulevard, and revenge-fully chopped up the head of the dealer, that had sold his wife those death-giving poisons. Appropriately, he brought along his hatchet so as to create a truly memorable, hatcheted corpse.

Then the man drove home, parked the truck he adored—one he had driven perhaps in his youth—and, feeling the world was at end for him, with a deadly .45, ended that world for him.

Remarkably, two hatchet homicides had been solved, through no brilliance at all on the part of Team 3's Detectives. It was just pure luck that led to the guilty parties; by a little man who hung around a bar; and a fellow who noticed an unusual old orange pickup, speed away from what he later learned, was a homicide by hatchet scene.

On the way home that Friday evening, Su told me the bank involved in her elder abuse case already had lawyers busy. The bank was attempting, she told me, to weasel out of paying back into the rich lady's account, a cool million bucks. She was sure the bank was stuck with making good, those fraudulent pay outs. There was but a small chance they could recover anything from the daughter, who was surely headed for prison.

At home, we found a note taped on our back door from a roofer. In the note, he apologized for the small leak at that plumbing vent pipe. He said he had got up on the roof and sealed around the pipe again. Well, we were both pleased by the contractor, promptly getting the right guy to fix the problem so quickly. We hurried off a very complimentary note to him, via the United States Postal Service.

That night, after we fixed dinner, ate heartily and cleaned up afterward, we put a video into our disc player and watched a movie on our big television set, mounted over our gorgeous fireplace. Of the forty or fifty movies she had to choose from, Su picked an oldie called, *An Affair to Remember.* The film starred Cary Grant and Deborah Kerr. Even I enjoyed watching that one, although I had seen it twice before and began to nod near the end of it.

Perhaps inspired by the romance in the movie show, and despite the fact we were getting to bed rather late, Su still wanted some loving. Well now, that was an idea I could hardly resist, what with she being so very beautiful and so fetching and so… oh, so wonderful in bed, too!

We woke up Saturday, the 3rd day of May, to hear rain pattering against our bedroom window again. That was unusual, because San Diego rarely got but tiny amounts of rain in May. For the first time in ages, Su and I wore our raincoats to our offices in Headquarters.

Su spent most of her time that Saturday, talking in person and on the phone with lawyers in the District Attorney's office. She was pressing the case of the fraudulent withdrawals from that elderly woman's bank account. It was the one with what seemed to me, to have an impossibly large balance, even with a million dollars or so stolen from it!

As for ol' Detective at Large Benjamin Franklin Abrito, about all I accomplished that day was to put some polish on, and fill in, some details on the files, of the two latest hatchet homicides. The longer I was involved in detective work, the more I realized a lot of it was paperwork—except it was mostly done without paper, on a computer.

Wow! Sister Lu and Jack Washburn treated us to a great

congratulatory dinner, for our successful remodeling of our home. We ate again, at Tom Ham's, on Harbor Island, that Saturday night. We had a table next to a window with a great view of lit-up buildings downtown, across the sparkling waters of San Diego Bay. Almost every minute we were there, we were entranced by sea craft of various sizes, cruising by the restaurant.

The largest vessel by far of them all, was an aircraft carrier, coming into our harbor from the wild and far spread Pacific Ocean.

Su and I both enjoyed top sirloin steaks, which was done perfectly. We finished our dinner with a treat of common apple pie, which was uncommonly thick and delicious.

Su had gathered a list of Garage Sales for us to visit on Sunday. We hoped to spy framed artwork that we thought appropriate somewhere in our home. If we didn't like the picture, perhaps an occasional frame would be fanciful enough for us to fill with a different picture. We hoped too, to find busts of famous people to mount on our library shelves.

As luck would have it, I found a new-looking, mechanic's tool chest with wheels. It had a bunch of drawers for tools and whatever. I could put a wooden top on it and a vise. Amazingly, the seller only wanted fifty bucks for it. Su and I together loaded it into the Expedition.

That would be a satisfactory replacement for the much larger, wooden bench I had envisioned. I could even roll it on its wheels, to wherever I would be doing some work.

Although we spent much of that day driving from one address to another, we didn't have much additional luck. We ended up with but a single beautiful portrait; that was of the gifted user of the English language, Abraham Lincoln.

"Four score and seven years ago, our fathers brought forth on this continent, a new nation, dedicated to the proposition that all men are created equal."

We also found two plaster busts. One was of an ancient young Greek man and the other was of a Greek Goddess; presumably she was Athena. They really would look impressive on our fire-place mantel.

Luckily, the 35th and Adams Bookstore was still open when we got there. We found two beautiful sets of encyclopedias. The Encyclopedia Americana's thirty volumes were old but looked new. They were impressively bound. The other set was the smaller World Book, of twenty volumes; it was also old, but bound nicely and in top shape. Encyclopedias are no longer printed; you have to go search for answers to your questions on the internet. But I grew up with encyclopedia books in my hand; I could hardly put one down, for it was endlessly interesting.

Su's primary interest in that 35th and Adams Street bookstore, wonderfully stocked with books, was to find three volumes on rental properties and another book on growing germaniums. She hoped to buy the ivy-type geraniums, to plant for them to climb, along our chain link fence, by her south kitchen window.

We finally loaded up our big Ford Expedition and headed home to add those books to our family library and the luckily found bench to the garage.

Our lawn was much abused, what with all those workmen tramping on it and with ladders poking holes in the sod, etc. So, I had to get that lovely grass back to its former beauty.

After we ate our dinner that Sunday night, and had cleaned the kitchen, I took one of the "Landlord books" Su had found. Sitting myself at the dining table, with the fanciful light lit over-head, I found it a great place to read and take notes.

Su also found a new book to read. She sat across the table from me.

Thumbing through the book, I found a chapter that immedi-ately intrigued me. It was about leasing such an apartment as ours, to a corporation. According to the book, very large compa-nies, with offices all over the nation or even the world, needed an apartment for a man—and occasionally, his family—to occupy while visiting the local office for training, as an example. In a year's time, the apartment might be occupied only once in a while.

A corporation, it said, could easily *pay the lease annually, and be done with it.* That meant there would be no struggle over rents, between the owner and renter, month after month. Also, such corporate employees as lived in the leased apartment, would most likely be mature and educated. They'd not likely have babies to worry about, falling into the swimming pool.

Su and I discussed that and she too, was intrigued with the idea of leasing to some large corporation, for the sometime occupancy of their employees.

She also said, with a very big smile on her beautiful face, that leasing out our first floor might actually pay off our mortgage! The interest rate on our loan was barely over three percent, so there would be not much advantage to paying it off early.

I vowed to her to first get the advice of an attorney, on how to go about getting such a lease. Second, I would dedicate every Tuesday of each week to finding a large corporation that would lease our first floor at our price. We were both already dreamily speculating on what an annual lease might bring us; maybe $36,000 to as much as $40,000!

With such figures bouncing around in our heads, I had to point out to my wife, that back in 1925, the cost of the lot and of the building of the house, was probably not so much as $8,000! Ah, there had since been so very much inflation in the world, as it was much to the advantage of governments, to cheapen their money. A government could sell bonds for $1,000 and many years later, pay the bond off with far cheaper money.

On Monday morning, we had just cleared off the breakfast dishes in our new dishwasher, when we heard the front doorbell ring.

I found a good-looking young lady there and three kids. The boy and two girls looked to be early teenagers.

They were all dressed nicely, and I was merely in blue jeans and a plaid shirt.

"How may I help you?" I asked, noticing a Chrysler van parked on the street there.

"You must be Detective at Large Abrito," the woman said. "Captain Morgan told me about the stunningly beautiful apartment that you may have for rent. My children and I are looking for a decent place now to rent. May we please see it?"

"Well, I don't yet know," I said. "But please, do come in and we can bring my wife into this. The truth is, we haven't quite decided what to do with it."

As the four of them walked in, their eyes went just everywhere, looking the place over. I thought they might suppose the main floor could be rented out.

Su was just behind me, I quickly saw, and she had to have been there, to hear what was said. She put her hand out to shake the woman's hand.

"I'm Mrs. Abrito," she told the woman. "Yes, please do come in. You must be Mrs. Buckner, I was told."

Then she turned to me. "Honey, I forgot to tell you that the Captain mentioned to me, that a lady with three children was wanting to rent a nice place. He told me she didn't want to buy a home at this time, because her children would, in a few years, be off to college and she wouldn't want to own a large house to rattle around in, all by herself."

"Mrs. Buckner," Su said. "The Captain had nice things to say about you and your children. He said you liked the high school here in South Park for them."

"Yes; that's true. Would you folks mind if we simply looked at your apartment, in case you should decide to rent it? Or, maybe a long-term lease, would be preferable," Buckner said.

"Honey," Su said to me, "it can't hurt to let them see our first floor, would it?"

Chapter Eleven

When Su and I returned to our offices on Wednesday, May 11th, I got one helluva shock. Sergeant Garcia informed me that during the past three days, seven hatchet homicides had been committed! Seven of those ghastly murders! One of them had been committed—so to speak—practically in my own back yard, in South Park. Aha, that was why we had heard sirens so close to our home!

Practically running to my desk, I turned on my computer to read about those hatchet jobs.

Those latest homicides were scattered all over much of the city. Going from north to south, I saw one had been committed on High Bluff road, east of Del Mar. Another was done on Carrol Canyon Road. Both of those communities were populated by wealthy folks.

There were two more committed in Clairemont. Two were committed in North Park and the last one, was done in South Park.

"Abrito," I heard our Sergeant say from behind me, "none of us have the slightest clue as to who in hell has done these killings. There is one difference in them from those previous. That is, whoever the slayer is, he or she does it with a single chop to the head, *but after he had killed them with a .32 caliber weapon.* Oh, except for the one in South Park, the victim was struck with a horizontal blow to their neck with the hatchet; but again, that was after she was dead.

"That was a young widow, that time. Her husband was killed in Afghanistan a few months ago. She must have got into the business of peddling drugs to maintain her house and feed her two-year-old little boy. The boy's grandma took the kid in. The grandmother lives in a condo, downtown," he told me.

"Sergeant, I would have thought there were far more drug dealers south of downtown, rather than north of it. Oh, I see; of course, the person committing these homicides could be a drug user and would necessarily only be familiar with the dealers he or she bought their drugs from."

"Hey Art, that's a good point," he said.

"Or maybe not, Sergeant," I said. "What's say Team 3 has a conference about these last seven hatchet homicides with our two Lieutenants? I'll have some ideas about these and surely others will, too."

"My friend Art," Sergeant Garcia said, "if you've got any ideas on these, you're all alone. The rest of us have of course discussed these killings endlessly and have come up with no ideas at all. Okay, I'll ask if we can come into their office."

In a few minutes the Sergeant was back, rounding up us five Detectives to have a visit with the Lieutenants in their glassed in, two-desk office. Their sofa, opposite their desks, was long enough that four Detectives sat on the seat of the sofa. The Sergeant and I sat on the sofa's arms, on each end.

"Lieutenant Brightwell and Lieutenant Alan, Detective-at-Large Abrito suggested to me that we meet like this, in the hope that we can come up with ideas on how to solve the latest string of hatchet homicides. Well Art, you can start us off," Team Leader Garcia said.

"Thank you, Sergeant," I said. "First, I'd like to suggest that someone take a map of the city and locate on it, where these latest homicides took place. Then he can draw lines from each one to the next. Now, that might just waste a perfectly good city map. That's true. But it might also have something jump right off the paper at you.

"Next, thinking about how scattered these hatchet homicides were," I continued, "I'm convinced that this time it wasn't a drug user, getting revenge, for getting hooked on that junk. No, I do believe these had to have been done by one of the Mexican cartels, rubbing out competition. And they may have just gotten started. That is, they probably do have a lot of murders yet to go."

"Damn!" Lieutenant Julie Brightwell exploded. "Abrito, without even looking at a map, I've gotta believe you're exactly correct. These last seven hatchet homicides, are too darn far flung, to be by someone who bought drugs, from so many peddlers. Okay then, does our star Detective have an idea of how to find the perp?"

Hey, I sure didn't expect any such compliment from her. Star Detective, indeed! I don't think that was a good idea on her part, because that remark slights the other Detectives; and unfairly so.

"Lieutenant, I must say, I'm no more a star here than anyone else. Every one of us is an eager star Detective, trying to stop whoever is committing these homicides," I told her.

"But yes, ma'am, I do have a notion, of how to go about finding the latest killer. Actually, it's pretty simple. Our Crime Lab now possesses the cell phones, taken from each of those murdered. The conversations made on those phones are not preserved, on the chip inside, but the numbers calling and called, are recorded there. You Lieutenants can get the Crime Lab to give us a list, in each individual case, of the phone numbers called and calling. We can, with various phone companies help, determine who those people are.

"Then, *we can bet, that one number which appears on each and all of those phones, is the perpetrator we are looking for!* Why? I'll tell you why. Simply because the man with that damn hatchet, wanting it to appear that a druggie did the deed, phones each victim to make sure where he'll be. Of course, he's pretending he's gonna buy drugs from him. We know those peddlers don't stick around in one place.

"How'd he get the phone number of each of his victims? I can't guess just how, but we all know, those cartels have an efficient intelligence network. Anyway, when we phone that cartel guy's number, our GPS ability will locate his position right then and we can go snatch him."

"*Well sonofabitch!*" Lieutenant Alan shouted. "By God, Arturo Abrito, you have a brilliant idea there! Hey Julie, let's you and I get over to that Crime Lab right now!"

The two Homicide Detail Commanders hurried off to the Crime Lab while we of Homicide Team 3 went back to our desks. Detective Ray Mason was assigned by the Sergeant to get a city map and start drawing lines on it. It was a wild chance, that those lines might reveal something.

No sooner had I sat myself down, when Sergeant Su Chi (as she went by yet), phoned me. She wanted me to drive her a high-rise office building downtown, to talk to an attorney for the lady who had been swindled by her daughter.

She maintained her maiden name on her business card, etc., since Officers married to each other, aren't supposed to serve together as we were, in fact, doing.

After parking in that building's underground garage, I accompanied her to the lawyer's offices. Wow! The place reeked of money. I sat outside of the glassed-in office, while Su took care of her business in there with the attorney. Then I drove her back to Headquarters, where I parked our Cop car in our designated parking spot.

After the nearly an hour I had been gone from the Homicide Detail, I found nobody of Team 3 there. They had high-tailed it to wherever GPS, had shown the Mexican Drug Cartel's assassin to be, at the moment. Lieutenant Brightwell had gone with them, I was told.

Okay, so I began studying one of the many cold homicide cases stacked up in the "Documents File" on our computers. This was one that the murderer was known, but was a bit hard to prosecute, since he had fled south, down Mexico way. The U. S. Border Patrol had been alerted to watch for the guy, if he returned to the States. But that case was four years old, so the culprit could have easily slipped back across the border, one way or another, without being detected. He could also have changed identities and of course, gone to another part of the United States.

In the file, there were four color photos of him. He was a blonde fellow, with straight yellow hair. Yet oddly, his eyebrows were brownish red. Ah, he had a narrow, well cared-for, mustache, that he must have kept trimmed… that was red.

Damn! All of a sudden, I was pretty sure I had seen him somewhere! Ah, during the remodeling of our house… yes, I was sure I recalled that man was briefly at our place, driving a rolling machine, packing down our carport's floors. I had no idea of what his name was.

Right away, I called our excellent contractor. He said he had sub-contracted that work, but he would get back to me shortly, with that fellow's name and his address.

Good to his word, he called me back within fifteen minutes. He told me the guy's name, that did a bit of rock-flattening work at our carports, was Jorge Garcia; he lived in the San Ysidro neighborhood, a part of the City of San Diego, practically under the noses of the Border Patrol! And I saw he had changed his name from Jose Garcia; which wasn't much of an alteration.

After getting my wife's permission to leave, I drove down to San Ysidro, to the address given me, for Jorge Garcia. When I got to that area, I asked a Patrol Officer there to back me up, in case I could find the man to arrest him. He readily agreed; he remembered that case, of the guy murdering his wife because she wanted to divorce him.

Both the Patrol Officer and I parked in the street in front of the sizeable apartment building in which Jorge "Jose" Garcia lived. We went around to the back of the building, where there was a sizeable parking lot. With the darnedest good luck, I saw the man getting out of his car there. I told my companion it was him.

We both pulled out our pistols and stopped the guy in his tracks. I placed him under arrest, we cuffed him, read him his rights, frisked him—and found him to be unarmed.

Getting his keys, etc., from his pockets—after I had him safely in the back of my Cop car, with the Patrol Officer standing guard —I went to his apartment. Inside, I could not see a single thing illegal. There were no weapons there and no drugs.

Thanking the other Officer for his assistance, I took the murderer down to our Headquarters lockup.

While there, I found out that Lieutenant Brightwell and Team 3 had returned also with the hatchet homicider a prisoner, who was then in the lockup.

Well, it turned out to be one very lucky day for Team 3, (and for Detective-at-Large Arturo Abrito), of the San Diego Police Department's Homicide Detail!

About Bill Barrons

Born 1926, in Cadillac, Michigan, the oldest boy of fourteen kids. Survived the Great Depression and joined the Marines the day after I turned 17. Could hardly wait to go fight those nasty Nazis and Japanese. Served 2½ war years in the Marines. Got married, went to college, had kids, re-joined the Marines in 1949, in time for the Korean War. I became a Marine Second Lieutenant but was a Platoon Commander only for a short while as my sick wife nearly died and I had to resign to care for my family. Became a Telephone equipment engineer with AT&T in Chicago. Then was a kitchen and home remodeling designer for 22 years. Retired at age 69 and began to research and write novels. At age 94, I'm still at it!

Bill Barron's Website: williambarrons.com

williambarrons.com

iCrew Digital Publishing is an independent publisher of digital works. We support the efforts of authors who wish to independently publish in the digital world.

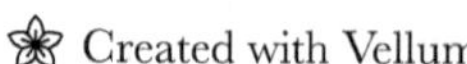 Created with Vellum

Books By William Barrons

Marine Corps Daze

The Nuworld at War

The San Diego Police Homicide Detail

The .22 Caliber Homicides

The Nude Beach Homicides

The Coldest Cold Homicides

The Forever Homicides

The Red Hot Homicides

The Homeless Homicides

The Rawhide Homicides

The Hellish Homicides

The Holiday Homicides

The Chief's Homicide

The Hatchet Homicides

The Cadillac of Detectives

Visit WilliamBarrons.com